SHE DRIVES ME CRAZY

ALSO BY KELLY QUINDLEN

Late to the Party

SHE DRIVES ME CRAZY

KELLY QUINDLEN

ROARING BROOK PRESS
NEW YORK

Published by Roaring Brook Press
Roaring Brook Press is a division of Holtzbrinck Publishing Holdings
Limited Partnership
120 Broadway, New York, NY 10271 • fiercereads.com
Copyright © 2021 by Kelly Quindlen

Library of Congress Control Number: 2020912124

ISBN 978-1-250-20915-3

Our books may be purchased in bulk for promotional, educational,
or business use. Please contact your local bookseller or the Macmillan
Corporate and Premium Sales Department at (800) 221-7945 ext.
5442 or by email at MacmillanSpecialMarkets@macmillan.com.

First edition, 2021 • Book design by Aurora Parlagreco
Printed in the United States of America

1   3   5   7   9   10   8   6   4   2

*For Mom, who always bounces back,
and for Quinn Patrick, our little game changer*

SHE DRIVES ME CRAZY

1

YOU WOULD THINK, BASED ON THE FACT
that I've played varsity basketball for three years now,
that I know how to score a basket.

You would be wrong.

"Zajac!" Coach screams, waving wildly at me. She's
only using my last name because she can't remember my
first name. "No more shots! Give the ball to someone
else!"

It's almost as humiliating as the air ball I lobbed up a
second ago. I play shooting guard, so I'm supposed to,
you know, *shoot*, but this is the third time I've taken a
shot that hasn't even touched the rim. The ball is usually so controlled in my hands, but tonight it's like I'm
chucking a giant potato through a wind tunnel.

The opposing team grabs the rebound and my ears
burn as I run back to play defense on the other side of
the court. I can't bear to look at my teammates. This

is technically just a preseason game, but it's against Candlehawk Prep, our rival high school, and right now we're trailing them by eighteen points. On our *home* court. If we lose this game, we won't have the chance to redeem ourselves until we play them in the Christmas Classic, which means these dickheads will have the upper hand for the next two months.

I dig my sneakers into the court and try to focus on playing defense. We're playing man-to-man, which is usually my strong suit, but tonight it's tripping me up because the opponent I'm guarding happens to be my ex-teammate.

She also happens to be my ex-girlfriend.

Tally Gibson was the first and only person I ever loved. She transferred to my school at the beginning of junior year with all the airs of the big city and a drive to prove herself on and off the court. The first time we talked, she tugged on my ponytail and told me I had the prettiest red hair she'd ever seen. The first time we kissed, it was like a flash fire ripped through me.

I was, in a word, entranced.

For her part, Tally only loved two things. The first was me. The second was being noticed. Tally wanted to *be* somebody, but she had a hard time making that happen at our school, where the girls' basketball team was about as significant as the knitting club. I knew she wanted more, but in my mind, *more* was always something that existed in the distant future, something we would eventually tackle together. I thought we were on the same page until the day she took me out to dinner and announced she was transferring again—and that she wanted to break up. The official letter welcoming her to Candlehawk Preparatory Academy was so wrinkled and worn that I could tell she'd been carrying it around for weeks.

I try not to look at Tally now as she bounds down the court in her new gold jersey, but it's like pretending the sun doesn't exist. She pulls her lips into her mouth like she's trying to keep a neutral expression, but I can tell she's thrilled with how this game is going. It validates every reason she had for transferring to a school with a better basketball program, a school where she could finally be noticed.

Tally takes her place near me at the top of the key, keeping enough distance to stay open for a pass from her new point guard. But then, almost like she can't help it, she glances at me.

You okay? she mouths. She's trying to look concerned, but it feels more condescending. I break the eye contact and turn away. I don't want her pity.

The other team's point guard has just about crossed the half-court line when the ref blows his whistle. My best friend, Danielle, has called for a time-out. Danielle is our point guard, varsity captain, and basically our makeshift coach because our official coach is clueless. She hustles over to me and speaks in an undertone before our forwards and center can join us.

"Dude." She gives me her trademark intense stare. "You gotta focus. *Ignore her.*"

Danielle knows how devastated I was after Tally broke up with me, and how I've just barely recovered. Between that and her competitive drive, Danielle is determined to win this game at all costs, even though we've lost to Candlehawk the last three years in a row. We lose most of our games, but it's never stopped Danielle from dreaming of a winning season.

"I know, I know, I hear you," I mutter to her. "You didn't have to call time-out."

Danielle huffs. "It's not all about you." She turns to our forwards and center as they join us. "Listen, do y'all recognize this play they're about to run?"

The rest of us stare at her. Danielle's mind is always working overtime, picking up patterns and rhythms the rest of us never see. Every once in a while, she completely zones out when she's thinking through something. Our friends called it Danielle Vision.

"The point guard does that hand-twirl signal when she wants the forwards to cross-swap," she says in a hushed tone. "They're gonna run out to the wings to pull the attention away from the top of the key—"

I'm trying to listen, but my eyes keep searching for Tally. She's standing in a huddle with her new teammates, doing that thing where she picks up her ankle and balances on one foot. The first time I teased her about that habit, during tryouts last year, she grinned crookedly and said, *Why are you watching me so closely?*

I wish I could get that moment back. Tally's arctic-blue eyes, her daring smirk, her eagerness to give this place—and *me*—a chance. She had yet to learn that playing for a losing girls' basketball team in a quirky suburban town made you a nobody. I had yet to learn that being a nobody was supposed to bother me.

"—Got it?" Danielle says bracingly, smacking me on the arm. And suddenly we're taking our positions and the ref is blowing his whistle, but I have no idea what I'm supposed to be doing.

It happens too fast: The opposing point guard makes the signal, the forwards cross-swap to the wings, and Tally runs to set a pick against Danielle. She plants her feet and crosses her arms over her chest, becoming a solid screen that Danielle can't move around. I chase after her, trying to keep up, but she rolls easily off Danielle and zips to the free-throw line to receive her point guard's pass.

By the time I catch up to her, Tally has already taken her shot. It sails crisply and cleanly through the basket in a perfect, nothing-but-net arc. The gold section of the crowd—which is pretty much all of it—roars with delight. One of their supporters waves a sign that reads *Tally it up!!!* It makes me want to vomit.

Tally grins as her new teammates rush to high-five her. They're now up by a whopping twenty points and my team has no chance of coming back. Danielle throws me a death glare, and I realize she must have warned me about the pick. I shrug defensively; she shakes her head and hustles to the baseline so we can pass the ball in for a new play.

It's in that one stupid second—between picking up the ball and passing it in to Danielle—that I lose it. One of the Candlehawk players who's hanging all over Tally cackles, "That girl didn't even see you move! She couldn't keep up with you!"

That girl. Like I'm some pathetic nonfactor who means nothing to Tally. She obviously didn't think I was worth mentioning to her new teammates.

"Hey, asshole!" I shout to the Candlehawk player. She turns around, scandalized. So do the rest of her teammates, including a bewildered Tally. "My *name* is Scottie!"

I hurl the basketball like we're playing dodgeball and I'm determined to take out their entire team. I feel one boiling second of satisfaction, but then—

Shrieeeeeeeeek. The ref blows his whistle and barrels toward me.

"Technical foul!" he shouts. "Unsportsmanlike conduct!"

The crowd starts booing me. The Candlehawk players throw me scathing, superior looks, except for Tally, who grimaces like I've become unhinged. My coach freezes where she stands, clearly unsure of what a technical foul is.

I can feel Danielle staring a hole into the side of my face, but I refuse to make eye contact with anyone as I hustle to the bench. The Candlehawk supporters are still jeering while our handful of home supporters are silent. I'm seething with anger, but there's a hot prickle of shame running down my spine, too. I take my seat on the bench and keep my eyes fixed on the floor.

* * *

We lose by twenty-three points. I know it's not all on my shoulders, but I can't help feeling smaller than the tiniest ant as we line up to shake hands with the other team.

Tally meets my eyes as we file through the handshake line. There's a look of secondhand embarrassment on her face, like she wants to recoil from me. I've seen that look only once before: last spring, when we went to our first real house party and the cheerleading captain had my car towed as a prank. I chased the tow truck down the street, fell and cut my knee open, and dissolved into sobs. Tally put her arm around me, but she seemed more concerned with shushing me than comforting me, especially once the crowd of onlookers grew. I remember feeling like I was both too much and not enough.

After that, I swore off the cool kids and their parties, but Tally tried harder than ever to join them. She never confirmed it, but I'm pretty sure the tow truck incident was the final straw that made her apply to Candlehawk. The humiliating nudge she needed to start over with something better.

"Scottie?" Tally calls when I'm slouching off to the locker room.

I freeze. "Yeah?"

She doesn't quite make eye contact. "Can you wait for me outside?"

I breathe in sharply. I know it's not a good idea, but I can't pass up this chance for a moment alone with her. "Sure, okay."

She nods and walks away. I continue on toward the locker room but stop in my tracks when some varsity cheerleaders swoop in from the larger gym next door. They must have just finished cheering for the boys' game. I feel that sweeping blush the cheerleading squad has provoked in me since the towing incident last year, so I crouch down and pretend to tie my shoe until the group of them has passed me.

* * *

Outside, in the senior parking lot, I hike myself up on the retaining wall where people like to smoke weed. Tally will no doubt find me here, since the Candlehawk players insist on parking in our senior lot anytime they play us at home. In a different world, Tally would have parked in this lot every day, right next to my old green

Jetta. Now she parks on the other side of town in a sea of Range Rovers and Escalades.

It's a cool October evening. The marquee in front of the school office is lit up in shining white, spelling out a reminder that it's Homecoming week, except someone has nicked the second *o* and replaced it to read HOME-CUMING. Our principal will pitch a fit tomorrow, but it won't stop people from messing with the sign. It's just one of those things kids around here do.

I live in the town of Grandma Earl, Georgia. We're famous for a gigantic emporium called Grandma Earl's Christmas 365, which old Mrs. Earl opened, like, a hundred years ago to sell Christmas decorations year-round. It became such a landmark that the town was eventually named for it. It's a little wacky, but I love this place. It's home.

Grandma Earl High School is the home of the Fighting Reindeer, which is why I have to wear a red-and-brown jersey on the basketball court. That color scheme doesn't look good on anyone, but especially not a fair-skinned redhead like me. That's one good thing about the lack of fans at our games: fewer people to catch me looking like a fire hydrant. Not that I've ever really cared. Or at least, I didn't used to.

Candlehawk is the town—or *township*, as they call it—next to ours, and they're kind of like Grandma Earl's douchey older brother: cool, cocky, and perpetually embarrassed to be associated with us. We share a border at the old railroad tracks, but things are much different over there: trendy, modern, full of organic coffee roasters and uppity farmers markets. The residents are low-key wealthy and high-key hipster. They show up to our rival games wearing navy beanies and $150 distressed jeans while our half dozen supporters show up in gardening shirts and cargo pants. And at halftime, no matter what the sport, their crowd taunts us about the time a Grandma Earl football player tackled his own teammate in a championship game. It's the reason Candlehawk sings "Grandma got run over by *her own* reindeer" whenever we play each other.

I hate that Tally has become a Candlehawk kid, but maybe I should have seen it coming. She was always obsessed with how things looked and who was doing the looking. Dating her felt like viewing my life through a photo filter. Sometimes I was swept up by how great we looked together; other times, I felt like the photo underneath wasn't good enough on its own.

The school's back door heaves open, jolting me from my thoughts. Tally comes gliding out, flanked by several players from her new team. Her face is bright and her laughter loud, but she draws to an abrupt stop when she sees me.

"Hey," I say evenly.

"Hey." She jams her hands in her leather jacket and shoots her entourage a loaded look. "Give me a sec, guys."

The Candlehawk girls trudge away with their eyebrows raised. They don't bother looking my way.

"Sorry," Tally mutters, coming toward me on the retaining wall. She nods at her retreating teammates. "They were trying to talk me into getting a fog machine for, um"—she glances away, shrugging—"for a Halloween thing I'm having."

I blink, trying to keep my expression steady. *A Halloween thing.* That's code for yet another party, one of many she's thrown since starting at Candlehawk. The lack of an invitation feels like a physical blow, but I know better than to have expected one. I try not to imagine what kind of costume she'll wear, the pictures she'll post. How many people will be in her house, taking shots in the kitchen where we baked cupcakes a few months ago.

"Tell people to watch out for that fireplace corner," I murmur. It's an intimate memory: During my first visit to Tally's house, while her parents were away, I'd cut my shin on the dark red brick protruding from her oversized fireplace. Happy to play nurse, Tally had kissed the pain away. She hadn't told me to shush that time. Probably because no one had been watching.

I think there's a glimmer of recognition in Tally's eyes, but she looks away before I can be sure. "Um—anyway. Some game, right? I've never seen you that pissed off before. I think you actually scared some of my teammates." She laughs, but it's hollow.

That prickle of shame runs down my spine again. I shift on the wall and ask, "Does it matter? I mean, do they know who I am to you?"

She chews her lip. "I don't know. Maybe from social media?"

I bristle. Tally deleted all her pictures of me the day after we broke up.

"So, probably not," I say pointedly.

Tally crosses her arms over her chest. "You didn't have to throw the ball at them. If they *do* know about you, that's not the impression I want them to get."

"Well, sorry I can't maintain a good enough image for you, Tally."

"Jesus, Scottie," she mutters, like I'm the most impossible person in the world. "You're being so over the top. It's just a *game*."

I feel like she's dumped a bucket of ice water on my head. It soaks through my skin and twists around my insides.

"Just a game?" My voice is shaking. "If it's *just a game*, why did you have to transfer to Candlehawk for it?"

Tally sighs. Dead leaves skitter across the concrete. "Okay, look, I don't want to fight. I should have known it was a bad idea to talk when you're all riled up after a game—"

"I'm not *riled up*," I say, trying to control my emotions.

Tally levels me with a stare. "Anyway." She reaches in her jacket pocket and pulls out a plastic button the size of a drink coaster. I know what it is even before I see the picture on the front.

"I wanted to give this back to you," she says, laying it in my palm.

It's my basketball button from junior year. A photo of me in my gaudy red-and-brown jersey, my eyes shining brightly. The school gives them out to athletes so our parents or friends can wear them to our games, even if it's usually just the football players who use them. Last year, Tally and I swapped buttons. I pinned hers to my backpack for the whole season, ready to tell anyone who asked that she was my girlfriend. No one did, but I was proud anyway.

Tally never wore my button, though. Maybe I should have taken that as a hint.

"I thought you would want it back," Tally says. "I know you'll get a new one this season, but it didn't feel right for me to hold on to it."

I blink rapidly and try to find my voice—

And just then, the back door heaves open again.

The Grandma Earl cheerleaders strut out. To my horror, the girl at the front of the pack is the *last* person in the world I want to witness this pitiful moment: Irene Abraham, the cheerleading captain. The girl who had my car towed at that party last year.

Irene is the quintessential queen bee: the most popular girl in our grade, a total lock for Homecoming Queen, and an absolute terror to us plebeians at the bottom of the social pyramid. She's a gorgeous Indian American girl with piercing dark eyes and an eyebrow scar of mysterious origin. A few weeks ago, my class voted her both "Best Smile" and "Best Hair" for senior superlatives. Rumor has it that when the yearbook staff asked her to pick one, she asked if she could have "Class Inseparables" with her notorious enemy, Charlotte Pascal, instead. She wasn't kidding.

I've only spoken to her twice in my life. The first time was in Driver's Ed, freshman year, before she ascended to the realm of popularity and was still nice enough to lend me a pencil. The second was last spring, at that party, when I accidentally spilled my cranberry mixer down the front of her white jumpsuit. She told me it wasn't a big deal, but an hour later she called the tow truck on me. Everyone ran out of the house to watch my car get dragged away while I went racing after it like an idiot. It wasn't until I tripped, skinned my knee, and saw everyone laughing that I started to cry. Irene merely stood in the center of the yard, hands in her pockets, with a cool expression on her face. The merciless, untouchable queen.

Irene stops short when she sees us. The whole squad stops behind her. One of the other girls asks if I'm okay.

"I'm fine." I stare pointedly away, willing them with everything I have to keep walking.

"Yeah, she's fine," Tally confirms. Her tone is apologetic, almost like she's saying *Sorry you have to see this.*

I can feel Irene's eyes land on me again, but I ignore her. What is she waiting for? She must get the hint, because she shifts her duffel bag on her shoulder and stalks toward the parking lot. "Are y'all coming?" she calls to her friends. "I've got shit to do."

They glance at me, but after a second they shuffle after Irene.

"I guess we should go, too," Tally says.

We. As if that's still a thing. I don't move. It's the only play I have left.

"I'm sorry that game didn't go how you wanted," Tally says. "Good luck with the rest of the season."

She hesitates, then plants a kiss on my cheek.

And then she walks away.

That's the moment I decide: I will do everything in my power to beat Candlehawk—to beat *Tally*—when we play them again. I will do whatever it takes to show her that leaving Grandma Earl—leaving *me*—was the biggest mistake of her life.

* * *

My trusty old Jetta is my baby. The seats have cracks in the leather, the cupholder fits a coffee thermos perfectly, and the interior smells inexplicably like crayons. It used to be my older sister's car, and when she passed it down to me, she stuck a four-leaf clover sticker on the gearshift to wish me luck. My mom's contribution was a Saint Christopher medal, for the patron saint of travelers, which now hangs from the rearview mirror and swings helplessly whenever I make a hard turn.

I throw my bag in the passenger seat and tuck myself into the driver's side. For a second I sit there holding my basketball button, gazing down at this person who no longer feels like me. Then I turn on the car, pull on my seat belt, and hook up my phone to the ancient aux cable.

I back out of my space and blare my music. Maybe playing "Purple Rain" loudly enough will soothe the bitterness in my stomach. I guide my car through the labyrinth of the senior parking lot, wanting nothing more than to get home.

Then I see Tally's car zoom out of the lot. The same red Ford Escape we used to make out in after school. I haven't seen it since the day she broke up with me. I can't help it: I crane my neck to watch her drive away.

It's because my eyes are glued to Tally's taillights that I don't notice it—

The car reversing out of its space directly in front of me.

CRUNCH.

I lurch forward in my seat as I slam straight into the other car's rear end.

2

IT TAKES A MOMENT FOR MY SENSES TO catch up with me. My heart is pounding so hard I feel like I've just dropped off the side of a cliff. My entire body is sweeping hot, and my palms are pooling with sweat.

The car I've hit is a black sedan, but before I can get a proper look at it, the other driver stomps out of the car with all the anger of a rabid bulldog.

It's Irene Abraham.

Fuck.

My shock transforms to fury. Go-*freaking*-figure. I know I wasn't exactly *looking* when I hit her, but I also know I had the right of way. She must have decided the rules didn't apply to her.

My adrenaline carries me out of my car before I can think about it. I slam my door and meet her in the middle. "What the hell?"

Her eyes flash when she sees me. Under her breath, she says, "You have got to be fucking kidding me."

I ignore her and check my front bumper. Miraculously, it's only slightly dented; I'll have to get it fixed, but it's still drivable.

Behind me, Irene is examining her own car. "Shit," she grumbles. "My parents are gonna kill me."

"Yeah, well, so are mine," I say, kicking at my front tire. I can feel tears building behind my eyes, but I fight against them. I hate the idea of crying in front of Irene Abraham ever again. I take a deep breath to steady myself, but when I turn around to check her car, the bottom drops out of my stomach.

Her rear bumper is a craggy, mangled disaster; the right half of it hangs off the frame, dragging against the pavement. There's no way her car is drivable like this. My anger suddenly turns to panic. If her car took the worst of the hit, does that mean it was my fault, even if I had the right of way?

I steady my breathing and look at her. "Damn it. I'm sorry."

Her dark eyes sizzle like I've just said something offensive. "Do you know *nothing*?" she snaps. "You should never apologize after a car accident. It's an admission of fault."

I'm so thrown off, I can only stare at her.

"Lucky for you, I'm not the type of person to fake a serious injury or some bullshit emotional trauma so I can sue you and your parents for all you're worth, but someone else might be. Use your head."

Anger flares inside me again. "You really wanna be giving *me* a lesson right now? You're the one who backed into me!"

"Why didn't you stop when you saw my car?"

"Why didn't you stop when you saw *my* car?"

We've created quite a scene in the parking lot. A bunch of people from our class run over, checking to see what happened. Even though school's been out for hours, there are enough kids here that our accident is impossible to hide.

"Are y'all okay?"

"Ohhh, your bumper's *fucked*."

"Aw, shit! Tow Truck Girl fucked up her car again!"

One of the cheerleaders hurries over, her eyes popping out of her head. It's Irene's best friend, the same girl who asked me if I was okay earlier: Honey-Belle Hewett. She's the great-granddaughter of the legendary Mrs. Earl. Her family still runs the Emporium, and she's exactly how you'd imagine a girl from a Christmas-business family to be. Sugary voice, cartoonish expressions, and a little out of it sometimes. Like a Care Bear magicked to life.

"Holy shit-balls," she exclaims, running straight for us. "What happened? Are you okay?"

Irene drags a hand down her face. "I have to call my mom. *Fuck*."

She stalks away on her cell phone, her brow still

19

furrowed with anger. Honey-Belle gives me a sympathetic look, but I turn away and pick up my own phone.

My mom shows up fifteen minutes after I call her. She smooths the hair back from my forehead and reassures me in her steady, measured voice. The whole world could explode and my mom would say, *Hmm, now how are we going to handle this?*

"Are you hurt anywhere?" Mom asks.

"No."

"Were you on your phone?"

"No."

Mom nods, searching me with her I-don't-miss-a-trick eyes. "Okay. Let's call the insurance company."

Irene's mom arrives soon after that. She's an attractive, sophisticated-looking woman, with curly dark hair and pristine lipstick, dressed in lavender scrubs with a name tag that reads DR. ABRAHAM. She has the same scrutinizing facial expression as Irene, like she could figure you out in a second. It looks like that's what she's doing to Irene right now.

"How did this happen?" she asks, cocking her head at Irene. Her voice is calm but commanding.

Irene huffs, crossing her arms over her chest. "I was backing out, and I didn't see her coming—"

Her mom cuts her off. "You weren't looking?"

"I was, but—"

"But you were lost in your head, imagining more cheer routines?"

20

Irene's mouth sets into a thin line.

"This is what happens when you don't *focus*," her mom continues. "You know better than to be careless. Make sure to take pictures of this bumper. Every angle!"

There's an unbearable stretch of time when our moms are on the phone with the insurance companies and Irene and I have nothing to do but pointedly ignore each other. When all is said and done, our moms exchange a nod and announce that we're both responsible—since both our cars were moving—but that Irene is primarily at fault since I had the right of way.

"That's not fair," Irene says, shaking her head. "She came zooming around the corner—she wasn't even looking—"

"How do you know I wasn't looking?" I say heatedly. "Besides, you're one to talk! This is the *second* time you've messed with my car!"

My mom frowns. "What does that mean?"

There's a hanging silence. I never told my parents the truth about how my car was towed last year; I lied and said I'd accidentally parked in front of a fire hydrant. I was too embarrassed to admit that I'd been bullied by the head cheerleader.

Now Irene and I stare at each other for a blistering moment. Her eyes are wide and anxious. It's the first hint of vulnerability I've seen from her.

"She . . . accidentally spilled coffee in my car once."

I'm not sure what possesses me to say it. This could

have been my chance for some much deserved payback, but I'd rather be Tow Truck Girl than Tattletale Girl.

"You've been in her car before?" Irene's mom asks. "You two are friends?"

We stare at each other for another extended moment.

"Mhm," Irene says, recovering. She gestures at my uniform. "I cheer for her team sometimes."

It's a good thing no one's looking at me, because my eye roll would prove that's a lie in a second. I have no doubt that Irene, as captain, *could* get her squad to cheer for us instead of the boys, but why would a cheerleading captain ever bother to challenge the status quo?

"Isn't that nice," my mom coos. "Well, that makes everything less awkward, doesn't it?"

Irene's mom chuckles. "Yes, what a relief!"

What follows is some of the worst mom-based embarrassment I've ever experienced. Our moms introduce themselves, then make corny jokes about how glad they are that neither one of them is an uptight, meddling mother who would blow this accident out of proportion.

"Imagine having to do this with a Candlehawk woman!" my mom says.

"That's a level of hell I don't need today!" Irene's mom laughs.

Irene and I say nothing, waiting for them to stop.

"Scottie, you look like a serious student," Dr. Abraham says suddenly. "What are you studying?"

"Mom, don't—" Irene tries.

"Uh . . . my favorite subject is history," I say.

"Is that what you want to study in college?"

"Totally," I lie. I've never seriously thought about it, but Dr. Abraham seems like the kind of woman who requires a confident answer.

"And what sport do you play? Is that a basketball uniform? Basketball's a wonderful sport. You see, Irene? You can be a serious student *and* a competitive athlete."

"I *am*," Irene says, with an air like she's said this a hundred times before.

"Cheerleading is very admirable, too," my mom chimes in.

Dr. Abraham nods politely, but she obviously disagrees. "Well, it seems everything is in order here," she says authoritatively. "We're waiting on the tow truck company, but then we'll be on our way."

I meet Irene's eyes at the words *tow truck*. She flicks her eyes away, but I catch a flash of guilt in them.

"Having your car towed *sucks*," I say with fake sympathy. "Happened to me once. I really feel for you."

I can almost see the steam coming out of her ears. It's so satisfying I could sing. But then—

"What a pain to be without a car in this town," my mom says. "How will you get to school, Irene?"

"My husband or I will drop her off," Irene's mom says with a wave of her hand. "It's easy for us. We're right over on Sleigh Byrne."

"Sleigh Byrne?" My mom gets a funny smile on her

23

face, and I'm suddenly dreading what she's going to say next. "We live on the next road over, off Bells Haven." She looks at me, and now I *know* what's about to happen.

"Scottie can give Irene a ride!" Mom declares, her eyes bright. "Please, please, we insist. It's the least we could do."

I try to catch my mom's eye to communicate what a terrible idea this is, but the damage is already done. Irene's mom lights up like this is the best plan she's ever heard. She smiles brightly at Irene and lifts her hands as if to say *How about that!*

Irene blinks and offers my mom a courteous, grateful smile, but I can tell she despises the idea as much as I do.

"Well, that's settled," Mom says, looking happily at me. "All's well that ends well, right?"

It's not until we've walked away from the Abrahams that I voice my horror. "Mom," I whine, "I can't stand that girl! I'd rather go to school naked than drive her anywhere!"

"I thought you said you were friends?"

"Uh . . . I mean, that might have been a *slight* exaggeration," I fumble. "But does it matter? The accident wasn't even my fault!"

Mom looks unperturbed. "No, it wasn't your fault, but it's still your responsibility. It won't kill you to give her a ride until her car's fixed."

In the end, I walk away from my first car accident with

a wounded ego, a dented bumper, and the looming dread of carpooling with the only person who could make my senior year worse than it already is.

* * *

My dad and younger sister are in the front yard, stringing up Halloween lights, when Mom and I caravan into the driveway.

I love our house. We've lived here since I was four. It's a quirky street, tucked away off a busy main road. The houses are as different as the people who live in them. There's the one-story ranch house where the Sanchez family and their three Labradors live. There's Mrs. Stone's green bungalow with the rocking chair porch, where she's always inviting people in for a cup of turmeric tea and a discussion of what their dreams mean. At the end of the street is my mom's least favorite house, the faux-modern monstrosity where Mr. and Mrs. Haliburton-Rivera host bougie parties we're never invited to. Mom and Dad call them "Candlehawk wannabes."

Our house is a lilac-blue classic with shutter boards and a tiny front porch. Instead of a garage, we have an old carport where we park our cars. There's a maple tree in the front yard that reaches as high as the second story and a row of bushes that guard the front porch. That's where Dad and Daphne are now, arranging the orange lights so they hang over the bushes the way Daphne likes them.

"What's the damage?" Dad asks when Mom and I join them in the yard.

"It's my front bumper." I grimace. "It's all dented in, but I was still able to drive it home—"

"I mean you, Scots," Dad says, bracing his hands on my shoulders. He looks me over with a worried frown, like he might be able to assess whether or not I'm concussed. This is one of the best things about my dad. I know he *will* be annoyed about the bumper, and that he'll insist on coming with me to the repair shop, but right now he's only concerned about me.

"I'm glad you're okay," Daphne says, hugging me gently. "Do you need an ice pack? There's one in the freezer from when I bruised my toe."

Daphne is the sweetheart of the family. She's only thirteen, but my parents like to say she's an old soul.

"I'm fine, Daph, thanks."

"How's your neck?" Dad asks. "Any whiplash?"

"Maybe a little whiplash," I say, and Dad starts feeling along the top of my spine. He's a chiropractor, so he's always quick to check my back if I tell him I slept funny or pulled a muscle in practice.

"Flat on the grass," Dad says, stepping back.

"What? We're gonna do the adjustment out here?"

"Daph and I are still working on the decorations," Dad says, like it's obvious. "Come on, you know the drill."

Mom and Daphne just stand there, amused, as I drop

to the grass and lie flat on my stomach while Dad starts cracking my back. If the neighbors are watching, I doubt they're surprised. My family's been known to do weirder shit in the front yard—like the time five-year-old Daphne insisted we eat breakfast out here with our winter coats on. In the middle of July.

"All right, that should do it," Dad says, giving my neck a final crack. "Feel better?"

I can only grunt into the grass in response.

We spend the next half hour finishing the Halloween decorations. It's dark outside, and we're limited by the lamps on the porch, but we're motivated to finish because Halloween is next week. It's tradition on my street for everyone to go all out with holiday decorations, even the stuck-up Haliburton-Riveras, who decorate in a style my parents call *tasteful Pinterest crap*. Our decorations, on the other hand, are cheesy as hell. We plant plastic tombstones all over the grass, Mom sets up a witch and vampire couple to look like *American Gothic* on the front porch, and Daphne wraps cobwebs all over the mailbox. My contribution is to arrange a group of skeletons around some hay bales. Last year, Dad made them look like they were doing the macarena. This year, I take a fat twig and place it in one skeleton's mouth to look like he's smoking. Mom rolls her eyes, but she lets it slide.

Inside, we sit down to a dinner of rotisserie chicken that Dad picked up on his way home from the clinic.

Mom and Daphne throw together a side of noodles and croissant rolls, while my task is to set aside a plate for my older sister, Thora, who's still at work.

"I texted Thora about the accident," Daphne says, helping herself to a double portion of noodles. "She's worried about you, Scottie. She wanted to come home right away, but she said the restaurant is a cluster-eff."

"Don't use that word," Mom says.

"I didn't, I said 'eff.' Thora used the real word."

"Still."

"Mom, most people in my grade use the f-word all the time."

"Doesn't mean you have to be uncouth, too."

"Yeah, wait until you're older to be uncouth," Dad says.

Thora works as a bartender at the best pub in town, The Chimney. She's saving money to rent her own apartment, but for now she lives in our basement with her two cats, BooBoo and Pickles, who keep getting into Mom's vegetable patch and digging up her arugula. The cats drive Mom crazy. Dad is cooler about them, but he's always more lax when it comes to Thora because he's technically her stepdad. Mom divorced Thora's birth father when Thora was a toddler, but she didn't marry Dad until Thora was seven.

"Scottie," Mom says when there's a lull in the conversation, "do you want to talk about what happened?"

I pick at the skin on my chicken, aware of everyone

watching me. I knew our evening of decorating fun would eventually give way to this conversation, but that doesn't mean I'm ready for it.

"Do we have to?"

Dad tilts his head at me. "Do we have to talk about why you were so distracted that you didn't notice a car backing into you? Yes."

I drop my fork. "I had a bad day, okay?"

"Because of the Candlehawk game?" Dad asks.

"Because of Tally?" Mom adds.

I feel lucky to have parents as loving and engaged as my mom and dad. They know about all the little things happening in my life, like when I have an exam I'm stressed about or a fight with Danielle that trips me up. But sometimes their involvement is so earnest and omnipresent that I feel like something can't happen to me without them wanting to pick it apart over the dinner table.

"We're sorry we couldn't be at the demo game," Dad says, ruffling my hair. "We know it's been a tough semester. It hasn't been easy for you without Tally."

"Losing your first love is excruciating," Mom adds sympathetically.

I'm not sure my parents ever liked Tally. They were sure to smile and hug her whenever she came over, but I always got the vibe that they were doing it for my sake rather than because they actually liked her.

"I promise it's going to get better," Mom coos. "But

that doesn't mean you can lose sight of everything else going on in your life. You've got your whole senior year ahead of you, with basketball and college applications and your wonderful friends—"

"I know, I know." Tears spring into my eyes. I try to swallow them down, but they drop onto my chicken. "I really am sorry about the car, you guys."

"Okay," Mom says quietly. "We'll let it go for tonight. Go upstairs and watch a movie. Daphne will take care of the dishes."

Doing the dishes alone is a pain—we usually split the cleanup—but the wonderful thing about Daphne is that she would never argue in a million years. She nods and clears everyone's plates, tossing me a small smile, and I take the stairs to my room without looking back.

* * *

I'm notorious for taking the longest showers in the family, but tonight is really something else. For a while I just stand there under the water, my aching muscles grateful for the heat. I wash my hair, loofah with Daphne's vanilla sugar body wash, and scrub my face after a good long cry.

Normally I would blow-dry and straighten my hair so it looks good for school tomorrow, but tonight I don't have the energy. I wrap a towel around my wet hair, change into my favorite long-sleeve tee and joggers, click on the string lights Thora got me last Christmas, and curl up in my bed. For the first time all day, I feel like I can breathe.

Mom was right to tell me to watch a movie. Aside from playing basketball, watching movies is my favorite thing to do. Tonight I queue up *10 Things I Hate About You*, the king of teen rom-coms. I can recite parts of it in my sleep.

A few minutes into the movie, Thora barges in. She's still in her bartending outfit, and her keys are in her hand, which tells me she literally just got home. She drops onto my bed, squeezes me tight, and fusses like I'm a poor kitten she's come across in the road. Daphne scurries in behind her, crawling up on my other side.

"Who hurt you?" Thora asks, still squeezing me. "Who do I have to kill?"

"Nobody." I laugh. "I'm fine. How was work?"

"The opposite of stimulating," Thora says, picking at the pink tips of her hair. "Seriously, how are you feeling?"

"It was a shitty day," I admit. "We played Candle-hawk in a demo game. They clobbered us. Then my car got clobbered."

Thora winces. "Candlehawk means Tally, huh?"

"Yeah. Their new star player. She gave me my button back."

My sisters trade a loaded look.

"What?" I ask, even though I know what they're going to say.

"She sucks," Thora says, rolling onto her back. "Like, really, *really* sucks."

"She didn't always suck. Not until she transferred to Candlehawk."

"I think she sucked before that," Daphne says. "Remember when she got mad at you for posting that pic where her hair was frizzy?"

"Remember when she didn't speak to you for a whole day because you refused to sneak into that concert with her?" Thora adds.

Here's the thing: I *know* Tally was tough sometimes, but it makes me uncomfortable to hear it from other people. It makes me question my judgment, because for a while there, I was *so* happy with her. Was I just oblivious? Or, worse, did I convince myself she cared about me when she really didn't?

"I know, I know," I say, dragging my hands down my face. "I promise she wasn't *always* that bad."

There's a pause where my sisters are clearly holding back their words, until Daphne says, "Well, I think she's an eff-head."

Thora busts out laughing, and I can't help but smile a little.

"Daph, you're a national treasure, you know that?" Thora says. Daphne beams.

"Can we watch the movie now?" I ask.

"Sure," my sisters say, and they snuggle up on either side of me.

Maybe an hour into the movie, my phone rings with a local number I don't recognize. I reject the call, assuming it's a telemarketer.

A moment later, it rings again.

"Scottieee," Thora whines.

"Sorry!" I fumble for the phone and answer it impatiently. "Hello?"

"Scottie?" a brittle voice asks. "It's Irene."

What the fuck.

I sit bolt upright, scrambling to pause the movie. My sisters stare at me, but I wave my hands for them to be quiet. Why the hell is this girl *calling* me? How did she even get my number?

"Hey," I say into the phone, trying to sound casual. I switch on the lamp and swing my legs off the bed. "I didn't expect you to call—"

"Didn't you, though?" she asks brusquely. "We have to plan for tomorrow. You know, since I have to *carpool* with you."

It takes me a moment to speak. "Right," I say tersely. "Obviously. I just figured we'd text."

"Calling's more efficient."

I clear my throat, trying to stop myself from screaming at her. "How's your car? What'd the mechanic say?"

She ignores the question. "What time are you picking me up in the morning? I usually leave by seven twenty-five."

I'm still trying to get my footing in the conversation, and it takes me a second to realize what she's asking. Seven twenty-five? Our school is only ten minutes away, and class doesn't start until 8:05.

"I usually leave at seven forty," I say pointedly.

She makes an impatient noise. "I have things to do in the morning. If I had my *own* car, I'd leave at seven fifteen."

"I guess you should have thought about that before you rammed your car into mine, huh?"

There's a stiff silence. "Are you picking me up at seven twenty-five, or not?"

I grit my teeth. "I'll be there."

"Great. I'll text you my address."

"Great. Isn't texting so efficient?"

A beat passes. "*Cute*," she says in the most acidic voice I've ever heard. Then she hangs up. I stare at my phone in outrage.

"Who the hell was that?" Thora asks.

"My nemesis," I say, only half joking.

"I thought Tally was your nemesis," Daphne says. Thora elbows her in the side.

"Scots," Thora says, grabbing the remote from me, "I don't know what this says about me, but your drama is becoming the most entertaining part of my life."

3

THE NEXT MORNING, I PULL INTO IRENE'S driveway a full five minutes late. I don't do it on purpose; the time just gets away from me. She's standing there impatiently, her long hair perfectly straightened, her makeup impeccably done. She clutches a giant silver thermos and holds her phone the way all pretty girls do: flat on its back like she might whisper gossip into the speaker any second.

I expect a snarky remark about my tardiness, but she's silent when she opens the door. She tucks her bags in the back seat and sets her thermos in my cupholder without asking. It feels invasive, especially in such a contained, intimate space. A space that I usually only share with the people closest to me: my sisters or Danielle or, until recently, Tally.

I reverse out of her driveway and turn up my music to drown out the awkwardness. My nerves are on edge, waiting for her to say something. I notice when she clears her throat. I sniff against the sharp, woody scent of her perfume.

When we turn onto the main road, I decide to break the silence.

"Sorry I was late." I lean back in my seat, pretending to feel at ease. "Hope it didn't inconvenience you."

She rakes a hand through her hair. "You weren't," she says flatly. "I usually leave at seven thirty. I told you seven twenty-five because I knew you'd be late."

For a second, all I can do is stare at her. "Wait, what?"

"You never got to APUSH last year until a second before the bell rang." She glances at me. "It's not an insult, just an observation."

My blood simmers. It's true that I always ran late to AP US History, but that's because Tally's locker had been right next to the classroom and I would loiter there with her until the last possible second. It's a reminder I don't need so early in the morning.

"So what?" I snap. "You've taken it upon yourself to keep a log of people's arrival times?"

She laughs breezily. "You're so easy to irritate."

I imagine how I must have looked to her, dashing into class late every day. Did she see me hanging all over Tally last year? Could she sense the cracks in that relationship before I could? Is that why she thought I was such a loser? A feeling of shame spreads through my torso.

"I'm better at getting to AP Euro on time," I say pointedly. "But I guess you wouldn't know that, since you didn't make it into the class."

It's a *really* snotty thing to say, but I want to get under her skin and I don't have many cards to play. It seems to work, because she puts down her phone and glares at me.

"I *did* make it into the class. I just didn't want to take it."

"What? Why?"

"Oh come on. AP *European* History? A class where you literally study how white people fucked up the world with the Crusades and colonization and small-pox? Yet there's no room in the budget to offer Asian or African History? Yeah, no. If that's the pinnacle of academic study our school has to offer, I'll fucking pass. Say what you want about Ms. Bowles's 'regular track' modern history class, but she makes a point of dismantling the whole European hegemony thing, and that's a much better use of my time."

I can't think of anything to say to that, not least because I'm trying to figure out what *hegemony* means.

Irene takes a pointed sip from her thermos and shakes her head. "But please, tell me more about how you're so much smarter than me. Not like I haven't heard it before. People love to assume they're better than you when you're '*just a cheerleader*,' as if I'm not completely fucking aware of the complicated identity that comes with my sport."

37

"I never said I was smarter than you," I say tersely.

She snorts. "Right. You only implied it. But *you're* the one who was dumb enough to get taken in by Tally Gibson."

My heart rate skyrockets. "What did you say?"

She raises her eyebrows. "Was I not clear enough?"

I jerk the car over to the side of the road. The car behind us blares its horn as it passes. Irene looks at me like I've lost my mind.

"Let's be clear about a few things." I'm so angry that my voice is trembling. "One: In case you haven't noticed, driving you to school is the last thing I want to be doing, so try to tone down the bitchy factor. Two: I might have covered for your ass yesterday, but I haven't forgotten your shitty tow truck prank, and I haven't forgiven you for it, either. Don't give me yet another reason to hate you. And three: Don't you *ever* talk shit about Tally to me. *Ever.*"

Irene is breathing hard, her face crinkled in fury. The scar in her eyebrow visibly shows. I'd like to thank the person who put it there.

"Understood," she says finally, her chest heaving. "But if you get to set some ground rules, so do I. And there's only one: Don't ever make assumptions about me again."

"Fine," I growl.

I pull back onto the road and turn up my music. We don't say another word for the rest of the drive.

When I park in my usual space in the senior lot, I notice with relief that Danielle's car is already here. I can't wait to escape and find her.

I'm scrambling out of my seat when it hits me: Irene Abraham is about to get out of my car . . . in the middle of the senior parking lot . . . where we're surrounded by classmates who know the two of us go together like a princess and a gremlin. People are definitely going to talk.

Irene gets out of the car first, snapping the door shut. I take a deep breath and open my own door.

The moment I stand up, I can feel all eyes on us.

The looks are coming from people all over the parking lot—the band kids, the potheads, the hipster Christian kids. Irene's group of friends looks up with their perfect haircuts and cocky smiles, most of them snickering. They make their way toward us as I fish my backpack and duffel bag out of the back seat.

"Yayyy, happy carpool day!" Honey-Belle trills, clapping her hands. She is impossibly chipper. Her DNA is probably made of cupcakes.

"So whose fault was it?" Gino DiNova calls. "Was it you, Abraham?"

Gino is hard to explicitly hate because he never says anything *actually* offensive, but he never says anything nice, either. Right now he's got his cell phone out, clearly taking a snap of my car, laughing like it's the funniest thing he's ever seen. I don't think I've even spoken to him before.

"Funny you're so interested, Gino," Irene says coolly, "considering you ran over Brinkley's mailbox last month."

That shuts Gino up. The group combusts with laughter and Honey-Belle pulls Irene into her side. I push past them toward the school entrance, feeling their eyes on my back. Not one of them says a word to me.

* * *

"How's your car?" Danielle asks the moment we meet at our lockers. I never texted her about it, but she must have heard through the grapevine. She looks sympathetic, which means she's gotten over my poor playing last night. I grimace and accept the coffee she hands me, while she accepts the baggie of apple slices I cut up for her this morning. We've traded breakfast like this since the first day of senior year.

"Bumper's all fucked up. But that's nothing compared to my ego." I take a sip of the coffee and brighten. "Whoa, second day in a row you've gotten the perfect cream-to-coffee ratio!"

"Told you I would," Danielle says smugly. Then her expression darkens. "I heard who the other driver was. I hope you smashed the shit out of her car."

The great thing about Danielle is that she would never say anything annoying like *Why didn't you tell me?* It's just not how we work. After Tally dumped me, I couldn't even bring myself to tell my friends. It was Daphne who texted Danielle, and within an hour, Danielle showed up at my house with a gallon of Rocky Road ice cream. She let me sob for half an hour, and then she and my sisters queued up a movie marathon of *John Tucker Must Die*, *She's the Man*, and a slew of other classics.

Danielle has been my best friend since fifth grade, when our teacher's alphabetical seating system landed us right next to each other: Zajac and Zander, the far-flung edge of the class roster. That same year, Danielle ran for class president under the platform of latter-half-of-the-alphabet rights. Pretty much everyone whose last name started with *M* or later voted for her, and after she won, we enjoyed a solid month of standing at the front of the line before our teacher got tired of it.

"Welp, I did. And now I have to drive her till her car's fixed," I say, nicking one of her apple slices.

Danielle stares at me, horrified. "*What?*"

"My mom set it up when she found out we live near each other. She felt bad that Irene wouldn't have a ride."

"That seems like a cruel and unusual punishment."

"Cruel, unusual, and completely on-brand for the year I'm having."

Danielle pointedly ignores the last one. I feel a twinge of embarrassment, knowing I sound pitiful.

"We need to give our moms a talking-to about meddling," Danielle says. "My mom barged in on my shower this morning because she came up with *another* idea I could write about for the Common App essay. And you know what it was? How I'm a great big sister to Teddy. As if admissions counselors care about that."

Danielle and her seven-year-old brother, Teddy, were both adopted. Danielle's mom is Black, like Danielle and Teddy, and her dad is white. Her parents met in a ballroom dancing club in college. Like, for real. Sometimes they spontaneously tango when we're hanging out at their house.

"Why is your mom so worried about this essay?" I ask, grateful for the change of subject.

"She's not." Danielle busies herself with chewing on her thumbnail. "*I'm* worried about it, so she's hovering. Everything I've read says you should avoid mission trips and personal heroes because those are the ultimate clichés. It's better to share an anecdote that reveals your personality. But, like . . . what am I supposed to say?"

We slam our lockers and lean against them, thinking. It's a nice escape from my new reality.

"You're one of the smartest people in our grade," I tell her. "You know so much about this application process, you could probably run the whole guidance department if you wanted to. Just like you're running our basketball team." I freeze, realizing the answer. "Wait! You can tell the story of how you've stepped up to be our coach!"

No one asked Danielle to take over our team. It's

just that Coach Fernandez isn't *really* a coach—she's the computer teacher who runs the robotics club. After our old coach retired last season, the school couldn't find anyone new to coach girls' basketball, so Fernandez agreed to sign on as Official Adult Person; otherwise, we wouldn't have had a season. She pops by practice maybe once or twice a week, but otherwise lets Danielle do her thing.

"It would make a great story," I continue enthusiastically. "You can paint yourself as our fearless leader!"

Danielle flinches like a mosquito landed on her. "No. That's so braggy."

"Dude, the *point* of an admissions essay is to be braggy. Isn't that why you do all the things you do?"

"I do them because I'm a long-suffering perfectionist." She shoots me a familiar smile: the one she uses to deflect attention off herself. It makes me want to hug her and shake her at the same time, because she's so wonderful but so determined to downplay it. It's like she hides herself under a lampshade so no one will see how brightly she shines. Even when she staged a coup in fifth grade for alphabet reversal—so those of us who were always at the end of the line finally got to be up front—she made me switch places with her so she didn't have to stand first in line.

I'm trying to think of another angle for her essay when we're interrupted by our two guy friends, Gunther Thomas and Kevin Todds. They're best friends the same way Danielle and I are; they even have lockers right next to each other. There's something about my friends and the alphabet.

"Look who's the talk of the town," Gunther says, slinging an arm around my shoulders.

I wince, all thought of Danielle's problems forgotten. "You guys heard, too?"

"A couple of the band guys were talking about it," Kevin says. "They didn't actually know your name, but we knew it was you because they described you as 'gay Ginny Weasley.'"

"Charming," I say with a scowl. "Glad to know I have such a powerful reputation."

"Better than Tow Truck Girl," Gunther says, and I punch his shoulder.

We've been friends with the boys since freshman year. Gunther is short and stocky, with thick brown hair and a blond birthmark on the crown of his head. He plays our mascot, the Fighting Reindeer, which means he spends a lot of time prancing around and charging people with his antlers. Kevin is a few inches taller than Gunther, with a round face and acne scars on his light brown skin. His big thing is music. He's been in marching band all four years, and he's trying to line up auditions for college conservatory programs.

"What's new with you, Danielle?" Kevin asks. "I heard you played well last night."

Danielle shrugs and tries to shift into a casual pose,

but she ends up stumbling into her locker. She's gotten increasingly weird around Kevin lately. Like, nursing-a-secret-crush weird. "Yeah, I played all right." She wrinkles her nose. "Better than you at mini golf, anyway."

Kevin presses a hand to his heart. "Damn. Low blow."

Just then, Irene and her entourage sweep into the hallway. It's one of those subtle things where everyone around us continues to go about their business, but you know they're aware of the popular kids entering their midst.

"There's your buddy," Kevin says with a sigh. "Revving up for Homecoming Court this weekend. Another day in the life of the princess."

"And now she's got Scottie to drive her pumpkin carriage," Gunther says, his eyes twinkling.

Irene doesn't look at me as she walks by, but I can sense other people staring at me, hoping for us to interact. I slam my locker closed and try to lose myself in conversation with my friends, but it's like an invisible string has tethered me to Irene and I'll spend the whole day linked to her no matter what I do.

* * *

Predictably, my day is smattered with interruptions from gossipmongers who want to know about the accident. I'm amazed at how many people suddenly know my name—not just the other seniors, but the juniors and underclassmen, too. Some of them are sincere when they ask if I'm okay, but most of them bring it up because they want to hear about Irene.

"Do you guys, like, hang out now?" a wide-eyed girl asks.

"Was she pissed at you for ruining her car?" another whispers.

"Does it feel like carpooling with a Kardashian?" a straight-faced freshman asks.

"*No*," I hear myself saying over and over again. "I literally couldn't care less."

I don't actually see Irene until the end of the day, when we have our only class together: Senior Horizons. It's a joke of a class with an albatross of a teacher. Mrs. Scuttlebaum is a grumpy, bitter old woman who wears the same tulip-patterned cardigan over every outfit. Her smoker's emphysema makes sitting in her lectures that much worse.

When Danielle and I walk into the classroom, a bunch of the guys, led by Gino, start laughing.

"Hey, Abraham, your Uber's here!"

"Can you drive me to the dance this weekend, Zajac?"

"Five stars, Zajac, five stars!"

I can feel my face burning, but I roll my eyes with a bravado I don't feel. Irene, however, crosses her legs and says, "I'd only give her three stars."

The classroom howls with laughter. Irene catches my eye and smirks, almost like we're sharing the joke.

There's a beat where it's silent, and then I say, "I'd give her zero."

The classroom erupts in laughter again. Irene tilts her head at me. She doesn't look angry, but I can't quite read her expression. I ignore her and fish my notebook out of my backpack until Scuttlebaum wheezes at everyone to shut up.

* * *

The most surprising thing happens at the end of the day, when I'm on my way to basketball practice. Danielle and I are walking down the hallway when my cell phone chimes with a sound that stops me cold.

That chime is set to only one person.

Tally Gibson: Why are you driving Irene Abraham around?

I can't sort out how I'm feeling at first. I mean, I'm stunned that Tally's reaching out at all, especially after our talk last night. But I also feel strangely validated. This is proof that she still cares about what I'm doing. That I'm in her head as much as she's in mine.

"Don't engage," Danielle warns, but I ignore her.

Me: How do you know that?
Tally Gibson: Saw it on Gino's Instagram.

Sure enough, when I open the app, Gino's Story is the first to pop up. It's a picture of Irene and me getting out of my car, her looking aloof and me looking grouchy. The caption says *Homecoming queen in her new chariot!! Gay Ginny Weasley for the win!*

Cool. So glad everyone in my universe, including my ex-girlfriend, is seeing this.

"Scottie," Danielle says in a way that means *Don't text her back.*

"I'll just give her the bare minimum so she lays off."

Me: It's just for a few days.

I don't want to tell her about my accident, even though she'll probably find out anyway.

Tally Gibson: Oh.
Tally Gibson: Am I not allowed to know the reason anymore?

"That freaking sociopath," Danielle says, glaring at my phone. "She is so manipulative. Ignore her. You don't owe her an explanation."

I can tell Danielle is getting riled up, so I pocket my phone and continue down the hall. But when we get to the locker room, I take advantage of the chaos to pull out my phone again.

Me: Why do you want to know?

Tally Gibson: Because it's not like you. What happened to hating her guts after the towing thing?

Me: I don't think my opinion of her is any of your business. Not anymore.

Tally Gibson: Wow, okay.

I think that's the end of it, but Tally sends one final text:

Tally Gibson: You should be careful. She can't be good for you.

And that's when it hits me: Tally is *jealous* of my perceived friendship with Irene. She's threatened by the possibility that I could change—scared that I could catapult to popularity even faster than her. The idea leaves me dazed.

When we spill onto the court, I have a bounce in my step. I'm playing as well as I used to—maybe even better. My energy is contagious, and suddenly the whole team is playing at our highest frequency.

I don't think it can get any better, but in the last ten minutes of practice, it does. The auxiliary doors open and, for the first time in my basketball career, we have a cheering section. Literally. Irene has brought her squad to watch us play.

I know she's not doing me any favors. She's only here because her own practice is over and she wants to hurry me along. Still, it feels validating to have an audience, and my teammates seem to feel the same way.

"Are they really here for *us*?" Shelby asks.

Liz Guggenheim, who we call Googy, shakes her head. "Nah, dude. They're here for Scottie." She turns to me, starstruck. "That car accident was the best thing you've ever done."

The whole team looks at me, their mouths twitching with glee. I feel like I'm flying close to the sun.

"Let's run the Hot Dog play," Danielle says, smirking. She passes me the ball, and I hesitate, realizing the gift she's giving me.

"You sure?"

"Make it sail, Scots."

We run the play with a palpable momentum. I zip around the court, and when Googy feeds me the ball, I send it swishing through the basket with a perfect jump shot.

The girls in the stands erupt. Honey-Belle actually *whoops*. Danielle looks at me like we've just found money on the ground.

"Carpool with Irene for as long as you can," she whispers, a gleam in her eye.

And for the first time, I think it's not a bad idea.

4

THE NEXT MORNING, I HUSTLE OUT THE
door with my shoes half tied. Carpooling home last
night was uneventful—we literally didn't speak—but I
don't expect the beast to slumber for long. I plan to be
outside her house way before our seven thirty departure
time, just to prove a point.

But when I pull into Irene's driveway at 7:23, she's
already outside. Of course.

"How long were you waiting?" I ask when she opens
the door.

She takes her time replying, setting her bags all over
my seat. "A few minutes."

It feels like she's saying that just to piss me off, so the
moment she's seated, I jerk the car backward with extra
force. Her coffee thermos spills over the cupholder.

"*Dude*," she says angrily.

"Whoops, sorry," I say breezily. "There are napkins in the glove compartment."

She wipes up the spill more carefully than I expected her to. "Can you turn your music down?" she grumbles. "It's too early for this shit."

"This is Fine Young Cannibals."

"I know who it is."

"Sure you do."

"Oh, you're right, you're the *only* person our age who's really into eighties music. I forgot how exceptionally unique you are."

Instead of responding, I turn up the music until I'm full-on blasting it. She literally scoffs and turns away from me. We don't speak again for the rest of the ride.

Still, that afternoon, before the end of practice, the cheerleaders show up again.

* * *

By Thursday, the whole school is swollen with Homecoming energy. Our principal announces that final voting for the Homecoming Court will take place during homeroom on Friday, so for the rest of the day, it's all anyone can talk about. I hear Irene's name even more than I have in the past two days, and since we're still carpooling, the attention on me intensifies proportionally.

"Homecoming Court is completely underutilized," Gunther muses at lunch. "We're not getting the max value. If there's kings and queens, why not add the scheming advisor or the greedy bishop? I can think of so many people I'd nominate."

We're lying on the cool grass outside the cafeteria, using our backpacks as headrests. The trees above us are still flush with leaves, but they're starting to turn orange and red. Most of the seniors are clustered in groups around us. A few of them are messing with the marquee again. It now reads IM COMING HO.

"What's the equivalent of a court musician?" Kevin asks. "That's what I'd want to be."

"Like a bard?" Danielle says. "Or a troubadour?"

"Troubadour," Kevin echoes, laughing. "What does that even mean? How are you so freaking smart all the time?"

Danielle bites her lip, smiling coyly. "I do this thing called studying."

"So do I, but you don't hear me tossing out words like *troubadour*. I swear your brain retains, like, everything you read."

We're interrupted by Charlotte Pascal, the varsity soccer captain, who approaches us with a couple of her teammates. The soccer girls are notoriously hot, all long legs and California hair. They're also our best athletic team, the only Grandma Earl sport that wins championships and local business endorsements. It's well understood that if you want to be somebody around here, you have two options: cheerleading or soccer. Basketball isn't even a blip on the radar.

Which is why I'm so confused Charlotte is approaching us. Before I can make sense of it, she pushes a homemade Rice Krispies Treat into my hand.

"Er—what—?" I try to say.

"Happy Homecoming," she says, her smile impossibly bright. "I hope you'll consider voting for me for Queen."

Neither the boys nor I reply; Charlotte Pascal is disarmingly gorgeous, and I'm pretty sure none of us has ever spoken directly to her before.

Danielle looks at the three of us and snorts. She squints up at Charlotte and says, "You know canvassing for votes isn't allowed, right?"

"Don't spoil the party," Charlotte says, wrinkling her nose. "It's just a little Homecoming treat."

Against my will, I look across the courtyard, where Irene and her pack have been lounging. She's watching Charlotte with narrowed eyes, her arms splayed across the bench, her henchwomen lurking around her in pleated skirts. Irene and Charlotte's friendship turned enmity has been the source of gossip for almost a year now, and it's only intensified since Irene pulled that "Class Inseparables" stunt during senior superlatives. Based on the way she's looking at Charlotte now, I'm surprised she made a joke about it at all.

Kevin is the first to regain his voice. "Thanks for the treat," he tells Charlotte. "Good luck with Court."

Charlotte gives him a flirtatious smile, glances over

the rest of us, and walks away. I notice she makes a point of avoiding Irene's corner of the yard. It's like feral cats delineating their territory.

"She is very . . . um . . . yes," Gunther says, gulping.

"She's stunning," Kevin says, and Danielle stiffens, "but she scares me."

"I swear I get a vibe from her," I tell them. It's a theory I've brought up before: that Charlotte gives off some queer energy. Tally was the only one who ever agreed with me, but she was more fixated on Charlotte's popularity than her possible sexuality.

"I doubt that," Danielle says. "She's been going out with that Candlehawk dude for, like, a year."

"Doesn't mean she can't be queer," I say.

"Whatever her deal is," Gunther says, "Charlotte's definitely more of a Lady Macbeth than a Homecoming Queen."

* * *

This time, when the cheerleaders show up for the end of our practice, they bring the boys' basketball team with them. There must be at least twenty people watching us now. It's hard to keep my cool, and I can tell my teammates feel the same way; even Danielle seems flushed. But after a few minutes of playing for a crowd, we start to feed off their energy. When we finish our scrimmage with a crisp layup from Googy, the group in the stands cheers loudly.

"This is insane," Danielle says as we're walking out of practice. "No one's ever given a shit about us before." She pauses to high-five one of the boys' players, then looks to me in disbelief. "Damn. I know you hate her guts, but Irene is really doing us a solid."

I shake my head, annoyed at how impressive the whole thing is. "She's not *doing* anything. She's just bored waiting for me to drive her home, and her minions follow her wherever she goes." I point over my shoulder to where the popular kids orbit around Irene like the sun.

Danielle clucks her tongue. "Poor Charlotte and her Rice Krispies Treats don't stand a chance of winning Queen."

We separate, heading to our cars. Danielle says something about going home to tweak her application essay since we'll be busy with Homecoming all weekend. I wish her luck and drop into my car, grateful that it's almost the weekend. I can't wait to get home, take a hot shower, and kick back with a movie.

But Irene doesn't get in the car right away. She loiters off to the side, talking to Honey-Belle with a serious expression on her face. I make a show of starting the ignition and flicking on the lights, but she ignores me.

After a full two minutes of this, I open the door and shout, "Excuse me! Can we go, please?!"

Irene holds up her palm to indicate I should wait. The

56

nerve of it sends me over the edge, and I pound on the horn so it blares across the parking lot.

Irene jumps and shoots me the ugliest look I've ever seen, but she finally steps away from Honey-Belle. She gets into my passenger seat like she's descending into the lowest level of hell. I can almost feel the negative energy crackling off her.

"That was really rude," she snaps.

"Yes, I agree, it *was* very rude of you to keep me waiting."

She shakes her head and jams her seat belt into the buckle. I switch on my music and cruise out of the parking lot feeling like I just won a boxing match.

But then Irene jabs the stereo off.

"What the—?!"

"I'm getting my car back this weekend," she says without preamble. "And Honey-Belle's picking me up tomorrow morning, so I won't need a ride."

I turn the music back on, too distracted by her audacity to understand what she's trying to say. "So?"

"So you don't have to drive me anymore."

That gets my attention. "Wait, really? What about tomorrow afternoon?"

"I don't go home on game days," she says shortly, like I should have known that already. "We get ready at school."

"So this is the last time I have to drive you?"

"Yes. I just said that."

I'm too delighted to be put off by her snark. Only a few more minutes of this tense arrangement, and then I'll be free forever. I'll never have to deal with this girl again.

We're quiet until I remember something that doesn't quite fit with the information she's given me.

"Hold on," I say. "You're not going home before the football game? But don't you have to get ready for Homecoming Court? I mean, like, don't you have to dress up for halftime?"

For a second I think she's gonna tell me it's none of my business. But then: "My mom's bringing my dress. I'll change after we finish our second quarter routines."

I snort. Does she ever *not* plan around her beloved cheerleading?

"So you're gonna be all sweaty in your dress? Why don't you just sit out the routines tomorrow night?"

Now she glares at me. "Would *you* sit on the bench during a big game just so you could look pretty in a dress?"

"No, but that's because what I do is an actual *game*."

She whips her head around. "What are you trying to say?"

"What? I just mean, like, you're not *actually* competing for anything. You're cheering on the competitors. There's no winning or losing for you."

She twists in her seat, more agitated than I've ever

seen her. "Oh okay, and this is coming from someone whose idea of 'competing' is lobbing a ball at a hoop? Cheerleading is more competitive than you can imagine. It's gymnastics meets acrobatics meets dance, with a shit ton of cardio work, not to mention the emotional intelligence it takes to read a crowd's energy—"

"And yet you're not actually winning or losing anything. It's just a performance. A performance you're doing *for someone else.*"

"It's not for *someone else*, it's for ourselves and our own physicality and—"

"It's for the boys' football team. Or their basketball team. Whichever *boys'* team is being worshipped that night."

"Wow, aren't you such a bastion of feminism, tearing down other girls because you think we're oblivious to misogyny—"

"Aren't you, though? Or is it just my imagination that I've never seen your squad at my basketball games before?"

"Have you ever *asked* for us to be there?" she counters. "I don't have time to hold your hand if you can't even be bothered to speak to us. I'm doing more than enough already, captaining two squads during overlapping seasons *and* trying to win Student Athlete of the Year."

This last part takes me by surprise. The Student Athlete of the Year award is just about the highest honor a Grandma Earl senior can win. The last few years, it's almost always gone to soccer or football players.

"You're trying for SAOY?" I ask.

"Don't say that like it's so fucking surprising."

"It *is* surprising. I've never heard of a cheerleader winning that."

"That's because no cheerleader ever has," she snaps, her eyes burning. "But we work just as hard as other student athletes, so why shouldn't we be considered?"

I shake my head and turn away from her.

"*What?*" she spits.

"It just seems like a waste of your energy," I say, knowing very well that I'm playing with fire here. "You're obviously going to win Homecoming Queen tomorrow night, which is a natural extension of being cheerleading captain, but instead of focusing on that, you're thirsting after an athletic award you stand no chance of winning?"

"Fuck you, Zajac," she growls. I only barely register her use of my name; it's jarring coming out of her mouth. "You have got to be the most arrogant, dismissive, judgmental person I've ever met—"

"And who are you to talk?" I say nastily. "You're just a stuck-up cheerleader who's high and mighty enough to think that Homecoming Queen is beneath her."

"Don't you *dare* try to tell me who I am—"

"Ah, right, I forgot I'm not allowed to 'make assumptions' about you. Since it's our last day together, though,

I'll leave you with one final thought." My words tumble out with a reckless, satisfying feeling. I know I'm crossing a line, but I can't stop. People have been singing Irene's praises to my face for *days*, but I know just how shitty she can be. "It's not *my* fault you're so fucking insecure about being a cheerleader or that no one, including your own mother, takes you seriously about it. So figure out your own shit and stop taking it out on other people."

The silence between us cuts like a shard of glass. Irene turns very slowly in my direction. Her jaw is clenched. Her eyes are dark fire. They're also, to my shock, slightly wet.

I'm breathing hard; she's hardly breathing at all. I don't know what else to do, so I twist the volume dial until it's all the way up, so loud that it pounds in my ears. Irene says nothing. She sits eerily still in the passenger seat, her arms crossed over her practice hoodie.

When we finally pull into her driveway, she throws off her seat belt and snatches her bags from the back seat. Just as she's about to get out of the car, she punches my stereo off. I can only gawk at her.

I open my mouth to say something, but before I can figure out what, she slams the door and stalks off into her house.

* * *

That night, my sisters and I curl up in Thora's bed to watch *Teen Witch* at Daphne's request. Pickles and

BooBoo prowl across our legs, restless. They haven't been allowed in Mom's garden for several days.

"I messed up today," I say when we're halfway through the movie.

"Did you hit another car?" Thora asks, and I shove her while Daphne laughs.

"No. I was an asshole to Irene."

"Nemesis Girl?"

"Yeah."

"Well, she's your nemesis. You're supposed to be an asshole."

Daphne frowns. "What happened?"

I tell them about our spat—and how ugly I was to her. "I don't know why I said that thing about her mom," I say feebly. "I don't usually go for people's weak spots."

"No, you don't," Thora says thoughtfully. "Sounds more like something your ex would do."

I stare at her. "Tally might be the worst, but she wouldn't do *that*. She's not outright malicious."

"Yeah, she would. I watched her do it to you for months. She got completely in your head, making you worry that you're not good enough. You've been a walking insecurity since you dated her."

I pause the movie. "You think I'm a walking insecurity?"

Thora looks straight at me. She never glosses over things. "Right now? Yes. And there's no reason you should be. You're smart and cute and really good at basketball. You should be thriving."

A trickle of bile runs down my throat. "No one else seems to think that."

"Who cares what anyone else thinks? What do *you* think?"

"Thora, do you *really* believe that no one else's opinion matters?"

"Absolutely." She shrugs like it's as easy as two plus two. "At the end of the day, I'm the only person living my life. Why should I answer to anyone else?"

"You obviously don't remember high school very well."

She snorts. "Of course I do. The unspoken social hierarchy sucks. But you know what I've figured out since then?" She dances her fingers in front of my eyes. "It's all perception, Scots. Making people see what you want them to see. If you want them to think you matter, start acting like they should *already know* that you matter."

Daphne nods. "Fake it till you make it."

"Exactly," Thora says.

I scratch BooBoo's ears, thinking. "You wanna know something stupid? Carpooling with Irene is the coolest I've felt all year. Like, it's the first time people have paid attention to me. Even Tally was jealous. How fucked up is that?"

"Tally was jealous?" Thora laughs humorlessly. "God,

that girl is a fucking case study. She's probably worried that you're secretly dating Irene."

I snort. The idea of that is unthinkable. "I would never. I can't stand that girl."

"Maybe Irene isn't as bad as you think," Daphne says. "Why do you hate her, anyway?"

I pause, considering. I never confided in my sisters about the tow truck incident. It would only open a can of worms if I told them now.

"She's just a jerk," I say. "She . . . kinda messed with me last year."

Thora's eyes flash. "What'd she do?"

I shake my head. "Nothing. Seriously, nothing. I just don't like her."

I can tell Thora wants to press me on it, but she doesn't. She plants a kiss on my head and goes back to watching the movie with Daphne.

You've been a walking insecurity . . .

Is that true? Judging by the constant ache in my chest, I have to believe it is. But when did I become this way? I didn't used to care about my social status; I was content to fly under the radar. But that was before Tally. It was also before the tow truck incident.

I always wanted to confront Irene about that prank. I wanted to scream that it was a completely disproportionate reaction to me knocking a drink on her. But the truth is, I was afraid it had nothing to do with spilling my drink. That maybe it was a cruel whim of hers, of all the popular kids', because I was more of a social pariah than I even knew. The queer, gangly ginger who had no right to be at their party.

After all, isn't that why Tally left me? Because she could see that, too?

5

FRIDAY IS THE START OF HOMECOMING
weekend. I wake up early, straighten my hair, and pull
on the Fighting Reindeer shirt I've had since freshman
year. Daphne hogs the bathroom mirror, painting bright
red *GE* letters on her cheeks. The middle schoolers are
always more excited than anyone for the Homecoming
game.

In a twist of irony, this is the earliest I'm ready to
leave all week. If I was picking up Irene today, there's
no chance she'd beat me to her driveway. I almost wish
she needed a ride just so I could rub it in her face. And
maybe so I could apologize for what I said yesterday.

Instead, I use the extra time to pick up coffee for my
friends. Sweet Noelle's, the best coffee shop in town,
has painted its windows for the game tonight. When the
barista sees me in my Fighting Reindeer shirt, she grins
and gives me a free chocolate muffin. I stuff my face

with it when I get back in my car, relishing in the privacy of driving alone again.

But when I pull into school a few minutes later, *alone* hits differently. People glance at my car, but when I'm the only one to get out of it, they turn away. I guess they don't care about me unless I'm shuttling Irene around.

I'm back to being a nobody, and I hate to admit it stings.

"Hey, happy Friday!" Gunther says when I show up with the coffee tray. "Why the special treat? Is it just because you love us?"

"Because I love you, and because I'm free." I drop my backpack and lean against Danielle's locker. "No more carpooling for me."

I thought it would feel euphoric to announce that, but surprisingly, I feel kind of bereft.

"Ding-dong, the witch is dead," Kevin says. He passes the coffees around, checking to see their descriptions first. "You sure you want this, Gunther?"

Gunther grimaces. He's on a black coffee kick because he thinks it makes him more sophisticated. "I guess. Send thoughts and prayers." He swallows the first sip like a kid taking medicine.

"And hazelnut with extra espresso for Danielle," Kevin says, passing her the cup. "What's the extra shot for today? The AP Lit test?"

"Yeah, 'cause I have to beat you," Danielle says, hiking her eyebrows at him.

Kevin laughs. "It's not a competition if you're the only one in it, Danielle."

"Still gonna leave you in the dust."

"We get it, you guys are smart," Gunther says, rolling his eyes. "Can we focus on the topic at hand? Scottie's back to being one of us."

Kevin and Danielle laugh. "I have to admit, I'm kind of bummed," Danielle says. "I was getting used to our cheering section."

"Yeah, I was ready for the cheerleaders to start cheering at your games," Gunther says. "Which means I'd get to, too."

"They'd never switch to cheering for us," I say.

"They might. I heard a bunch of the cheerleaders talking about how good y'all are." Gunther pauses, and for some reason his cheeks flush pink. "Honey-Belle said you're her *she*-roes."

Danielle and I laugh, but before we can respond, my phone chimes with that dreaded tone.

Tally Gibson: Glad to see you're free of her.

"How does she *know* these things?" I whine, showing my friends the message.

Danielle huffs as usual, but Kevin pulls out his phone. "Damn," he mutters. "Gino needs to get a life."

He shows us Gino's Instagram Story: a video of Irene and Honey-Belle getting out of Honey-Belle's Jeep. The caption says *No more Uber service, back to riding with the elites!!*

"The 'elites'?" Danielle says with disgust. "God, they practically parody themselves."

"Weren't you just saying you enjoyed their cheering section?" Kevin teases, and Danielle shoves him.

I don't say anything. A hot wave of embarrassment flushes over my body. I'm mortified that Gino would write that. I'm even more mortified that Tally saw it.

* * *

During first period, we have a special extended schedule so the video journalism kids can broadcast their latest news segment. It's Homecoming-centric, with a choppy story about the football team's practice regimen and interviews with the student gov kids about their decorating plans. The last segment is about Homecoming Court. Ten people from my grade are nominated for the King and Queen spots, and one of the Cleveland triplets, who have their hands in everything that goes on here, nabbed interviews with them.

"*Yeah, I mean, it's an honor,*" one guy says.

"*I'm so excited, just so, so excited,*" a peppy girl grins.

Charlotte Pascal is up next. "*To get this kind of recognition from your peers, it's just—what more can you ask for?*"

And then Irene's face pops up, and I squirm uncomfortably in my seat.

"*Are you so excited?*" the Cleveland triplet asks.

"*Yeah, it's a trip,*" Irene says with a casual flick of her hair. She sounds like she couldn't give two shits.

"*Are you nervous?*"

Irene blinks. "*For the game, yeah. I'm concerned about getting our routines right. We've been working our asses off, and right now I'm splitting my time between football and basketball cheerleading, with different sets for each—so I want to make sure we do everything right on Friday night.*"

"Why didn't they bleep out 'asses'?" my civics teacher asks. "And what's with this girl's answer?"

"She's cheerleading captain," one of my classmates says.

"So?"

"So that's all she ever talks about. Her friend Honey-Belle says she's running for Student Athlete of the Year."

"As a *cheerleader?*" someone sneers.

The shot changes to another nominee, but I stop listening. An unwelcome feeling stretches over me, like I'm starting to understand Irene Abraham even if I don't want to.

* * *

Practice that afternoon is dead. The whole team seems to understand that our short-lived glory is over. When we finish for the day with no one in the gym but ourselves,

70

the mood is sour and defeated. Googy tries to lighten things by asking me to hit Irene's car again. Nobody laughs.

When Danielle and I walk outside, my irritation spikes. There's a number of fans already tailgating by the football field and I'm bitter to realize they'll never show up for one of my games in the same way. No wonder Tally wanted to transfer.

Danielle and I swing by her house to get ready for the game. During dinner with her family, my mood finally brightens. Mr. and Mrs. Zander ask about basketball, about the dance tomorrow night, about college applications. Teddy sits at the table with his legs knocking excitedly, dressed in a reindeer onesie that he insists on pairing with an alien headband.

"Hold on," Mrs. Zander says when we're about to leave. I think she's about to compliment our homemade Grandma Earl T-shirts, but instead she eyes Danielle's makeup with suspicion. "Who you dressing up for?"

"Nobody," Danielle says, too casually. "It's the Homecoming game, Mom."

"I used to love Homecoming weekend," Danielle's dad says, oblivious to the undercurrent of tension between his wife and daughter. "Everyone was so distracted with the pomp and circumstance that my friends and I were finally able to play Dungeons & Dragons in peace."

"I've never seen you try a smoky eye," Danielle's mom continues. "Scottie, who's she trying to impress?"

I shake my head. "Nobody. As far as I can tell, Danielle's just in love with basketball."

Danielle hikes her eyebrows as if to say *Ha, see?*, but I know her well enough to pick up on the nervous way she's messing with her jacket zipper. She's probably thinking about seeing Kevin on the field when marching band performs during halftime.

The stadium is swelling with people by the time we join the admission line. The drums are booming, the sky lights are bright, and the air smells like hickory. I remember Tally squeezing my hand last year, promising we could escape to her car if we got too cold. Candlehawk's Homecoming game is tonight, too, and she's probably loving the thrill of a bigger stadium, the brighter lights, the news crews planted on the field to film their student body.

It's cold on the metal bleachers. The band is stationed behind us, blasting their trumpets and pounding their drums. The cheerleaders are down on the sidelines, calmly going about their warm-up stretches in the midst of the building excitement. If I squint, I can just make out Irene, a dark ponytail directing the rest of the team. She's obviously in her element. Not that I care.

The game starts a few minutes later. Our players sprint onto the field through a handmade banner of an old lady in a football helmet. The cheerleaders dive straight into their routines, amping up the crowd until we're in a full-blown frenzy, and I hear the echo of Irene lecturing me about cheerleaders' emotional intelligence.

A few minutes before halftime, the other team fumbles the ball and one of our guys runs it back for a touchdown. The crowd is roaring, riding the wave of the play. The cheerleaders pop up to run a victory routine. Irene is at the front of their formation, directing the pyramid before she goes to take her place.

I look away, watching the football players switch out the offensive and defensive lines. Then everyone gasps.

The cheerleader at the top of the pyramid has fallen off.

There's a prolonged pause, followed by a rumbling of anxiety from the crowd, as the cheerleading coach and sports medicine team rush to the sidelines. The cheerleaders break out of their pyramid and hover around the girl, blocking everyone's view. The announcer's voice wavers as he says, "Hold on here, folks, looks like we've had an incident on the sidelines . . ."

After a long, suspended moment, the huddle clears and the girl hobbles to her feet. Irene presses close to her, talking to her as the sports medicine guys heave her forward on one foot.

"And thank goodness, it looks like she's okay," the announcer says, his voice hearty again. "Sprained ankle, from the looks of it. Yet another sacrifice these cheerleaders make to support our young men."

"Sprained ankle, shit," Danielle mumbles.

"They're not cheering just to support the '*young men*,'" I say, annoyed.

"I mean . . . yeah. But the point is, I hope that girl's okay."

I don't answer. Irene has disappeared, leaving the cheerleaders in disarray on the sidelines. I don't see her again until the Homecoming Court parades onto the field during halftime. She glides along between her parents, easily visible because of her long dark hair. I wonder if her mom has been here all along to watch her routines, or if she only came to escort her for Court.

When they announce Homecoming Queen, no one is surprised to hear the name Irene Abraham. She smiles as she accepts the crown and flowers and poses for pictures with her King. To anyone else, it must look like she's radiant with happiness, but my instincts tell me she's berating herself for the cheerleading stunt gone wrong.

6

ON SATURDAY, DAD AND I GET UP EARLY TO take my car to the Sledd Brothers Auto Shop. They promise us the bumper is an easy fix, but with the amount of business they've had lately, it's going to take several days before I get my car back. My parents will have to drop me off at school until then. When the mechanics tell us the estimated cost, I feel weird knowing that Irene's insurance policy will pay for it.

The rest of the day is devoted to getting ready for the Homecoming dance. Mom and Daphne chirp about it all afternoon, bombarding me with ideas for how to do my hair as if I know what the hell they're talking about. Finally, Thora takes pity on me and sets up a hair and makeup station in the basement. She hangs my suit on the door for "inspiration," queues up music on her portable speaker, and brews a fresh pot of coffee to keep us in the zone. Daphne plops down beside her, offering input, and I sit still and silent, letting my sisters take the reins.

Thora and Daphne move effortlessly through Girl World. They speak a common language I've never understood, with shimmery words like *contouring* and *bandeaus* and *bralettes*. It's their birthright, this ability to be like any other girl. I've never had the same birthright, and I've understood that since long before I heard the word *gay*.

Maybe that's one of the reasons I liked Tally: She had no qualms about moving through both worlds. Now I have to straddle the two without her.

I breathe easier when Thora and Daphne agree on a hairstyle and reassure me of how stunning I'm going to look. Daphne hands me a coffee and smiles a giddy, ecstatic smile. Her own coffee looks too big for her little hands, but she takes a practiced sip and smacks her lips together the way Thora does.

* * *

From the moment I walk into the dance, my heart hurts. All I can think about is Tally and how this should have been our perfect senior Homecoming. I'm so preoccupied that I miss half the things Danielle and Gunther are talking about. There could be a wild bull chasing me down and I wouldn't even notice.

But speaking of, there's Irene.

She's dancing with a group of friends, and she looks

genuinely happy, but I don't care. Danielle, meanwhile, is trying to act like she's not eyeing the stage every other second. Kevin is up there, bleeding his red guitar, his black twists catching the light above him. He's dressed in slacks and a button-up shirt, but still wearing his trademark string hoodie on top.

Over by the punch bowl, Charlotte Pascal is making a show of pouring little paper cups for her friends. When one of them shifts to the side, I see a silver flask in Charlotte's hand.

I catch Gunther's eye and nod toward the drinks table. He watches for a second, then raises his eyebrows and asks, "Feeling thirsty?"

We sidle up toward Charlotte. Before we can say anything, she speaks to us out of the corner of her mouth.

"It's only for people who voted for me."

Gunther side-eyes me. "We both did," he lies.

"Everyone keeps saying that, and yet that bitch is wearing my crown." She skirts her eyes judgmentally over my suit. I feel my face flush. "Dollar donation on Venmo," she says finally. "Title it 'senior fundraiser.' Loop around the table and come back at the end of the song."

Gunther and I peel off to the end of the refreshments table, where we pull up our phones to Venmo Charlotte. There's been a whole slew of payments in the last few minutes, all of them referencing the fundraiser with various emojis tacked onto the end.

We loop back after the song ends. Charlotte slides two cups down the table, still not looking at us.

"Eugh," Gunther says, taking a sip before I can. "This tastes like the inside of my mascot costume."

I swallow some down and feel my throat burn. The taste is definitely nasty.

"Gross," I say, licking my lips. "That's way more vodka than punch."

I never drink—or at least, I haven't since the party last year—but it feels good to have something to do. The alcohol hits me right when the slow songs come on. Couples are grabbing each other to sway and brush foreheads and make out, and I remember Tally at prom last year, whispering silly jokes in my ear.

I hear Thora's words in my head again. Was Tally really all that bad? And if she was, why do I feel so sad and lost without her?

I slip away from the crowd without caring where I'm going. The locker-lined hallway is a welcome breath of air, moonlit and empty. I sink to the floor and rest my head against the cold locker behind me.

Impulsively, I grab my phone. Tally's Instagram Story has been updated with a post from Candlehawk's Homecoming dance. It's a snippet of some girl pretending to spank some guy while the crowd cheers them on. Tally's laughter blares through the speaker, sweet and exultant.

My throat is tight before I can stop it. I tuck my

phone away and wipe my eyes. Then I just sit there, trying to make sense of how this happened, how I lost Tally and myself in the same fell swoop.

I'm about to get up when a pair of girls comes clacking down the hallway. They're swishing in their dresses, whispering sharply at each other. I don't have time for anyone else's drama, especially tonight, so I'm about to dash out of there when I catch the sound of a voice I've been hearing all week.

"I'm not in the mood, Honey-Belle," Irene is saying. "I've got enough on my plate right now."

"One dance isn't gonna hurt you," Honey-Belle insists. "It'll be good for you. Come on, you just won Homecoming Queen! You deserve some fun."

"With the girls you've been picking out? Fat chance."

My heart jolts unexpectedly. Did I just hear right? *Girls?*

"You're picky as hell," Honey-Belle continues. "What was wrong with Madeleine Kasper? She's one of the cutest sophomores—"

"You know I can't date a sophomore—"

"Stop being so uppity. There's someone out there for you. You just need to open your eyes and receive what the universe wants you to have!"

I can't move. There's a faint ringing in my chest. It's bizarre to hear Irene chatting away with her best friend like this—almost like I'm seeing behind a curtain—and

I still can't get over the girls thing. Is it common knowledge that Irene Abraham likes girls? Did I somehow miss that memo?

"I can't worry about dating right now," Irene says. She sounds tired. "Mom's on my ass about paying them back for that stupid insurance deductible, but she still doesn't know I used my savings on cheer camp last summer. Unless I quit cheerleading and find a job, there's no way I'll be able to—"

"You can't quit cheerleading," Honey-Belle cuts in. "This is the first time one of us has a real shot at SAOY! How many years until another cheerleader even comes close to that?"

"Tell that to my mom," Irene says.

"She'll come around," Honey-Belle says, kicking a heel up against the lockers. "She knows how important this is to you. Did you tell her about Benson yet?"

"No. What's the point, when they're not gonna let me go?"

"But that cheerleading coach wants you, Irene!" I put the pieces together: Benson University is a school in Virginia, and it sounds like Irene might have a spot on their cheerleading squad. "And I know you want to go there, even if you're trying to act all cool about it." It sounds like there's a small tussle and I imagine Honey-Belle trying to smother Irene with a hug and positive vibes.

"You know I can't go there without a scholarship. My parents would never agree to that when I could go to an in-state school for much less. The Benson coach said she can fight for me if I win something as impressive as SAOY, but what if I don't?"

"Don't think like that. You have a real shot."

"I hope so." She sounds downcast, defeated. "Charlotte's already trying to sabotage me. She's going around telling everyone that even if cheerleading is quote, unquote, 'a legitimate sport,' that I'm obviously not a good captain if I'm letting girls fall during our routines."

"That jealous, snaggletoothed heifer," Honey-Belle says, and I have to choke back a laugh. It's the first time I've ever heard her angry.

"Plus, I can't figure out whether winning Queen helps or hurts my chances," Irene continues. "Do people think girls are less athletic when they win a You're Pretty Award?"

"Absolutely not. You're a boss. Everyone knows that."

"Maybe," Irene says. She doesn't sound convinced. "I don't know, Honey-Belle. I have to win SAOY to afford Benson, and I can't win SAOY if I'm not cheering, but I can't pay for this deductible unless I quit the squad and get a job."

"You have to tell your parents," Honey-Belle says. "Just explain it to them. Give them a chance to understand."

"They won't understand, especially my mom. She'll make me quit the squad and work at her practice to pay them back. She'll finally have some real leverage to use in her favor."

Irene's voice is different than I've ever heard before. It provokes a feeling in me that I can't quite name. It takes a moment to realize it's sympathy. She has a lot more on her shoulders than I thought. That doesn't excuse how shitty she's been toward me, but still. I feel for her.

Irene sighs, Honey-Belle soothes her, and they finally leave. I wait it out for a minute before I follow suit.

* * *

When the dance ends, it's collectively decided that the night will continue at the Christmas Emporium. It's a well-known secret that Grandma Earl students have been hosting after-parties there for decades. Plus, Honey-Belle has a key to let everyone into the Santa room, where the Earl-Hewetts keep their stock of Santa Claus statues that kids take pictures with when they're drunk.

Kevin drives us since he's the only one who didn't partake in the "senior fundraiser." Gunther takes the front while Danielle and I sit in the back seat, holding Kevin's guitar case across our laps. Gunther helped himself to another two rounds of fundraiser while I was out in the locker hallway, so he's giggly and goofy. He won't stop laughing about how he has to pee.

The Emporium garage is open when we arrive. People are milling about in their suits and dresses, half inside the Emporium, half outside in the parking lot. The air is cool and smells like dead leaves and campfire.

As my friends walk off to survey the Santa statues, I take a moment to drink water and mull over something that's been fermenting in my brain. It fizzled to life sometime in the last hour, after I overheard Irene and Honey-Belle at the dance. It's a wild, ridiculous idea, but I can't shake the feeling that it could be exactly what I need to solve my problems. I mean, didn't my sisters tell me to fake it till I make it?

I make the decision and march toward Irene before I lose my nerve.

She's standing with a small crowd of friends who look up as I approach. It's outside the prescribed social norms for me to seek them out, but right now I don't care.

"Irene," I say loudly.

"Yeah?" she says, an edge to her voice. She crosses her arms over her apricot dress and eyes me warily.

"I need to talk to you." I give her a meaningful look. "It's important."

I've never been so bold before. But why shouldn't I be, especially now that I know all her weak spots?

She follows me out back behind the Emporium, where the long-forgotten train tracks are. There are fewer people out here; it'll be easier to have a private conversation. I scoot onto the track incline and wait as she folds herself down next to me.

"Well?" she prompts.

I tuck my knees up, wrapping my arms around my pant legs like this is the most casual conversation I could imagine.

"I heard you and Honey-Belle talking in the hallway," I say, looking her square in the eye. "I had no idea you were into girls."

There's a flicker of alarm in her eyes, but she sets her expression and gives me a steely look. "Why are you *always* in the wrong place at the wrong time?"

Of course she wants to blame *me* for her decision to have a private conversation in a public place. "I was already in that lane," I say coolly. "You're the one who failed to check if the coast was clear."

She laughs bitterly. "Clever. Love the metaphor."

"Right? It just came to me in a burst of inspiration."

Irene shakes her head and combs her fingers through her hair. For the first time, it reads to me as a nervous habit instead of vanity. I expect her to deny everything, or to threaten me, but her response is something else entirely.

"If you're planning some sort of payback for what I did to your car, then just get it over with."

I'm so surprised I sputter out a laugh. "What?"

She searches my eyes. "What do you want, Zajac?"

"Do I strike you as the blackmailing type? That is seriously fucked up. I'm not talking about that at all. I would never out you."

In the moonlight, her eyes relax the slightest bit. "So what are you talking about?"

"I think we can help each other. How much is your car insurance deductible?"

"What?"

"Just answer the question, Abraham. How much?"

She sets her mouth. "A thousand."

"Wooooof." It's higher than I expected, but still within range for this plan to work. "And how much do you have right now?"

"Not enough. Why do you care?"

"I have a fat wad of cash from my summer job. Enough to cover your deductible." It's true: I worked hours and hours at the Chuck Munny Cineplex, the vintage movie theater in town, sweeping up popcorn and watching old films. I'd been keeping the cash as extra spending money, especially since I'm planning to attend college in-state for free, but now I have a much better way to use it.

Irene narrows her eyes. "And why would you give that money to me?"

"Okay, listen." I clear my throat. This is the part that could either go beautifully or disastrously. Once I put this out there, she'll be able to put me on blast if she wants to. But I have an instinct that she won't.

"Everyone at Grandma Earl *and* Candlehawk thinks my team is a joke," I say. "That *I'm* a joke. But you have the clout to change their minds. I want to get the team some attention so we'll start playing better and beat Candlehawk in the Christmas Classic." I pause, remembering Tally's tinny laugh on my phone while I sat by myself in that empty hallway. "And as you have no doubt realized, Tally Gibson did a number on me. I want to make her jealous and I think I know how. The most she's paid attention to me lately was when she heard I was giving you rides. If she sees me hanging out with you for real, she'll lose her mind."

Irene hikes her eyebrows. "So you want to pay me to hang out with you?"

My heart thumps wildly beneath my suit jacket. "I want to pay you to date me."

There's a swell of silence.

Then Irene laughs into the cold air. "Date you?" she says shrilly, like I've just suggested the craziest thing in the world. "As in, pretend to be your girlfriend? You're not serious right now."

"I absolutely am."

"Is this some kind of *Can't Buy Me Love* fantasy?"

I'm momentarily stymied. "You know that movie?"

She rolls her eyes. "God, you really do think you're unique," she says under her breath. "You're telling me you actually want to pay me to make you more popular? You do realize that's not a *thing* anymore, right?"

"Bullshit it's not a thing. Or are you telling me the cheerleaders and basketball guys have been showing up to my practices out of the goodness of their hearts?"

"So you're trying to use me."

"I'm manipulating a situation so we both benefit. You *need* the money if you want to keep cheerleading and win SAOY. This might get your mom off your back, don't you think?"

She breathes. I can see the wheels turning in her head.

"So you *do* want to out me, in a sense," she says flatly. She sounds the least bit vulnerable.

This is the part I was worried about. "Only if *you* want to. You don't strike me as the kind of person who lets others determine her narrative. If you want to do this, great, we'll announce it however you want to. If you don't want to, that's fine. I'll walk away and never bring it up again. I won't even tell my best friend."

She wraps her arms around her calves. "I wouldn't care if you told Danielle."

I blink. "You know that my best friend is Danielle?"

She stares at me like I've grown another head. "Yes? Everyone knows your best friend is Danielle. I voted for y'all for 'Class Inseparables,' for fuck's sake."

I'm at a loss for words. I was sure she knew nothing about my life—at least not until we got in that fender bender. "Oh. Well . . . I voted for you and Charlotte Pascal."

Irene snorts. It's the first time she's appreciated one of my jokes.

"You should know that I don't take coming out

lightly," I say delicately. "But I do think you can use it to your advantage, especially when it comes to getting more votes for SAOY. People are *all* about the queer trend right now. They'd bottle our hormones and sell them if they could."

Irene side-eyes me. "You're more cynical than I realized."

"It's true, and you know it. What would you have to lose?" I hold out my hands like I'm offering her the world on a gold platter. "You already won Homecoming Queen. Your cheer routines are amazing, minus the little mishap last night, which I'm guessing only happened because you were distracted with worrying about having to quit cheerleading. And now you can push boundaries by not *only* being the first cheerleader to win SAOY, but by openly 'dating' a girl in the months leading up to it."

"Do you think I'm not pushing boundaries already?" she asks sharply. "How many desi cheerleaders do you know?"

I shrug, trying to play it cool. "Just you, I'm pretty sure. So why not go big or go home?"

She purses her lips. "For how long?"

"Until we play Candlehawk in the district championship in February."

"*Four* months?"

"It's not as long as it sounds," I insist. "Look, if you can get your squad to cheer for us, it'll have a huge effect on our playing. We'll beat Candlehawk in the Christmas Classic, and then we'll ride that high straight into the championship, by which time you will *surely* have snagged a nomination for SAOY."

She shakes her head stubbornly. I have no choice but to pull out the big guns.

"Or . . . ," I say innocently, "you could quit cheerleading for four months while you work off your debts to your parents. Not sure that would help you win SAOY, though, which means you'd have no shot at going to Benson."

I feel shitty about leveraging her dream, but I need her to say yes. My heart is almost beating out of my chest at this point.

Irene runs her finger along her mouth, thinking. "Will you give me the money up front?"

"Yes."

"And you won't tell anyone we're doing this?"

"Not if you don't."

She smooths her bottom lip again. It's actually very distracting. "I can't believe I'm considering this."

"Neither can I," I admit. "But I also can't believe you've converted me into a secret cheerleading fan who will probably vote for you for SAOY. I guess this is just an unprecedented week."

She looks at me, her eyes twinkling the tiniest bit. "Fine," she says, extending her hand for me to shake.

I grip her warm, soft palm and squeeze. A rush of excitement shoots up through my arm. This is the first thing to go right in a long, long time.

"How do we start?" Irene asks.

"You got your car back from the shop, right?"

"Yes."

"Good." I smirk. "First step: *You* drive us to school on Monday."

7

IRENE PICKS ME UP AT 7:22 ON MONDAY morning. I know the exact minute because she calls three times in a row while I'm blow-drying my hair.

"I'm coming!" I bark into the phone.

She clucks her tongue and hangs up without a word.

When I step into the driveway, there's an unforeseen complication. Thora is standing beneath the carport, keys in hand, glowering at Irene's car.

"Uh . . . good morning," I say to Thora.

"Is it?" Her eyes narrow. "Mom told me I need to give you a ride because your car's still at Sledd Brothers, but it looks like Regina George got the same memo."

Irene stares between us through the windshield of her car. She looks impatient.

"I thought I'd told Mom I had a ride." I swing my backpack over my shoulder, trying to look like I'm in a hurry. "Sorry about that, but don't worry, I'm all set!"

I step away toward Irene's car, but Thora grabs me by the arm.

"Do you wanna explain why your *nemesis* is giving you a ride?"

"Um, it's kind of complicated, I'll tell you tonight—"

She holds my arm tighter and waits.

I'm not sure how to explain this to her. I knew I'd have to convince my family more than anyone that Irene and I are dating, but I thought I'd have a few more days to prepare for it. And Thora is the *last* person I want to start with. She's way too shrewd for this shit.

"There's been an . . . unexpected love development."

Thora snorts. "With *her*? She hit your car last week. And you said she bullied you last year."

I shrug. "Forgive and forget, right? People change."

"Scots. Have you lost your mind? This bitch is gonna mess you up just like Tally did."

The car door swings open. Irene steps out, whipping her sunglasses off with a move that suggests she's ready for a death match. "Hi," she says, her voice level and cool. "This bitch's name is Irene."

Thora turns on her heel to face her. She's several inches taller than Irene, but Irene holds her own and returns the glare Thora's giving her. I hover between them, my pulse quickening.

"So you're the one who's messed with my sister *twice* now," Thora says, dangerously calm. She prowls around the hood of Irene's car, examining it. "Hmm. Seems like your ride is good as new. Wouldn't it be a shame if my hand slipped?"

She holds up her car key and mimes like she's going to scrape the driver's side door.

"Thora, don't—" I say.

Irene sets her mouth. "I would deserve it. So if that's what you need to do, go ahead."

She takes a step back, clearing a path toward her car, and my brain short-circuits. This is the first admission of guilt I've heard from her. Thora narrows her eyes even further.

"We're running late," I say, striding toward the passenger side. "Thora, please, we need to go."

"Why did you bully my sister?" Thora asks.

Irene's eyes flicker toward me. She has the grace to look ashamed. "I made a mistake."

"A mistake," Thora says with a hollow laugh. "Bullying isn't a mistake. Have you apologized?"

By the way Irene exhales, I can tell how humiliating this is for her. "No, I haven't."

Thora doesn't reply at first. Then she tilts her chin and says, "I'm surprised you can stand with a spine that weak."

Irene's cheeks color. "I'm working on it."

There's a prolonged silence. Thora stares directly at Irene, unabashedly assessing her. Then she turns to me. I can tell by the fold of her mouth that she's relenting. For now.

"You call me if she fucks with you," Thora tells me. She sends one last glare at Irene, then slides past us and makes her way into the house.

Irene gets back in the car without another word. I'm still reeling as I drop my bags in the back seat. When I take a peek around the trunk of her car, the rear bumper looks good as new.

* * *

Irene's car is spotlessly clean and sweet scented; there's a vanilla air freshener attached to the AC and the windshield looks like she scrubs it regularly. There's a single elegant cheer ribbon hanging from the rearview mirror. She's playing music, but it's too soft for me to hear.

"Your sister looked like she was trying to burn me with her eyes," Irene says in a clipped tone. "If you'd come outside on time, we could have avoided that whole stupid altercation."

I snort. "You know how else we could have avoided it? If you'd never messed with me in the first place."

"I said it was a mistake."

"Some mistake."

Irene pops a stick of gum in her mouth. She drums her fingers anxiously on the steering wheel. "If we're going to be *in love*, can you please try to run on time?"

"Can you please try to act like the kind of girl another girl might fall in love with?"

I expect another retort, but a shadow crosses over her eyes. "I don't need this on top of everything else today."

I avoid looking at her. Maybe I should be reveling in her discomfort, but all I can feel is empathy. I may hate her, but I wouldn't wish homophobia on anyone.

"It won't be that bad." I tap my fingers on the console like this is all very nonchalant; I don't want her to think I care. "No one really said anything when I came out. Just try to act like it's something people should have known all along."

Irene doesn't say anything. The silence between us feels heavy. She clears her throat and says, "Play a song."

I think I've misheard her. "What?"

"Play a song," she says impatiently. "You've got one for every damn mood, don't you? So play something upbeat. Something that's—I don't know—"

I know what she's trying to say. *Something to get me through this.*

I scroll through my library, hovering over a few options, until I find the perfect track. Perfect because it's so ridiculous. I connect to her Bluetooth, press PLAY, and wait for her reaction.

BUM. BUM BUM BUM—

I can tell the exact second she recognizes it, because she gives me that look.

"*Really?*" she asks.

I shrug and turn the volume up. "Oh come on. 'Eye

of the Tiger' is everyone's favorite pump-up song. It has major don't-fuck-with-me energy."

"It has cheesy-sports-movie energy."

"Yeah, and you love sports. You're an *athlete*, remember?"

"Screw you," she says, but her heart's not in it.

"Fine," I say, taking pity on her. "What's your favorite song?"

"I'm not telling you that."

"Favorite movie, then. We'll do the soundtrack."

She shakes her head. "No, this will work." She flexes her hands on the steering wheel. I pretend not to notice that her knee is shaking. Is this *really* a good idea?

When we pull into the school parking lot, my hands are sweating. Irene kills the ignition. "Are you ready?" she asks. There's a slight quake in her voice.

"We don't have to go through with this if you don't want to."

She turns to me with her jaw set. "I wouldn't have agreed if I didn't want to."

We stare at each other across the console. It's almost like a game of chicken, where one of us is hoping the other will back down first. I know it's not too late to call this off, but I don't want to. I think of my team. Of the haughty Candlehawk players. Of the shame I felt when everyone laughed at my car being towed away.

Most of all, I think of Tally.

"Fine," I say. "Sell this with all you've got."

She snorts, tucking her keys into her bag. "You're forgetting that I spend half my time performing. It's *you* we need to worry about."

I ignore the jab and push my way out of the car. We stand up at the same time, side-eyeing each other across the roof. Already, I can feel the attention on us. Heads are turning our way.

Irene meets me at the front of the car and grabs my hand in the loosest grip imaginable. "I'm only doing this until we get to your locker," she says under her breath. "God, your hands are sweaty."

"And yours are as cold as your heart," I snip back. "Just smile and work your hot-girl magic."

She takes a deep breath. I ignore the nervousness in her eyes as I take a deep breath of my own.

And then she's pulling me along like a puppy dog, strutting her way through the parking lot with a winning smile on her face. I keep my eyes locked ahead of me and grin as wide as I can. Everything's a blur, but I know we're having the desired effect: People are stopping to watch us.

"The fuck?" Gino laughs.

"Are they *together*?" some girl shrieks.

"Since when are you gay, Abraham?" someone else calls. Irene twitches reflexively, but she keeps her head held high.

When we reach the senior locker hall, the effect is magnified: the shocked whispers and hissing gossip are almost enough to give me cold feet. Without meaning to, I clasp Irene's hand tighter.

I don't know how she's handling this with such poise. Several people are blatantly gawking at us. One guy has the nerve to snap our picture. Charlotte Pascal actually stops in the middle of FaceTiming her Candlehawk boyfriend to turn our way and say, "You're fucking kidding me right now."

Irene ignores her and continues through the chaos like a queen in a fucking parade. I've got to hand it to her: When she sets her mind to do something, she goes full throttle.

It's not until we reach my locker, all the way at the end of the hallway, that I realize I've been holding my breath. I relax my shoulders and loosen my grip on Irene's hand. I didn't realize how tightly I'd been holding it.

Danielle watches us approach. Whereas everyone else in our class seems to be jumping at this piece of gossip, Danielle's eyes are narrowed like she just caught Teddy sneaking candy.

"Fascinating couple," she says as Irene steers me to my locker.

Irene all but drops my sweaty hand and wastes no time in wiping her palm on her skinny jeans.

"Jesus. Can you get her some gloves or something?" she asks Danielle.

"What the hell are you two doing?" Danielle says.

"You can't tell? We've fallen for each other," Irene says, batting her eyelashes at me.

"Give it a rest," I tell her.

"Fine." She resumes her usual tone. Now that we're past the rest of the hallway, her nerves are on display again. "I'll see you later. Oh, and if anyone asks, which they definitely will"—she lowers her voice and leans closer to me—"*you* asked *me* out."

I scoff. She shakes a hand through her hair, and then she's gone, wading back through the sea of onlookers.

I try to avoid Danielle's pointed stare, but she moves to block me from my locker. She won't even hand me my coffee.

"Scottie. What. The fuck."

"What?" I say innocently. "Just trying something new."

"Are you blackmailing her or something?"

"Why does everyone assume I'm blackmailing?"

"What's your angle here? Do you realize the entire hallway was staring at you?"

I give her a smug smile. "Yes. And hopefully Tally has seen their Stories by now."

Danielle's jaw drops. "Seriously, Scottie? God, I know you're upset about the breakup, but this is *really* going off the deep end. Does Irene even like girls?"

I pull her around the corner so we can talk more quietly. "Yes," I tell her firmly. I recount the conversation I heard between Irene and Honey-Belle, plus the conversation Irene and I had at the tracks.

"But you're doing all this just to make Tally jealous?" Danielle whispers, shaking her head.

"Come on, give me some more credit than that." I whip out the homemade blueberry muffin I brought for her this morning. We both know it's her favorite. She purses her lips but finally hands over my coffee.

"Tally is just the tip of the iceberg," I explain. "You said it yourself that driving Irene brought so much attention to our team. Didn't you see how well we played when she kept bringing a whole cheering section to our practices? You *know* more people will show up now that they think I'm dating her, especially if they cheer at our games. It's exactly the confidence booster we need. We're going to beat Candlehawk in the Christmas Classic, and then we're going to slaughter them in the district championship. Can you argue with that, Captain?"

For once, Danielle is speechless. I've got her on that one.

* * *

When I look back someday, my "coming out" with Irene will really be something for the books. For the first time in my high school career, people are straight-up *fawning* over me. I feel it between classes, in the cafeteria, and even in the bathroom, where some random freshman lets me cut in front of her in line. It's like the secondhand celebrity I felt after our car accident, but magnified times a thousand.

Nearly everyone has something to say about it. The Cleveland triplets corner me in the library and demand to know how I asked Irene out. I'm only slightly offended that, just as Irene predicted, they assume *I* did the asking. A few straight kids congratulate me for helping Irene to acknowledge her sexuality ("You guys are *so* brave") while the queer kids pat me on the back for swelling our ranks. Even Gino pulls me aside before economics to admit I have more game than anyone suspected.

Gunther and Kevin seem wary of me. When our physics teacher takes us outside to launch the catapults we've been building this month, the two of them make a show of examining the grass and the weather conditions before they finally ask me what's going on.

"So you're really going out with her?" Gunther says, loading peanuts into the catapult.

"Why is that so hard to believe?" I ask. I know I could tell them the truth if I wanted to, but it seems safer to limit the secret to Danielle.

Gunther shakes his head. "She's really hot."

"And I'm not?" I shove him playfully, pretending the insinuation doesn't hurt. I think back to the few times Tally told me I was hot. I never quite believed her.

"You know we think you're pretty," Kevin says, bending down to make notes in our lab notebook. "But wouldn't it surprise you to hear I was going out with her? The last person I went out with was Nina Bynes."

Nina Bynes is a sweet but dorky girl who pulls her books around in a carry-on suitcase. Gino refers to her as the flight attendant. For the three weeks Kevin went out with her, people kept telling him to buckle his seat belt. Gino wouldn't stop joking that Kevin's tray table was up.

"I know what you mean." I sigh, digging my shoe into the dirt. "She is, as the kids say, 'out of my league.'"

I kneel down to trigger the first launch. The sun is blinding and I have to squint across the soccer field to aim for the plastic hoops Mrs. King set up in the distance.

"I didn't realize she was into girls," Gunther says. "I'd heard that rumor, but I thought it was just Charlotte Pascal starting shit."

I look up at him. "Wait. What rumor?"

"That she and Charlotte hate each other because Irene made a move on her last year."

I'm distracted by this sudden development, but before I can say anything, Honey-Belle appears at my side.

"Hi, Scottie," she says brightly. "How's my favorite girlfriend-in-law?"

I blink. "What?"

"Oh come on," she says, cheesing hard. "Irene's my best friend, and now you're her girlfriend, which makes us in-laws."

If I didn't know any better, I would think she was messing with me, but she seems entirely earnest.

"Hi, Honey-Belle," Gunther says in a high-pitched voice. His cheeks redden. "You look nice today."

She cocks her head at him. "Thanks, Grover."

Kevin snorts under his breath. Gunther glares at him.

"I wanted to tell you how happy I am for you," Honey-Belle continues, touching my arm. "You're just what Irene needs, even if I didn't see it before. I mean, the sexual tension was *obvious*, but I never sensed the true affection underneath."

I stare at her, at a loss for words.

"You and Irene had that much sexual tension, huh?" Kevin asks, elbowing me.

"Oh, it was overflowing," Honey-Belle says seriously. "So thick you could spread it like peanut butter."

"I think maybe you're misinterpreting—" I begin.

"But it's really cute to see you together now," Honey-Belle plows on. "When I asked Irene about it, she could barely look me in the eye. She only gets like that when she's shy."

"Right," I say.

"Anyway, I'll see you later, Scottie. Bye, Kevin. Bye, Grover."

She skips away, leaving Kevin to laugh at Gunther and me.

* * *

Later that morning, I receive a single text that validates this whole damn thing.

Tally Gibson: You're really dating her?

I feel so smug in that moment, it's a wonder I can tolerate myself. I'm smirking when I text her back.

Me: Yeah, so?

Only a small, distant part of my brain pays any thought to how Irene is handling this. From what I can tell, it's benefiting her: I overhear someone in the cafeteria line whispering that her coming out makes her "more relatable." When I see her in Senior Horizons that afternoon, she looks for all the world to be as regal and untouchable as ever. She shoots me a smile that to everyone else probably looks flirtatious, but to me seems to say *This is such bullshit and these people are idiots and I might kill you but I haven't decided yet.*

I smile back and even toss in a wink. I can almost feel her straining not to roll her eyes.

* * *

When I get to practice that afternoon, my teammates give me more shit than anyone. "So you've finally moved on from Tally?" they ask, and I can feel how it's a victory for them as much as me.

"Irene is hotter anyway," Googy says, "but I don't know how we should feel about you trading basketball for cheerleading. Didn't wanna stick with athletes?"

"Cheerleaders *are* athletes," I snap.

"Oooooh," the girls say, trading looks.

"Enough about Scottie's love life," says Danielle, who seems like it's taking everything in her not to blurt out the truth. "We need to focus. Let's run Marshmallow."

I play better than I have all season. Danielle's eyes are shining when I nail my third three-pointer. And sure enough, near the end of practice, Irene and a dozen others show up to watch.

* * *

"You're a solid actress," I tell Irene when we walk to her car that evening.

"Mm," she says disinterestedly. "Wish I could say the same for you."

"What? My acting's been great."

"False. That wink in Senior Horizons was completely over the top."

"You loved it."

"Yeah, okay," she says dryly.

Whatever she says, I can tell she's as pleased—and as tired—as I am. We get into her car and flop against our headrests, sighing at the same time.

"Coming out is exhausting," Irene says suddenly.

I look over at her. Her eyes are glazed and she's breathing slowly.

"For what it's worth, I think you handled it well," I say neutrally. "Was anyone a dick?"

"A few people asked how you 'turned me.'"

"Morons."

She stretches back, yawning. "I just wish people could be more creative with their ignorance."

I laugh without meaning to, but I stifle it by turning it into a cough. "Does this mean you have to come out to your parents?"

She answers like she's swatting a fly. "My parents already know."

"They do?"

She blinks at me. "Why is that so surprising? Don't *your* parents know?"

"Yeah, but . . . I didn't realize you were this far along in your, you know, *journey.*"

"Ah yes, my big fat gay journey," she says with false reverence. "Just because I didn't tell our whole school, doesn't mean I'm not open at home. It's not just white kids who come out to their parents."

I set my mouth. "I didn't say that."

"And yet your ears are turning red," she says, eyebrows raised.

"I'm just surprised because . . . I don't know, your mom . . ."

"Has a constant stick up her ass?" Irene rolls her

head against the headrest. I notice the damp baby hairs at the back of her neck. "Yeah, she's a piece of work, but she's a good person. She donated to PFLAG after I came out."

I don't know if I'm pushing my luck, but I try anyway. "So why does she hate cheerleading?"

Irene's eyes flicker toward me. I try to show that I'm asking sincerely, but I don't know if it's working.

"She thinks it's a dead end," she says finally. "When I first started cheering back in, like, fifth grade, she thought it would just be another extracurricular, so she was supportive. But then I got serious about it and she couldn't understand why. She wants everything I do to lead to something in my future."

"But you want to cheer in college. Doesn't that count as the future?"

"Yeah, for four years, but then what? My parents play the long game. Especially Mom. She wants me to focus on academics and, like, things that lead to a stable career. She's an optometrist. My dad's a researcher at the CDC. They both went to Georgia Tech and they want me to go there, too." She exhales a long breath. "They think they're way more progressive than my grandparents, but they're not. Their definition of success is pretty narrow."

"And your definition of success?"

She side-eyes me again. "You really think you're entitled to my personal story, don't you?"

I shrug. The truth is, I'm starting to build a composite

portrait of this girl, and some of the pieces don't add up. "Fine. Don't tell me. But I do have something that might brighten your mood."

She hikes her eyebrows, waiting. I dig through my backpack's front pocket until I find the check I wrote out last night.

"Here," I say, handing it over.

She takes it carefully and studies the paper. I try not to think about what it represents: $1,000 of my hard-earned money. Hours and hours of scraping gum off theater seats and pouring sodas for preteens.

But on the other hand, it's my ticket to ensuring we beat Candlehawk.

"Your signature is atrocious," Irene says. "This *S* looks like a bowling pin."

I ignore the jibe. "You're good to deposit that whenever. Just, you know. Keep good on your word."

She looks at me seriously. "I always do."

"Then we have nothing to worry about, do we?"

Irene sighs and tucks the check into her sweatshirt pocket. "Let's get the fuck out of here," she says, and she drives me home.

8

HALLOWEEN PASSES IN A BLUR OF CANDY
corn and costumes. My friends and I celebrate at the
Chuck Munny, where they're showing *Hocus Pocus* on
the big screen for three-dollar admission. I secretly hope
we might run into Tally—she always loved the Munny
and would hang out with me at the concession stand while
I worked on slow days—but when I check her Instagram,
she's posting from a haunted house with her new friends.

My family learns of my new "relationship" on the
first night of November. Mom and Dad and I are getting
ready for college scholarship night, a boring info dump
hosted by the school guidance department, when Thora
throws a grenade into the mix.

"College night is for all the seniors, right?" she says,
even though she already knows the answer. "I guess that
means you'll meet Scottie's new *girlfriend*."

Dad freezes in the act of pulling on his Crocs. Mom stops lint rolling the cat hair off her jacket.

"Girlfriend?" they say at the same time.

I glare at Thora, but the damage is done. I explain as sparingly as I can, but they manage to wrangle Irene's name, description, and practically her star sign from me.

"But this is the girl you got in the car accident with!" Mom says, beaming. "And you said you didn't like her . . . Now how about that for life playing a joke on you!"

"It's like they say, Scots," Dad chimes in. "Beautiful things can grow out of shit."

"Buck, don't say 'shit' in front of the girls," Mom says, glancing at Daphne.

"Mom, I'm in seventh grade," Daphne says exasperatedly. "Today I heard one of my *teachers* say 'shit.'"

"What? Why?"

"He was talking about Candlehawk."

"Oh, well, that's different."

"Come on, we're gonna be late," Dad says. "I want to meet Scottie's new *amour*!"

"Are we sure we're happy about this?" Thora asks. "I'm concerned Scottie might be suffering from Stockholm syndrome."

"Like Sweden?" Daphne says.

"No, like *Beauty and the Beast*. Scottie is in love with her captor."

"Oh, Thora, don't be a sass monster," Mom says,

swatting her. She steers me toward the door and I shoot one last scowl at my sister. Her timing could not have been worse. I still don't have my car back, which means I'll have to ride with Mom, Dad, and their incessant questions.

I find Danielle and Mrs. Zander as soon as we enter the school auditorium. "Help me keep them away from Irene," I whisper under cover of the parents talking. "Thora spilled the beans."

Danielle rolls her eyes but finds us a row toward the top of the auditorium, sequestered away from most of the senior class and their parents. Mom and Dad make jovial conversation with Mrs. Zander, but their eyes keep wandering over the newcomers like they expect Irene to appear at my side any moment.

Thankfully, she doesn't. I'm not even sure she's there until I spot Honey-Belle's bright blond braids in the middle of the auditorium. Irene is seated next to her, whispering into her ear, both her parents tucked into the seats next to her.

The info session takes about forty-five minutes. I basically hear what I already know: that my plan to attend Georgia State University will definitely make me eligible for in-state scholarships. I pretty much zone out after that, but when the guidance counselors touch on athletic scholarships, I watch Irene straighten in her chair. I wonder if her mom notices. I wonder if her mom even *knows* Irene wants to cheer in college.

They wrap up the session with an audience raffle. We do these a lot in Grandma Earl, always offering local treats like a coffee mug from Sweet Noelle's or a pack of toothbrushes from Hermey Orthodontics. In Candlehawk they raffle off iPads, stock market shares, and dinner with the mayor. One time they gave away a French bulldog.

When the session finally ends, I'm out of my seat before the lights come on. "Time to go!" I say brightly, shooing my parents along.

"But your girlfriend!" Mom says.

Mrs. Zander gasps. "Scottie has a new girlfriend?"

It takes everything in me not to face-palm. Danielle looks resigned, but she saves me. "We'll meet Irene next time, guys. I think she was—um—sick today?"

"Aw, what a waste," my dad says. "I've been storing up so much Embarrassing Dad Energy."

Danielle and I move our parents along, but they're still casting looks over their shoulders; even Mrs. Zander has joined in with the nosiness. We spill into the lobby with the hordes of other Earlians. And just when I think we're about to be free—

Dr. Abraham walks straight into us.

"Ancy!" Mom trills.

"Wanda!" Irene's mom says.

Of course they remembered each other's fucking *names*. And now they're *hugging*.

"This is my husband—" Mom says.

"And this is my husband—" Dr. Abraham says, pulling Irene's dad out of nowhere.

"And this is our dear friend Harmony Zander, Danielle's mom—"

The only good thing is that Irene is nowhere to be found. Maybe she went off with Honey-Belle somewhere. Maybe she's already left in her own car—

"Oh for fuck's sake," a voice mutters next to me.

Yeah. Irene is still here.

"Why didn't you keep them moving?" she says, gritting her teeth. I should have noticed she'd walked up next to me. Her cedar perfume is getting too familiar.

"Keep them moving?" I mock. "I'm not walking a pack of dogs, Abraham."

"Oh girls!" the moms squeal. "Look at you together!"

There's nothing to do but smile and pretend to be thrilled with this family introduction. Mom and Dad beam at Irene; Irene's parents beam at me. Mrs. Zander literally claps. Danielle hides her laughter behind her hand.

"Let's get your picture together," Irene's dad says, pulling out his phone. He's slender and speaks with an accent. He has Irene's mouth.

"Oh, we don't need to—" I start.

"No, Dad, we're fine—" Irene tries.

But of course the parents have their way. There are suddenly five phones trained on us, because even Mrs. Zander is getting in on the mix.

"Why are you standing so stiffly?" Irene's mom chides. "Hug each other! Do something!"

Irene and I trade looks.

"Um, we're not really into PDA," I say.

"Yeah, we're not huggers. It's so tacky," Irene adds.

"Really?" Danielle says. I recognize the twinkle in her eyes: She's about to have some fun. "But I see you hug all the time. I *love* watching you hug. It's like all the love in the universe coming together."

I'm ready to throttle her.

"Come on," my mom says. "Just one little hug and we'll leave you alone."

And that's how Irene and I end up with our arms around each other, forcing smiles for the cameras. Her shoulder is warm. Her hair tickles my face. I find myself holding my breath.

"Oh! Don't move!" another voice shouts at us. "It's for the newspaper!"

The goddamn Cleveland triplets have walked into our picture party. Now all three of them are snapping photos that will no doubt end up on social media.

But maybe that wouldn't be so bad, I think, *because Tally will see them.*

"Okay, that's enough," Irene says, releasing me. "It was lovely running into you all, but I have to, um, finish my Senior Horizons homework."

"Same," I say.

And with that, we bolt.

Mom and Dad are predictably eager on the drive home. They won't stop talking about what a cute couple we make. They spend as much time talking about Irene as they do about the actual college session.

"It's good to see you with someone who deserves you, Scottie," Mom says. She reaches behind the passenger seat and squeezes my hand. "I like how genuine that girl is."

I snort without meaning to. But if I think about it, I guess Mom is right. Irene has never been anything but herself.

* * *

I finally get my car back that weekend, thank God. It's a lot easier pretending to date my nemesis when we don't have to spend every morning and evening trapped in a speeding metal box together.

Our first regular season game takes place in early November. Danielle works us hard at practice, and I work myself even harder at home, refining my shots in the driveway each night. Googy leads the charge to make posters publicizing the game but is forced to take hers down after she paints a pair of basketballs inside a bra.

Nevertheless, word gets out: There's a sudden buzz about the girls' basketball team because of my relationship with Irene. When she unilaterally changes the cheerleading schedule so the squad will cheer for our games instead of the boys', the buzz only increases further. To seal the deal, I give her my team picture button before school one morning.

"You actually expect me to wear this?" she asks, regarding my button like it's the most heinous thing she's ever seen. "It's just so *corny*."

"God, prima donna, just wear it on your backpack. It'll make you a walking advertisement for my team."

The button has the desired effect: On the evening of our first home game, the bleachers are packed with students and fans. It's the largest crowd we've ever drawn—maybe the only thing that counts as a *crowd* at all. When my teammates peek through the locker room door, they return with radiant expressions on their faces. The only one put off by the show of support is Danielle.

"I can't play with all those people watching me," she says nervously. She starts to disappear into herself, sinking into the locker room bench, almost like she's going into Danielle Vision. "So many people. So many eyes."

"You'll be great," I assure her. "You've been killing it at practice with people watching."

"That's, like, twelve people," she says, staring at the lockers. "This is our whole grade."

"Hey." I shake her shoulder. "I don't mean to be insensitive, but buck up. Either you want us to be dynamite—which means more people cheering for us—or you want us to suck. You can't have it both ways."

She swallows and lets me pull her off the bench. "Fine. Just—don't let the announcer call my name."

"I literally have no control over that," I say, laughing at her.

"Shhh," she says, walking to the door robotically.

When our team runs onto the court, there's a huge roar from the crowd. I find myself blushing in a good way. Irene and her squad are stationed at the sidelines, working their magic. I almost wish she would turn around and throw me a knowing smirk.

Googy wins the tip-off, and the ball lands in my hands, and before I know it, I'm sailing down the court like I own the damn thing. Before the other team has time to finalize their defensive formation, I pass the ball to one of our open forwards, who sinks an easy jump shot.

The crowd cheers. I high-five a slightly less nervous Danielle, and as we run to the other side of the court to play defense, I can't help grinning.

* * *

We win that first game, and then our second game the following week, and somehow we end up rolling into an undefeated season. November becomes a flurry of practice-practice-game, practice-practice-game, and I'm high on the rhythm of it, the sweet exhaustion I feel after each practice, the crisp, bright air on my cheeks when Irene and I break out of the gym every evening.

A few weeks into the season—and my new "relationship"—I get word of an opportunity I've been itching for.

"Charlotte Pascal's house," Gunther says abruptly when we plop down for lunch. "Have you heard?"

"No?"

"It's all anyone's talking about. She's throwing a party over Thanksgiving break."

"So?" Danielle asks.

"So I think we should go," Gunther says bracingly. "I'm in the mood for another 'senior fundraiser' to liven up my social scene."

Danielle half turns to Kevin. "What do you think? Are you gonna go?"

"Yeah, why not?" Kevin says, shrugging. "It's something new. The only other party I've been to was with band kids and it was . . . underwhelming."

"I heard Charlotte's still dating that Candlehawk bro," Gunther says through a mouthful of sandwich. "Honey-Belle was telling me about it."

I study him. "Since when do you and Honey-Belle talk?"

"We talk sometimes," Gunther says, his voice high-pitched.

"Does she still think your name is Grover?" Kevin asks.

Gunther ignores him. "She said the guy's a total toolbag. He told Charlotte he'd only come to her party if she invited his Candlehawk classmates, too."

My ears perk up. "All his Candlehawk classmates?"

"Why does that—" Danielle starts to say, but then she stops. Her expression darkens. "Scottie, *no.*"

"What?" Kevin asks.

I scratch the back of my neck, trying to seem casual. "I was just wondering."

"She's wondering whether *Tally* will be there."

"What? Why?" Gunther says, licking the mustard at the corner of his mouth. "You're dating Irene now."

"Yeah, I know, I'm just considering whether she would be there," I say carefully. "I mean, I'm not above making her jealous."

Kevin snorts into his Gatorade. Danielle squeezes her eyes shut like she's praying for patience. I don't care; I have a new mission.

I find Irene after lunch. "Hey," I say, leaning up against her locker. "Did you hear about Charlotte's party?"

Her eyes turn stormy. "What about it?"

"It's next weekend, once break starts." I lower my voice. "Our first public outing together."

"I'm not going to Charlotte's party," Irene says, slamming her locker.

I follow her as she stalks off, grabbing hold of her backpack to slow her down. My basketball button stares up at me. "Um? Why not?"

"Because I despise her. Which you already know. *Everyone* knows."

"Candlehawk people will be there," I insist. "*Tally* will be there."

"Who cares? We can flaunt our sexy relationship in front of her at the Candlehawk game. I thought that was your goal."

"No," I say, getting heated now. "We agreed this was part of the deal: You helping me make Tally jealous."

Irene spins around by the Language Hall. She pulls me into a room two doors down.

"This is a teachers' lounge," I say as she snaps the door shut.

"Only the language teachers use it, and they all have third block classes."

I squint at her. "You've come in here before?"

She ignores the question. "I'm not going to Charlotte's house."

"You don't have to talk to her," I say impatiently. "For God's sake, there'll be a million people there. You can hang with me and Danielle and Honey-Belle."

Irene looks ready to incinerate me with her stare. "Don't push me on this, Zajac."

"What's your problem with Charlotte, anyway?" I ask, even though I know the rumor from Gunther.

Her eyes flash. "That's none of your business. You're not entitled to know or understand how I feel about people."

I straighten my back, keeping my eyes hard on her. "This was part of the deal."

Irene stands tall, holding her ground. "If you can't bend on this one thing, the deal is off. You don't get to treat me like some escort for hire. I understand that to you I'm just some 'hot girl' with social capital, and for the most part, I've let you get away with that, but this is too far. I'm a person with feelings and boundaries. Get your head out of your ass and respect that, or we're done."

She wrenches the door open and sweeps out of the room, and I'm left standing in her wake, completely dazed.

* * *

Irene and I give each other a wide berth after that. We hardly acknowledge each other and she stops coming to my practices, prompting the Cleveland triplets to grill me about our "trouble in paradise."

The week leading into Thanksgiving break arrives with a flurry of tests and project deadlines. Rain lashes down, darkening the sky outside our school windows, and the ancient tree behind the library is stripped of its vibrant red leaves. It's our first glimpse of winter branches, bare and clawlike.

The Thursday before break starts, we're in Scuttlebaum's class, whiling away the minutes as the rain pelts against the window. Danielle is sketching new basketball plays on the corner of her notebook. Gino's on the opposite side of the room, flicking paper footballs every time Scuttlebaum turns her back. Irene is sitting with her head in her hand, picking at her nail polish and staunchly avoiding my eyes.

Scuttlebaum is prattling on about her favorite show, *The Masked Singer*, when she abruptly switches gears and grabs a stack of papers off her desk. "I've got your homework graded," she announces. "Scottie, here."

Scuttlebaum never says *Please pass these out*. She just gestures vaguely and says *Here*.

I take the stack of papers obligingly and start to pass them around the room. That's when I notice Charlotte Pascal trading a note with her friend Symphony Davis. They're scrawling furiously back and forth.

Just when I'm about to deliver the last pieces of homework, there's a ruckus as Scuttlebaum confiscates Charlotte and Symphony's note.

"Sending notes, Ms. Pascal?" She stands imperiously at the front of the room. "Hmph. Let's see what's so interesting that it couldn't wait until class ends . . ."

She narrows her beady eyes and wheezes into reading. I stop where I stand, the last two homework pieces in my hand.

"*If she thinks she'll even set foot on my property, she's delusional,*" Scuttlebaum starts, her voice grating. My classmates shift in their seats; everyone can tell this is gonna be good.

Scuttlebaum changes her voice to indicate Symphony's reply. "*But you said everyone's invited to this party.*"

"Not a predatory bitch like her."

Everyone gasps, wide-eyed with glee. There's a rumble of *Oooooh* around the room.

"Why would you say something so crass?" Scuttlebaum scolds Charlotte, but she continues reading.

"Girl, jeeze, L-O-L what did she even do to you?"

My instinct about the "bitch" they're talking about grows clearer. I can't help but notice Irene's face darkening on the opposite side of the room.

"Ugh, I don't even wanna talk about it. We were at that party last year and she started—"

There's a collective anticipation in the room; it seems like everyone has figured out who Charlotte's note is about. Something we've all been wondering for months is about to be revealed—and the look on Irene's face is one of terror.

Scuttlebaum opens her mouth again, and my heart drills in my chest, and then—

In a flash, someone snatches the paper out of Scuttlebaum's hand.

And that someone is *me*.

Before anyone can register what happened, I spit my gum into the note and crumple it up in my hand. I lob it into the trash can with a crisp, clean shot. The room goes so quiet I can hear someone cracking their knuckles nervously.

Scuttlebaum's eyes are popping. I feel like I'm staring

down a basilisk. I do the only thing I can think of: shrug and back away from her, acting like I've just done the most innocent thing on earth.

"Good timing," I say casually. "That gum just lost its flavor."

There's an outbreak of gasping and giggling. I collapse into my seat, with Scuttlebaum glaring at me like a tomato-faced demon.

"Detention, Ms. Zajac," she snarls. "How about tomorrow, just to delay your break from starting?"

I don't care about the punishment, even though Danielle will be on my ass about missing practice. Everyone is staring at me, and I know my face is flaming red, but the only person I manage to connect with is Irene.

She stares across the room at me with the most curious expression on her face. I hold her eyes for a moment, then look down at my homework, perfectly graded with an A+ on top.

* * *

By the time I finish practice that day, the entire senior class seems to have heard about my wildly stupid gesture. A record number of people show up to watch the end of our practice, and I can't figure out why until I see that Irene is back in their ranks. Danielle, who has barely spoken to me since practice started, looks resentfully delighted.

Irene approaches when I'm yanking off my ankle

braces. I can feel every eye in the gym on us. I don't look up until the last second.

Her dark hair is in its usual high ponytail, her tank top soaked with sweat, her biceps swelling the slightest bit.

"They think we're going to have some dramatic reconciliation," she tells me.

"Gross."

We hover on the spot. Then Irene says, "Let me walk you to your car."

We leave our nosy classmates behind and make our way out to the parking lot. We busy ourselves with zipping up our jackets and chugging our water bottles. It's not until we're standing by my car that Irene speaks.

"You didn't have to do that, Scottie."

It's the first time she's said my actual name, and I feel it like a sudden warmth in my chest. I have to look away from her eyes. "Trust me, I didn't plan to."

She clears her throat. "Is she really gonna make you stay late tomorrow?"

"It won't be too bad. She wants me to deep-clean her whiteboard."

"I used to love doing that. The smell of that cleaning spray."

We fall silent. The air is crisp, cold, clean. The marquee across the way reads HAPPY WANKSGIVING.

"What would I have to do at Charlotte's?" Irene asks.

I laugh through my nose. "Are you asking because I

proved myself to you, or because her nasty note said you couldn't come?"

Her mouth twitches. "Both."

"God, you're stubborn."

"And you're not?"

I roll my eyes. "We wouldn't be at Charlotte's long. We'd just 'make an appearance,' hang with our friends, make sure Tally got a good look."

Irene shifts her duffel bag, watching me. "You really think she's worth all this effort?"

I chew my bottom lip. "I know it's petty."

"Yeah," she agrees, but not like she's judging me. There's a silence until she speaks again. I can tell by her expression that she's going to relent. "If we get there and I say we need to leave, we leave. No questions asked."

"Deal." I stick out my hand for her to shake.

She quirks an eyebrow. We clasp hands for a brief, firm moment. It's weird that her hands are starting to feel familiar.

"See you tomorrow, asshole," she says, turning on the spot.

"I'll send you a love letter from detention," I call after her.

9

THE START OF THANKSGIVING BREAK MEANS
no school but extra basketball practice. I don't mind;
I'm so amped at the prospect of destroying Candlehawk
in a few weeks—especially after Tally sees me with Irene
this weekend—that I practice harder than ever, getting
to the gym earlier and staying later than my teammates.

Daphne and I spend our downtime in the beginning
of the week watching movies. Thora joins us as often
as she can, but The Chimney is busier than usual with
the holiday, so she's swamped with shifts. On one of the
mornings she has off, the three of us drive to the Chuck
Munny to catch a double feature of *Clueless* and *Never
Been Kissed*. When we leave the theater, I have a text
from Irene.

Irene Abraham: Planning my outfit for the party.
Wearing red. Do not match me.

I can't help but laugh.

On Thanksgiving Day, we feast on our usual turkey, stuffing, and cranberries. Thora brings leftover mead from the restaurant and my parents actually let me try some. Daphne sulks and takes extra helpings of pumpkin pie.

"This blows," Daphne says, stabbing her fork into her pie.

"Don't say that word," Mom says.

Thora takes advantage of the distraction to sneak bits of turkey to Pickles and BooBoo. Dad totally notices but pretends not to. After we finish the dishes, we flop on the couches and watch a quiet show about Alaskan fishermen. It's perfect.

"Scottie, we've been meaning to tell you," Dad says during a commercial. "We're so proud of you for moving on from Tally. You're giving your all to basketball and your new relationship. It's a real lesson in resilience."

Mom strokes my hair back from my forehead. "We always knew you'd bounce back."

I make a joke to deflect their praise. I'm careful not to catch my sisters' eyes; they'd see right through me. I feel a twitch of shame knowing that I'm going to be dangling my fake relationship over Tally on Saturday night, but I shut that feeling down. I've worked too hard to get to this point.

* * *

If you had told me a month ago that I'd be rolling into Charlotte Pascal's party with a crew comprised of Irene, Honey-Belle, and Danielle, I would have laughed in your face.

And yet here we are.

"You owe me," Irene says as we traipse up the front walk. She whispers it close to my ear so Honey-Belle won't hear. Part of me wishes she would just tell her about our arrangement.

"Owe you?" I ask with a demure smile. "Hardly. Did you forget you're doing this because I impressed you with my big, chivalrous, note-stealing gesture?"

"Yeah, so gallant," she says dryly.

Charlotte's house is wild when we walk in. There are people everywhere with Solo cups, making noise and posing for pictures. Gunther and Kevin stand against the foyer wall, watching everyone like they're not sure what to do with themselves. They're both dressed up— at least, their version of dressing up. Gunther is wearing his best graphic tee and Kevin has a military-style jacket over his usual hoodie.

"We just came from dinner," Kevin says, hugging us hello. He squeezes Danielle around the middle and she goes exceptionally quiet. "Partridge Pizza."

"Brought some leftovers if you want them," Gunther says, passing a box toward us. "They have the best garlic sticks."

129

"Thanks," I say, reaching for the box, but Kevin holds up his hand.

"You might wanna check this guy's breath first," he says with a grimace.

"It's not that bad," Gunther says, but now that I'm closer to him, I can definitely smell a strong, funky garlic smell.

"Oh *woof*, that's bad."

"Told you," Kevin says. "Dude put raw garlic bits on there."

Irene watches this interaction with her nose wrinkled. When I turn away from the garlic sticks box, she grabs my elbow. "*Thank you*. I would have refused to talk to you all night."

"Well, as it is, *darling*, maybe you can escort me to the kitchen."

"The way they flirt is so cute," Honey-Belle whispers to Danielle.

"I completely agree," Gunther says, standing as close to Honey-Belle as possible while keeping his hand over his mouth.

Irene starts to head for the kitchen, but I hold her back.

"*What?*" she whispers.

"You need to hold my hand. We're here to sell this to Tally, remember?"

"God, you're a psycho," she says, but she takes my hand anyway.

We make our way through the throng of people, all

of whom stare at Irene and then at me. By the time we reach the center of the house, my heart is trilling, expecting Tally's face to appear any moment. I scan the room out of the corner of my eye, but I don't see her anywhere.

"Well?" Irene prods.

"She'll show up. Let's get a drink."

It's hot and crowded in the kitchen, but the sea of people parts for us until we find the island with the drinks stationed on it. I grab the vodka and lemonade to mix myself a drink.

"What do you want?" I ask Irene.

"Water."

"Ha, ha. I'll make you one of these."

"No, I just told you. Water."

She butts me aside, grabs a Solo cup, and fills it from the sink. She sticks a lime wedge on the rim of the cup so it looks like a mixed drink.

"What?" she says, seeing my expression. "Do you think I want people giving me shit for not drinking?"

I shake my head. This girl never ceases to surprise me. It's a welcome distraction from worrying about Tally.

"So Danielle totally has a crush on Kevin," Irene says.

My heart stops. "What? No she doesn't."

"Please. It's visible from a mile away."

"That's—it's not—"

She quirks an eyebrow.

"Fine," I grumble. "But keep your mouth shut about it."

"Who am I gonna tell? Besides, I like Danielle."

I'm about to respond when her face changes. Her eyes widen, her breath stops. "Shit," she says, looking over my shoulder. I try to turn, but she plants a hand on my arm.

"What?" I say, wrenching free of her grasp.

I spin around. My eyes find the stoners passing a joint, the soccer girls flirting with the baseball players, the kid throwing up in the corner, and—

Tally.

In the middle of the room.

Making out with another girl.

All the air is sucked out of my lungs. It feels like my heart's been flattened by a slab of concrete.

It's a girl I've never seen before, so she must not go to Grandma Earl. Probably a Candlehawk girl, based on the way she's dressed. And she's *pretty*. Tally is kissing her with so much enthusiasm it's almost like she's trying to eat her. Everything inside me sears with pain.

There's a warm hand on my shoulder.

"Stop watching," Irene says, pressing firmly until she can spin me around.

"But I—"

"No, Scottie," she says, holding me in place. Her voice is softer than usual. "Don't torture yourself."

We make eye contact. She actually looks concerned, but I don't have the emotional bandwidth to care. I slip free of her grasp and hurry to the back patio.

At the last second, when I close the door, I look back to see Tally watching me.

* * *

I'm not sure how long I sit there for. It's so cold that I'll have to go inside soon, but my heart is aching and I don't know how to make it stop.

Shouldn't I have expected this? I mean, I've been pretending to move on, but why wouldn't Tally *actually* move on? Is she dating that girl, or merely hooking up with her? Is she kissing lots of pretty girls at parties?

The back door snaps open behind me. Irene stands there, fiddling with the long necklace that hangs over her scarlet sweater. She purses her lips like she's trying to decide something.

"Don't tell me you've come to gloat," I mumble. "I've already realized my plan has backfired. I don't need you to rub it in."

She sits next to me, kicking her wedge boots against the steps. "It's truly heartwarming how you always expect the best from me."

"So you're *not* here to gloat?"

"I'm here to tell you that your ex-girlfriend looks like a *terrible* kisser, and the only person I feel sorry for is that poor girl whose face she was chewing on. Seriously, that was heinous. Did you even *like* kissing her?"

I'm not sure why I answer. "I thought I did."

"It sucks you had to see that. She could have done that somewhere private. She knows you're here."

I drop my head into my hands, tugging at the roots of my hair. "She was watching me for my reaction."

"I know. I saw her."

"Thora thinks she's manipulative," I admit.

"No shit. It's almost like she gets off on it or something." She snorts derisively, sounding more like herself again. "Fucking weirdo."

Without meaning to, I laugh.

"To be fair, though," Irene says, and her voice changes to something more serious, "you *were* trying to manipulate her, too. She just got there first."

I glare at her. "So you *are* gloating."

"No. I'm trying to point out that this competition isn't going to make you happy."

"Since when do you care about my happiness?"

"Don't be such a victim, Zajac. I've been playing this girlfriend role with you for a month now. I'm allowed to make observations."

I exhale and turn away from her. I can't even begin to consider whether this "competition" is still worth it; I'm in too deep now. But I've clearly underestimated Tally. It doesn't matter how carefully I set up my shot: She will always hit the basket first.

"It might cheer you up to know that Tally is either really drunk or really high, or potentially both," Irene says. "She had her grubby paws on everything in the kitchen. Literally pushed me out of the way to grab the tortilla chips."

"So?"

"So maybe she doesn't even like that girl. She's just messed up right now."

"Yeah. Maybe."

Irene watches me out of the corner of her eye. I can feel her piercing stare. Part of me wishes she would stop. The other part is just grateful to have someone out here with me.

Irene takes a long sip of her water. We're both quiet. The air is biting.

"Let's mess with her," Irene declares.

I look over at her. "What?"

Her eyes are narrowed. There's a gleam in them. "Yeah," she says, more to herself than to me. "I've got an idea."

* * *

Inside, we find my friends hovering in the hallway. Irene wastes no time in marching up to them.

"Gunther," she says, and he freezes. "Where did you put those garlic sticks?"

He points wordlessly to the pile of jackets in the corner. The Partridge box sits on top of them. Irene opens it, wrinkles her nose, and walks away.

"What is she—?" Gunther stammers.

We follow her around the corner, back into the

kitchen. Just as Irene said, Tally is standing there, munching away on a bag of pretzels. Her eyes are glazed over, but she looks up when Irene enters with the garlic sticks.

"What are those?" Tally blurts out.

Irene turns to her, feigning surprise. "Garlic sticks. Why?"

Tally's eyes light up. "Can I have some?"

Irene sets the box on the counter and steps in front of it like a lioness guarding her pack. "No, I don't think so," she says with fake sweetness. "They're not mine. I don't know if I'm allowed to give them out."

I know Tally well enough to understand what a delicious challenge this is for her. Not only because someone is trying to deprive her of something, but because that someone is a popular girl she's resented for a long time.

"Really," Tally says dryly. Her hatred for Irene practically crackles on the air. "And who put you on guard duty?"

Irene shrugs. "I just like to play by the rules. Don't you?"

My heartbeat quickens. It's a showdown like the Wild West, and the crazy thing is, I want Irene to win.

Tally lunges around her and grabs a garlic stick. Irene pretends to be affronted, but I don't think the fury in her eyes is fake.

"Mmm," Tally says, chowing down. She cocks her head. "I can see why you were hoarding them."

"Yeah, you can see right through me," Irene says coolly. She turns and stalks off, but not before catching my eye.

Tally eats another garlic stick before she licks the crumbs off her fingers and struts back to the center of the party. My friends and I watch intently, trying to figure out what's supposed to happen next. Where was Irene going with this?

And then, as Tally slithers up to the pretty girl she was making out with earlier, it hits me.

"Oh shit—"

Tally leans in to kiss the girl again. For a blistering moment they're wrapped together, mouths open, Tally devouring her, and then—

"AUGH!" the girl gags, rearing backward. She covers her mouth with her hand.

Tally looks stricken. She tries to say something in the girl's ear.

"Back off!" the girl says, lunging away from her. "God, that smell!"

The whole party is watching now. A bunch of people are laughing; one girl has her phone out to record the humiliation. Some guy yells, "Come on, Gibson, brush your teeth for once!"

Tally freezes, mortified, before turning on her heel and fleeing the room. I watch with my mouth hanging open, dazzled by the brilliance of Irene's scheme.

"Shit," Kevin says, his eyes wide. "That was the best thing I've seen in years."

"You gotta hand it to Irene," Danielle says, shaking her head. "She knew exactly how to push Tally."

* * *

We stay just long enough for the party to reach its peak. Tally never returns, leaving the Candlehawk girl behind. Danielle and Kevin melt into conversation with a bunch of other smart kids who won't stop talking about college applications. Gunther, to my surprise, manages to capture Honey-Belle's attention. They sit at the kitchen table, whispering and laughing at each other, so oblivious to everything around them that Gunther doesn't flinch when someone spills beer on his shoulder. If Honey-Belle can smell the garlic on Gunther's breath, she doesn't seem to mind.

"Pretty diabolical plan," I tell Irene when I find her in the hallway.

She shrugs. "I can be evil when I want to be."

"And here I thought you had no control over it."

"Ha ha."

"So we've slain one beast tonight. Where's the other?"

Irene scans the vicinity, searching for Charlotte. "I don't know. I keep waiting for her to strike."

"Maybe she doesn't care that you're here. She's too busy hosting."

"Believe me, she cares. She's probably plotting with her soccer henchmen."

"Hench*women*."

"Hench*people*."

I shrug and gulp down the beer in my hand. I feel much more relaxed now that Tally is out of sight. "Whatever. I think you're being paranoid," I say, bumping her with my shoulder. My skin tingles, but I ignore it.

"You're being arrogant. You don't know Charlotte like I do."

Unfortunately, Irene proves to be right. It's only a few minutes later that the music cuts off and the party splits into silence again.

Charlotte Pascal, with her gorgeous auburn locks and shrewd green eyes, climbs atop a chair. Her boyfriend gives her a hand up, even though she doesn't need it. He looks pompous and bored.

"Hel-*lo*, everyone," Charlotte says in her usual affected tone. "Thanks so much for coming over tonight. People from Candlehawk, thank you for making the drive." She pauses. "And everyone else, please remember to vote for me for Student Athlete of the Year."

"Oh god," Irene mutters under her breath.

"Speaking of SAOY . . ." Charlotte's expression turns malicious. "I know we have at least one other candidate here tonight: the newly gay Irene Abraham."

Heads swivel in our direction. A trickle of nervous laughter runs around the room. Most people here are too chickenshit to challenge Irene's social position, but they obviously don't mind another popular girl doing it. The expressions on their faces are thirsty. The Cleveland triplets actually stand on their tiptoes to get a better look.

Irene stiffens and leans the slightest bit into me. Her elbow brushes mine. I lean my weight toward her without thinking about it.

"I'm *so* very happy for anyone who finds their truth," Charlotte drawls on. "It's so important to celebrate diversity in this day and age. But I also think that truth should be authentic, and I'm a little concerned that Irene Abraham is *anything but.*"

My blood simmers. Across the room, Danielle catches my eye. I can tell we're on the same page about this: We can shit-talk Irene all we want, but at this point, no one else can.

Charlotte gestures elaborately at the TV in the center of the room. Her Candlehawk boyfriend has connected his laptop to it, and at a signal from Charlotte, he pops a video onto the screen. At first it's just a still frame: Irene, dark hair and hazy eyes, smirking at the camera.

He presses PLAY.

Charlotte's voice blares from behind the camera. "*You are sooo drunk! Admit it. You're drunk.*"

"*Am not,*" Irene says on screen, but she's slurring. She's not looking at the camera; I can't tell whether she knew she was being filmed. Charlotte laughs hysterically off-screen. The video must be at least a year old, before their friendship blew up.

140

"*You were totally hitting on me earlier*," Charlotte says. "*You get so gay when you're wasted.*"

"*Whaaat? Don't be weird, Char. I'm not gay.*"

"*There's nothing wrong with being gay*," Charlotte's voice replies. But the way she says it makes my skin crawl; it's almost like she's baiting Irene.

"*I know that*," video-Irene slurs. "*I just happen to be straight.*"

"*Are you sure?*"

"*Half the people at school are only 'gay' because they think it makes them more interesting. They're so desperate. It's embarrassing.*"

"*So you'd never hook up with a girl?*"

Video-Irene snorts. She rubs a hand down her face. "*I'm not saying I wouldn't. But you know it wouldn't mean anything to me.*"

The video ends. Candlehawk Boyfriend unplugs his computer and smirks at Charlotte. There's a ringing silence as everyone turns in our direction. I've never felt so exposed, and the video wasn't even about me.

The real Irene is stock-still next to me. Her cheeks are flushed with dark patches. I wait for her to recover and deliver her usual acidic retort, but for the first time since I've known her, she's mute. On impulse, I grab her hand and tug her away, through the hallway and outside to the sharp, cold air.

10

THE NIGHT IS QUIET AND BARE: A VACUUM OF sound. It must be chilly, but I don't notice it, either because I've been drinking or because my blood is boiling, or maybe both. I hold Irene's hand until we make it past Charlotte's front walk. She stops cold and pulls her hand away.

We square off, facing each other. Her chest is heaving; her eyes are daggers.

"I'm sorry," I say quietly.

She glances away. "Like I said." Her voice is eerily calm. "You're arrogant to think you understand my enemies better than I do."

I swallow. "You're right."

Danielle and Honey-Belle catch up to us at the car. Honey-Belle falls all over Irene, petting her hair and asking if she's okay.

"I'm fine," Irene says flatly, holding Honey-Belle at arm's length. "Please stop smothering me."

"Charlotte Pascal is trash," Danielle says. Her eyes take on that destructive look she gets on the basketball court, but she looks unexpectedly at Irene. "You'd better be sincere about being gay, though. You can't fake liking girls for votes."

"Of course she's sincere," Honey-Belle snaps. "You don't know the process she's gone through—you can't imagine the internalized homophobia—"

"My best friend is gay, too, Honey-Belle," Danielle says loudly. "So you'll understand if I want to make sure she's not being led along by this whole thing."

Irene snorts derisively. She falls back against the car, shaking her head. "'Led along.' That's an interesting way to put it."

"What does that mean?" Honey-Belle asks.

Irene and I lock eyes. I prepare for her to throw this whole arrangement away, and in that moment, I almost want her to. This scheme has caused more trouble than it's worth. For both of us.

But as usual, she surprises me.

"Nothing." She sniffs. "Let's just get out of here. I'm tired of thinking. I'm tired of acting."

Honey-Belle nods sympathetically. Danielle sets her mouth, but she glances toward me, deferring.

"Okay," I say, trying to anchor myself. "Let's go. But someone else needs to drive."

"I can," Honey-Belle says. "I didn't drink anything."

I nod, hand her my keys, and slink into the back

seat. When Danielle slides in next to me, I meet her eyes sheepishly. "Did you tell the boys we won't be back?"

"Yeah," she says shortly. She was getting such good quality time with Kevin, but she gave it up to check on my fake girlfriend and me. Not for the first time, I feel unworthy of her friendship.

Irene tucks herself into the passenger seat in front of me. I watch her expression in the side mirror as we pull away from the curb. She looks utterly defeated. I know it's not directly because of me, but I still feel the weight of it.

It wasn't your fault, Mom said the day of the accident, *but it's still your responsibility*.

I speak before I can think twice about it.

"Maybe we should keep hanging out, just the four of us."

Danielle stares at me like I'm malfunctioning. Irene maintains her stony silence. But Honey-Belle, God bless her, gasps with delight.

"I love that idea! Like a girls' sleepover?" She gasps again. "We could have a self-care night in my Jacuzzi!"

Danielle's interest piques. "Wait, hold on. You have a Jacuzzi?"

"Yeah, with seven types of bubbles and color-changing lights!"

Danielle bites her lip. She's always loved Jacuzzis. I catch her eye, and she sighs in resignation. "Fuck it, I'm in."

"Great!" Honey-Belle trills.

"Irene?" I ask hopefully.

Irene clears her throat and shifts in her seat. "Fine."

Honey-Belle cheers and spins the car in the other direction.

* * *

The Hewett house is very much what you would expect of the Grandma Earl Christmas Emporium heirs. It's like a gingerbread house come to life, with swirls of color and light. I can hear the thrill in Mrs. Zander's voice when Danielle calls to say we'll be staying here tonight.

"*Is it true they have a hidden library?*" Mrs. Zander asks. Danielle hastens to click the volume down on her phone, but we can still hear her mom's excited voice. "*Teddy wants to know if they really have a ball pit in the basement!*"

"We do!" Honey-Belle beams. "Your brother can play here anytime!"

Danielle blushes and hastily tells her mom goodnight.

After that, it's a matter of figuring out swimwear for the Jacuzzi. Irene has her own bathing suit she keeps at the Hewetts' house—it's as red as the devil, which doesn't surprise me in the slightest—and Honey-Belle has a flowery bikini she's outgrown that fits Danielle's petite frame well enough.

But as for me?

"How about this top, Scottie?" Honey-Belle asks,

handing me a flaming orange racerback that clashes horribly with my hair. It looks too big for me, but maybe the racerback will keep it in place. I pull it on and turn around to show the others.

"You look like a carrot," Irene says, snorting. Her hands are at her hips, her bare stomach shining in the lamplight. I catch myself staring and turn toward Danielle instead.

"*Baywatch* thinks she's funny," I say, jerking my thumb toward Irene.

"She is," Danielle says.

Honey-Belle leads us through the merry house with its twinkling lights and pink-cheeked nutcrackers until we reach a sunroom with a Jacuzzi squat in the center. It's one of those aboveground whirlpools with an insulated cover, which Irene and Honey-Belle pull off the top in a way that suggests they've done this a million times before.

"It's . . . *bedazzled*," Danielle whispers to me. There's no need for her to point it out: The glinting gemstones catch the light on every part of the outer shell.

I can't help laughing, because the more I hang out with Honey-Belle, the less any of this surprises me.

Honey-Belle fiddles with the controller until the hot tub roars to life, the jets *glug-glug-glugging* while bubbles pop at the surface. We sink into the hot water and stretch against the four sides of the tub.

"This is heaven," Danielle says with her eyes closed.

"Screw that party, we should've been doing this the whole time."

Irene sinks low enough for the water to reach her chin. Her expression clouds over, and I think she must be ruminating on Charlotte's cruel gag. I feel another stab of guilt in my chest.

Honey-Belle must be thinking along the same lines, because she affectionately scratches Irene's head and says, "How about we play How's Your Heart?"

Irene laughs. "*You* can, Honey-Belle."

"What is it?" Danielle asks skeptically.

"It's what it sounds like," Honey-Belle says brightly. "Everyone goes around and shares how their heart feels right now. Mom and Dad and I play it all the time."

Danielle meets my eyes with a look that says *This can't be real.*

"I'll start," Honey-Belle says, undeterred. "My heart feels happy from talking to Gunther tonight. He's so sweet and interesting." She bites her lip demurely. "I didn't know he was so funny."

"Is he, though?" I mutter to Danielle.

Danielle doesn't hear me; she's staring keenly at Honey-Belle. "How do you admit that so easily?"

"What? That I like Gunther?"

Danielle twists her mouth, self-conscious. "Yeah. What if he doesn't like you back?"

Honey-Belle shrugs. "That's up to him, not me. I always say when I like things so the universe will hear me clearly. Actually, that's how Irene and I became friends! I told her I liked her aura. It's shimmery and bold, as I'm sure y'all have noticed." She shakes Danielle's forearm. "Why, do *you* like someone?"

"No, no, definitely not." Danielle clears her throat. "I was just asking hypothetically."

"That's too bad, because there's probably lots of guys who like you. You're a natural leader and you're super brainy and, to top it all off, you have Cleopatra eyes. You could rule a whole kingdom with a scepter and a necklace of rubies."

Danielle blinks rapidly. "Er . . . thank you."

"Anytime." Honey-Belle beams. "Your turn: How's your heart?"

"Um." Danielle shifts to spread her arms wider. "My heart feels anxious. It's like I'm always on the edge of something. The next test, the next big game, the next college acceptance letter. I have a hard time being happy where I am."

I've never heard Danielle speak like this. A surge of affection shoots up through my chest. I want to reach across the hot tub and hug her.

"That sounds mega stressful," Honey-Belle coos. "Thank you for sharing and helping to cement our bond of vulnerability. Okay, Ireenie, you're next."

Irene, who has been taking all this in as quietly as I have, shakes her head. "Not tonight, Honey-Belle."

"Oh come on. We can tell you're upset about the party."

"I'm fine."

"Your aura has gone dark and spiky," Honey-Belle says pointedly.

Irene dips her head back so she's looking at the ceiling. "Fine. My heart feels betrayed." She pauses. "I'm also hungry."

Honey-Belle smiles. "I was waiting for that. Nachos?"

"God, yes, please."

"Coming right up. Danielle, will you help me?"

"What?" Danielle says. "But it's so warm in here—"

Honey-Belle stares meaningfully at her and does an obvious head cock in my direction; she clearly wants me to have a moment alone with the angsty Irene.

"Yeah, yeah," Danielle grumbles, following Honey-Belle out of the Jacuzzi. "Y'all better have jalapeños . . ."

Irene and I are left in a loaded silence as their voices trail out of the room. We ignore each other from opposite sides of the hot tub until a full minute has passed.

"It's your turn," Irene says suddenly.

"What?" I ask, even though I know what she means.

She stares expectantly at me, unimpressed with my feigned ignorance. I roll my eyes and stretch my arms across the top of the tub.

"I feel—"

"No," she cuts me off. By the look on her face, I can

tell she's enjoying my discomfort. "Not 'I.' You know the format."

I glare at her. "*My heart* feels mixed emotions."

"Like?"

"I guess you could say there's a *tiny* part of my heart that feels bad for subjecting you to Charlotte. And *maybe* my heart feels guilty about it."

Irene squints across the haze. "And here I thought you couldn't admit to being wrong."

"I guess you made an incorrect *assumption*, then, huh?"

The ghost of a smirk flits across her mouth. I think we're going to leave it at that until she says, in a reckless sort of way, "You know I was lying in that video, right?"

We blink at each other across the roiling, gurgling water. I hesitate, knowing it's risky for me to call her out. I take the plunge anyway.

"You had feelings for her, didn't you?"

The way she tightens her mouth tells me everything.

"But she didn't like you back . . . ," I say, putting the pieces together, "and she's obviously a sociopath, so she knew how to use it against you . . . Let me guess: Did she make out with you 'for fun' and act like you were crazy for reading into it?"

Irene's expression darkens. Her chest rises and falls beneath the water. I force myself to keep my eyes above her neckline.

"The first time we hooked up was the same night she took that video," Irene says.

"You're shitting me."

"I'm not."

"So you knew she was filming you?"

"I was too drunk to care." She pauses. "I drank a lot back then."

"And now you don't." It's not a question. I'd inferred as much after watching her sip water all night.

She turns away and glances up at the dark skylight. "Did you and Tally sleep together?"

The question knocks the breath out of me. For a long beat, I can't answer. "Now who thinks they're entitled to personal history?"

Irene doesn't laugh. Her eyes burn into mine. "Did you?"

I look away from her. "Yes."

We're silent. The Jacuzzi bubbles simmer and pop.

"Did you and Charlotte sleep together?"

Irene brushes a finger against her chin. "Only when we were drunk."

"And she has the nerve to pull that shit on you tonight?"

Irene is quiet. Then she says: "Charlotte hates me because I loved her."

"That doesn't make any sense."

"Says the girl who can't figure out whether she wants to bone or murder her ex-girlfriend."

I fall silent.

"Charlotte is the reason I have this scar." She touches her eyebrow, smoothing it over like one day she can make it full again. Even in the dim light of the hot tub, I can see the break in her skin.

"We went to this Candlehawk party last year," she continues. "It was the craziest shit I've ever seen. Pills everywhere you looked, girls feeling each other up while people watched, some guy sobbing in the corner because he was so tweaked out. All I wanted was to go home and be together, just the two of us, but Charlotte caught a glimpse of Prescott from across the room, and that was the end of it."

Prescott. The Candlehawk boyfriend. The pompous jerk who assisted Charlotte tonight.

"She asked him to drive us to her house. He was so wasted he could hardly stand up straight. I refused to get in his car, or to let *her* get in his car, but Charlotte was so messed up she started fighting me. She kept yelling about how I was in love with her but could never have her, and I was a jealous loser, and that it was totally pathetic and—" she cuts herself off. "I tried to grab her, but she shoved me off. I smashed into this huge cabinet and cut my face on the corner."

I think of the lore surrounding her eyebrow scar. *She got too drunk at a party. She swam into the side of the pool when she was wasted. She fell off the bed when she was having crazy, anonymous sex.* What a cruel, bastardized version of the truth.

And then I remember the many times I wanted to thank the person who put that scar there. It makes me sick to my stomach.

"Charlotte's an asshole," I tell her. "She should be thanking her lucky stars you stopped her from getting into that car."

"But I didn't," Irene says. There's a tinge of regret in her tone. "I was drunk, too, and all I could focus on was my face bleeding. I let her go off with him and he got pulled over a mile from his house. He should have gotten a DUI, but his parents were friends with the Candlehawk police chief, so they let him go with a warning. Charlotte was escorted home, her parents freaked out and told Coach Banza and the other soccer coaches, and she got benched for the first five games of what was supposed to be her big debut year."

"And she blames you for this?"

Irene smiles wryly.

"But you tried to stop her!"

"She thinks I should have tried harder. And I don't know, maybe I should have. But sometimes it just hurts too much."

I let the story settle around us. "I'm sorry I made you go tonight."

Her eyes take me in. "You didn't *make* me do anything. I knew what I was stepping into."

"Still. I'm sorry I didn't take it seriously when you told me how toxic it was between you."

"It's fine, Scottie," she says, brushing my apology away. The way she says my name is comfortable and worn. "I'm not the only one dealing with a toxic fallout."

My heart pangs, remembering Tally at the party tonight. "Yeah. I guess."

I want to talk more, but Danielle and Honey-Belle barge in with their tray of nachos. Irene sits up and forces enthusiasm, and I remember what she said leaving Charlotte's tonight. *I'm tired of thinking. I'm tired of acting.*

For once, I don't call her on it. We kick back in the hot tub and feast until we're wrinkled as prunes.

* * *

When it's time for bed, Honey-Belle surprises us by offering her bedroom.

"Oh no—" Irene and I say together.

"Really, I want you to have it!" Honey-Belle insists, grasping our hands. "Danielle and I can sleep in the bunk bed room."

Behind her, Danielle struggles to hold a straight face. I can see the laugh fighting to burst out of her.

"Honey-Belle, don't be a martyr," Irene says urgently. "You love your bed."

"And I also love you," Honey-Belle says, tugging on a loose tendril of Irene's hair. "*And* your girlfriend."

Irene looks pointedly at me, but I'm at a loss for how to get out of this one.

"Sounds cozy," Danielle pipes up. "You guys can snuggle up and whisper sweet nothings while you fall asleep. What could be better?"

I shoot her the most intense death glare I can muster, but she just grins.

"So it's settled, then," Honey-Belle says brightly. "Let me get you some cozy pj's to make the snuggling even better."

* * *

Sometime later, I find myself standing in the middle of a bedroom that is unmistakably Honey-Belle's. There's an entire wall of stuffed animals, most of which are unicorns. I count nine different music boxes atop the dressers, desk, and nightstand. The sleigh-style bed is covered with a fluffy yellow comforter beneath a high white canopy.

Irene moves to stand on the opposite side of the bed, eyeing it like a sewer she's dreading climbing into. I step up to my side and wait. There's a swell of silence as we delay the inevitable.

"Fuck," I say finally.

"Hmph," she snorts in agreement.

"You couldn't convince her to put us in the bunk bed room? She's *your* friend."

"This is *your* stupid scheme, and I didn't see you making any effort."

I shake my head. "It's impossible to argue with her. It's like upsetting a baby."

"Don't patronize her."

"I'm not, but you know what I mean."

"You definitely are, but whatever." She snatches her pajamas out of her duffel bag in a way that suggests the conversation is over. I lay my borrowed pair out on the bed. We both go still. There's another swell of silence.

"Nervous to change in front of me, *snookums*?" I ask.

"Do you always project your neuroses onto other people?" She slips her towel off her body and I roll my eyes so I won't accidentally look at her bare skin. She turns away to change, but glances back at me at the last second. "Don't you dare creep on me."

"Right, 'cause that's what I'm thinking. I'd rather creep on a bunch of boys."

"Funny," she huffs, spinning around. She starts to pull off her bathing suit straps; her back muscles move in the dim light. I wonder how it would feel to press my lips to the nape of her neck—

No. Stop.

I squeeze my eyes shut and turn hastily around. I slip into my borrowed set of pajamas—a soft blue shirt with a ribbon at the collar and a pair of candy cane-striped bottoms. The only sound is the heavy *thwap* of our damp bathing suits hitting the floor. My heart won't stop thumping in my neck.

Just as I'm pulling my hair out of my shirt, Irene clears her throat.

"Are you finished?"

"Yes."

She turns around. Her eyes flicker briefly over my pajamas, but she doesn't say anything, just gathers her toiletry bag. I stay quiet as she slips out of the room.

I'm not going to wash my face or brush my teeth alongside her, so I plop down on the bed and wait. I glance at her phone lying innocently on the bedside table and try to imagine what her pass code might be. I tell myself it's probably 666, but the joke doesn't amuse me the way it normally would. It's been a weird, confusing night.

The last person I shared a bed with was Tally. It was summertime and her parents were out of town. We held each other beneath the sheets, and my heart pulsed at every touch of her skin. But that was months ago—long before she made out with another girl at a party, long before I set up a dating ruse to make her jealous.

Would I have rejected her for having garlic breath tonight? I know the answer immediately: *No. I loved her too much.*

But would she have rejected me?

"I knew you were the type to fall asleep without brushing your teeth first. Gross."

Irene comes swooshing back into the bedroom, her loose pajama shirt hanging over her black joggers. I swallow down the unexpected emotion in my throat and try to level a retort her way.

"Are you wearing a retainer?" I shoot back. "God. Please don't breathe in my direction tonight."

"I'm sure you'll smother me with a pillow if I do. You'd better hurry if you want to beat Honey-Belle. She takes forever in the bathroom."

I grab my things and hustle out of the room, glad for an excuse to be alone again. I use the spare toothbrush Honey-Belle gave me, noticing how Irene has squeezed the toothpaste so it perfectly curls at the empty end. Freaking weirdo. I wash my face and take several deep breaths to clear my head.

When I slip back into Honey-Belle's bedroom, Irene is tucked beneath the covers, playing on her phone. Her hair hangs long and wavy, the sides of it brushing her glasses. I had no idea she wore glasses.

"You'd better not touch me," she says as I crawl into bed.

"In what universe would I touch you?"

"You look like a hand-grabber. Or a footsie freak."

"No chance, weirdo." It's a lie: I was always grabbing for Tally's hand when we shared a bed. I *really* hope I don't subconsciously try that tonight. "What are you holding?"

The slightest patch of color blooms in her cheeks. She keeps her eyes glued to her phone. "Nothing."

It looks like an old T-shirt, or maybe just a rag. She has it tucked under her arm in a way that suggests regular habit.

"Doesn't look like nothing."

"Shut up," she mutters, but she doesn't say anything more.

"No, really," I say, rolling my head toward hers. "What's the story?"

She's silent for an annoyingly long minute. "It's my mom's old shirt. She let me nap with it when I was little."

"Why?"

"Because it was soft," she says irritably. "Why do you care?"

I shrug, unperturbed. "I just think it's funny when you're weird."

"Everyone's weird." She rolls away and turns off the light. "Goodnight. Touch me and you die."

The way she says it, it's almost like she's trying to make me laugh.

"Sweet dreams to you, too."

It takes me a while to fall asleep. I can feel Irene struggling, too. It feels too intimate, too revealing, to sleep alongside each other like this. I'm too attuned to her breathing cycle, to the sound of her cheek finding the cold part of the pillow. I'm too aware of the smell of her hair, only inches from my face.

11

I WAKE UP TOO EARLY, LIKE 7:00 A.M. EARLY.
The blue-white light is peeking through the curtains,
and the room is quiet and calm. Irene is sleeping on
her stomach, her mom's old shirt clutched against her
side. Her wavy hair fans across the pillow. Of *course* she
looks attractive even when she's asleep.

I slip out of bed and sneak down to the kitchen, hoping to find some bread I can toast, but I'm not alone like
I'd hoped.

Honey-Belle is there, sitting cross-legged at the table,
scrolling through her phone with her hair sticking up at
odd angles.

"Scottie!" She beams. "How'd you sleep? Did you
like my air purifier?"

"We didn't use it," I say apologetically. In the back
of my brain, I notice how weird it is to say *we*. I help

myself to the bread box and find cranberry jelly in the refrigerator.

"I'm so glad Irene has you now," Honey-Belle tells me when I sit down. "She needed a win after everything that happened last year."

My ears perk up. "You mean with Charlotte?"

Honey-Belle winces. "I know she might seem hung up on her, but I promise she likes you. I can tell. She talks about you all the time. 'Oh, Scottie has two sisters. Scottie killed it at practice yesterday. Scottie loves this song.'"

I almost choke on my toast. "Really?"

"Don't be a goof," Honey-Belle says with a little laugh. "It's nice to see her with someone who takes care of her. Irene is super loyal. If you're one of her people, she'll do anything for you. And I'm sure you've figured out that she's a total romantic, even if she denies it. I mean, her favorite movie is *Dirty Dancing*. She plays that song from the end over and over again. So cheesy."

The irony of Honey-Belle calling something *cheesy* is not lost on me. "Right."

"Oh my gosh," Honey-Belle says suddenly. "You know what we have to do? A double date! You can set me up with Gunther!"

"Oh . . . yeah?"

"It'll be perfect! How about next weekend?"

* * *

We leave as soon as Danielle and Irene wake up. The rival college football games are on today and we want to watch them with our families. Irene rushes us out so she can catch the Georgia/Georgia Tech game with her dad, but first, she pours a thermos of coffee. For each of us.

The moment we drop Danielle off, I turn to Irene and word vomit.

"Honey-Belle cornered me into a double date. You, me, her, and Gunther. I was so shocked I couldn't say no."

Irene's head rolls slowly in my direction. "So?"

"So . . . that's . . . you're fine with that?"

She sighs wearily. "We've already dug ourselves this deep. Might as well go a little deeper."

I tap my fingers on the coffee thermos she poured for me. She knew to add cream, but not sugar. She takes a relaxed sip of her own thermos and stretches back in my passenger seat like she's done it a million times.

And I realize, with a tightness in my chest, that she has.

"You snored like a monster last night," I sputter. "Like a dragon. Or a *T. rex*. Or maybe a mastodon."

She shrugs. "I was tired."

"Yeah, well . . . it was annoying."

"Sorry," she says like she couldn't care less.

"And you kept stealing the covers. Like, every half an hour. I even shoved you at one point, but you were oblivious."

Irene side-eyes me. "Okay, are you done now?"

There's no venom in her tone; she merely sounds tired. The way I only let myself get with my sisters or Danielle. The way I never let myself get with Tally.

"Well, it's . . . it was annoying," I repeat feebly.

Irene draws a deep breath. "Can we press pause on the I-hate-your-guts game? The banter is juicy and all, but it'd be nice to let my guard down. Especially after last night."

My chest constricts again. "Fine."

"So what else did you and Honey-Belle talk about? Did she show you her vintage Furby collection?"

I hate the way we're talking like casual friends. I hate knowing what she looks like when she first wakes up. I hate that she's still wearing her glasses in front of me.

I want to tell her that Honey-Belle said she talks about me all the time. I want to ask her what it means. What any of this means.

But I can't go there. I can't. Tally made out with another girl in front of me last night, and then Irene and I shared a bed, and I don't know how to process any of it.

"We made plans for the double date," I say with a shrug. "It sounds ridiculous, but whatever."

"It won't be that bad. Hopefully we'll get a good movie out of it." She drops her head back and watches the scenery fly by like she doesn't have a care in the world. "But *you're* driving."

* * *

I'd thought Irene's reputation might take a hit after Charlotte's antics, but if anything, people at school seem even *more* obsessed with her. Some of them—mostly the cheerleaders and their followers—insist that Irene is a victim in this situation. "It's nobody's truth but her own!" I hear one girl ranting to her friend. "How dare anyone judge her journey?!" Other people, led by the soccer girls, are convinced that Irene is manipulating the whole school for the purpose of securing a SAOY nomination. "Like, does she think we're some kind of convenient identity she can just shrug on and off again?" the queer soccer goalie says to anyone who will listen. "There's no way in hell people will buy into this bullshit."

The only people who know the truth—which is somewhere in the middle of these opposing sides—are Irene, Danielle, and myself. Irene doesn't seem particularly bothered by the constant gossip, and Danielle is too antsy about the upcoming Christmas Classic to pay any attention. As for me, I'm preoccupied with checking my phone every other second. I'd thought Tally might text me after the party, but she's been silent.

On the first weekend of December, Irene and I go forward with our double date with Gunther and Honey-Belle. It doesn't seem like a bad idea now that we need to cement ourselves as a "real" couple, especially because I know Honey-Belle will talk about it at school the following week. That should get the haters off our backs.

So that's how I find myself swinging into Irene's driveway on a Friday night, dressed in my best date clothes with my hair straightened to perfection. I'm right on time to pick her up. By which I mean, I'm only four minutes late. She doesn't even bother complaining about it.

We drive to the Chuck Munny in near silence until Irene takes the liberty of plugging her own phone into the aux cable.

"Um?" I say.

"Um?" she mocks, batting her eyelashes.

"Play something good, at least."

"Sorry, but I don't have your eighties-dad playlist on Spotify."

"Oh, aren't you just *hilarious*."

When we get to the theater, Honey-Belle and Gunther are already there, chatting inside the concessions area. Irene takes my arm as we swoop up to them.

"Such a great night for a date, right?" she says. "I had to force Scottie off the couch. She was enjoying our snuggling a little too much." She pinches my cheek and I try not to swat her off. "You know how she is. Such a cornball."

Gunther smiles uncertainly. "Yeah, I guess." He puts an arm on the small of Honey-Belle's back. "Can I treat you to an Icee?"

After they turn around, Irene drops my arm like a heavy weight.

"That hurt," I whisper, rubbing my cheek.

"Bitch-baby," she mumbles, scanning the menu board. "Are we getting anything? I could go for a soda."

"We can split one," I say without thinking.

There's a twinkle in her eyes. "Fine," she says, shoving me along. "But two straws, horndog. I don't want your germs."

Once the four of us have our snacks, we make our way to the only theater in the building. Tonight they're showing *Say Anything . . .* , the eighties classic with John Cusack and Ione Skye. It's my absolute favorite, but I don't dare tell any of them that.

The seats are packed when we walk in, so we split up between two rows. Gunther and Honey-Belle snag a couple of seats in the middle and Irene and I grab a pair of seats diagonally behind them. We settle back and kick our feet up at the same time.

It's kind of weird, sitting next to her in a dark theater, especially once we start trading Sour Patch Kids back and forth. My fingers keep accidentally brushing hers when I reach into the box. I ignore the warm tingle across my scalp.

"I have to pee," Irene says toward the end of the movie. She moves to stand up, but I grab her arm.

"You can't go right *now*! He's about to do the boom box thing!"

"I've seen that clip a million times." She rolls her eyes in the blue light of the screen. "It's so cheesy."

"*Cheesy?* Are you insane?"

"Zajac, I will piss in your lap if you don't let me go."

Sure enough, she misses the iconic moment when John Cusack holds the boom box outside Ione Skye's window, serenading her with "In Your Eyes" at dawn. I get goose bumps up and down my entire body. Without meaning to, I imagine Tally holding a stereo outside my window, determined to win me back. I wonder if I'd run out to her.

"I feel so much better," Irene whispers when she returns.

"I can't believe you missed that."

"I sure as hell wasn't going to miss the scene where her dad gets caught embezzling. That's the best part."

I shake my head in the darkness, but Irene merely shrugs and steals the soda cup from my hand.

* * *

Gunther and Honey-Belle are holding hands when we exit the theater. Irene catches my eye and pretends to gag when they're not looking. It almost makes me laugh.

"What a night for romance," she says as we're driving home. "Honey-Belle and Gunther, Ione Skye's dad and prison . . ."

"You're such a cynic."

"Am not." She chews on another Sour Patch Kid. She insisted we buy a second box before we left the Munny. "I just always hated that stupid boom box moment. It's melodramatic for no reason."

I whip around to scoff at her. "It's one of the most iconic images in American cinema. It's fucking perfect."

"It's empty and self-indulgent."

"It's *romantic*. It's tender and poignant and star-crossed—"

"It's a waste of time. Grand gestures don't mean anything in the place of actual effort. He should have just talked to her. You know, actually *communicated* instead of performing some fantasy version of love. He just wanted to be all up in his feels."

I glare at her. "Says the girl whose favorite movie is *Dirty Dancing*."

Irene falls silent. Even in the darkness, I can see her embarrassment. "How do you know that?"

"I have my ways."

"Seriously." She reaches over to pinch my arm, and I yelp. "How do you know that?"

"God, relax, I'm trying to drive! Honey-Belle told me, okay?"

Irene blows out an irritated breath, but I can hear the self-consciousness beneath it. "What else did she tell you?"

"That's between us."

"Scottie."

"Fine, you really wanna know? She said you talk about me all the time."

Irene snorts. "Oh did she now . . ."

"*Are* you talking about me?"

She narrows her eyes. "What, you think I'm, like, gossiping? I spend half my time with you now. You're obviously going to come up in conversation."

"She said you talk about my favorite songs."

Irene laughs in the back of her throat. "More like I complain that you play the same five songs over and over."

I look over at her as we turn back onto the main road. "So you're not . . . like . . ."

"Obsessed with you?" She snorts and strains against the seat. "No. Were you worried I was catching feelings?"

"No," I say hastily.

"Okay, good. Because I'm not."

"Good. Neither am I."

We fall silent. I turn the music up. She turns it back down.

"You don't have to act like the idea is so horrible, though," she says. "You sound like you've contracted bird flu."

"That's not what I meant," I say quickly. "It's just . . . this is purely a business arrangement."

"I am well aware, Zajac." She crosses her arms over her chest. "I wouldn't want to date you, anyway. You love drama too much."

"What? I don't love drama."

"You totally do."

"In what way?!"

"Um—" She gestures meaningfully between us. "This way? Paying someone to be your girlfriend so you can emotionally manipulate the ex who doesn't care about you? Talk about a performative gesture. It's exactly the kind of thing I *hate*."

I feel my heart rate rising, my cheeks flushing. "You're really pushing my buttons, you know that? What was it you said after Charlotte's party—something about how I was arrogant to think I understood your enemies?"

She pops her lips. "Point taken. I'll stay in my lane."

"Thank you."

When we pull into her driveway, she takes her time getting out of my car. She even hands me the last few Sour Patch Kids.

"Okay look, you know something?" She hovers outside my car door, her hands in her jumpsuit pockets. "I don't understand your motivation with this whole thing, but I do think it's . . . *endearing* . . . that you still believe in love. Even if it's of the melodramatic-gestures kind."

I narrow my eyes, pretending to be suspicious of her. "This candy really got to you, huh?"

"What?"

"'First they're sour, then they're sweet,'" I recite.

She drops her head back, disgusted with me. "Wow. That was actually the worst."

"Good thing you're making a pretty penny off it."

"Honestly, I need a pay increase."

I smirk. "'Night, Abraham."

"'Night, Zajac."

She rolls her eyes and snaps my door closed.

12

THE MORNING OF THE CHRISTMAS CLASSIC game, I wake up to a FaceTime call from Danielle, who's still in bed with her hair scarf on. "I'm freaking out," she says scratchily. "My stomach's twisted up like a pretzel. Tell me I'm allowed to quit the team."

"Don't ask me, ask our captain," I say, rubbing my eyes. "But just know, she's a hard-ass."

"Ha ha."

We get out of bed and go to our respective toilets, in our respective houses, and carry on our conversation.

"I can't even pee," Danielle groans, screwing up her face. "I hate sports. I hate them. I'm only meant to be a bookworm. I am Hermione and I will never be Cho Chang."

"You're *both*," I promise her. "I'm nervous, too, but I have a great feeling about tonight! Aren't you at least a *little* excited?"

She groans some more. We hang up after she promises to play upbeat music during her shower.

My sisters bolster my confidence when they barge into my room singing "IT'S GAME DAY! IT'S GAME DAY! FUCK CANDLEHAWK, IT'S GAME DAY!"

"Daphne!" I gasp theatrically. "Did you just curse?"

They smoosh me into a hug. Thora plants kisses all over my head, and I can't do anything but laugh.

"I'm wearing your old practice jersey to school!" Daphne says. "My friends are gonna be so sick of me talking about you!"

"I'm renaming our lunch special The Eleven," Thora says, referring to my jersey number. "You're gonna kill it tonight, Scots!"

Irene picks me up before school. We've planned that she'll be the one to drive me to the game's after-party, which will hopefully be a blowout celebration after we win. She's wearing my picture button affixed to her shirt today, and I do a double take when I see it.

"For real?" I ask, not even trying to keep the delight out of my voice. "I got upgraded to your actual wardrobe?"

She shrugs; the corners of her mouth twitch. "It's a special occasion. I can suffer through it for one day."

At school, I'm greeted with a roar of noise. People high-five me in the hallways and tape good-luck notes to my locker. The Cleveland triplets beg to take a selfie with Danielle and me. Even Gino goes out of his way to be seen talking to me in the cafeteria line.

By the time the bell rings at the end of the day, I'm feeling so hopeful and assured that I actually hug Irene when I see her.

"Oh," she says, tensing up beneath my hug. "So this is a thing now?"

"We did it," I tell her. "There's no way in hell we're gonna lose this game."

She laughs, and for maybe the first time since I've known her, it's a bright and authentic laugh. "You know something, Zajac? For once, I agree with you."

* * *

The bleachers are jam-packed with fans when my team hustles onto the court. It's the fullest I've ever seen our gym, and the vast majority of the crowd is wearing red. Dozens of people sport the trademark reindeer ears that are usually reserved for big football games.

"Holy shit," Danielle whispers, her eyes wide. "There's even more people than last time."

"Which means we'll play even better," I tell her as we claim our spots on the team bench. "We're gonna win tonight, I promise you. Look at their players—they can't even fathom how this happened!"

Down the line from our bench, the Candlehawk players in their shiny gold jerseys are regarding the bleachers warily. Whereas my team is casually stretching and grinning at our show of support, their players are frozen in place. Tally looks more devastated than the rest of them put together.

Our starting lineups meet at half-court for the jump ball. Danielle and I take our places on either side of the center, which means I'm only a few feet from Tally—the closest I've been to her since Charlotte's party.

Tally catches my eye for a fleeting second. It's hard to read the expression on her face, but it's something close to regret. It's almost like she wants reassurance from me. Her blue eyes are asking if this is a fluke.

I purse my lips and look away from her, and in that moment, I realize I'm the one who has the power now. It feels incredible. And yeah, maybe I feel kind of disgusted with myself for that, but I don't dwell on it.

At the last second, before the ref tosses the ball into the air, I lock eyes with Irene. She's standing with her pom-poms behind her back, her hair up in its perfect ponytail, her stance confident and balanced. Her squad is lined up neatly behind her, watching with bated breath. She catches me looking and winks. A weird surge of affection shoots up my chest.

The ref tosses the ball up, and the game begins.

* * *

A few minutes into the second quarter, I know for certain we're going to win. It's impossible to deny our momentum, our energy, the electricity rolling off our fans. Danielle sinks two jump shots in a row, her anxiety completely evaporated. Googy snatches a rebound straight out of Tally's hands. I have two steals in a two-minute period and can literally hear my family screaming my name.

And in the third quarter, when we're leading by sixteen points, I intercept a pass that Tally meant for her point guard. It's a breakaway steal that has me racing down the court, the crowd's applause thundering in my ears, the ball sure and steady under my hand. I make an easy layup and loop my way under the basket with a grin so big my cheeks hurt. Gunther, dressed in the Fighting Reindeer costume, bursts onto the court and scoops me up in a hug, and everyone screams with laughter, even after the ref threatens a technical foul.

In the end, we win with a solid eleven-point lead. To me, it feels like we've won Olympic Gold. The noise in the gym is so loud it makes my head ache, but I can't do anything but smile and hold on to Danielle, who's so happy she's actually crying.

When we line up to shake hands with our opponents, I don't even look twice at Tally. In that moment, I'm so far beyond her that I forget it's her I've been trying to beat all along—and that I still have a ways to go. I break free of the lineup to find my family, Danielle's family, Gunther, and Kevin pouring out of the stands to hug us.

And behind them, fresh off her victory routine, is Irene.

"Amazing what a little confidence can do, huh?" she

asks me in the midst of the madness. Her eyes are alight; her whole face is shining. My button is pinned to her cheerleading uniform.

I can't focus enough to answer her; I'm being grabbed on all sides by my teammates, my family, my friends. But I do know that the smiles we're giving each other are as real as the points on the scoreboard.

* * *

The scene at the Emporium is wild. Outside, by the tracks, people are lighting sparklers. Inside the garage, the air is stuffy and warm. Honey-Belle has lit up the string lights, Gunther is pouring eggnog into holly-green cups, and someone has inflated the lawn-decor Santa Clauses. Everything is crowded and intimate and alive.

Danielle is euphoric. She's switched her game shorts out for her favorite Adidas joggers, but she's still wearing her jersey like a badge of honor. I notice she's washed her face and put on makeup, too. Her eyelashes, which are naturally long, look even thicker and prettier in the dim light of the garage. And maybe it's my imagination, but it seems like Kevin is noticing.

Honey-Belle is in hostess mode, her cheerleading uniform bedecked with a sparkly feather boa. She congratulates me for the fifth time and squeezes me so hard it hurts my neck. Gunther grins at her like a puppy dog.

For the first hour of the party, my teammates and I are treated to hugs and drinks and replays. Somebody sticks reindeer antlers on my head and tells me I was the MVP, and I blush without caring that my cheeks turn the color of my hair. I hardly speak to Irene, but I have this sense that she's letting me have my moment. When I spot her on the other side of the garage, still sporting her cheerleading uniform, she grins and gives me another uncharacteristic wink.

"Hey!" Honey-Belle shouts at the room. "Hey! Cut the music! I want to make a toast!"

The thumping bass stops and people press closer to the center of the room. Gunther passes Honey-Belle an eggnog cup that sloshes over the rim.

"Where's Irene?" Honey-Belle shouts. She looks at me. "Scottie, where's your girl?"

Something about it makes my face warm; I can't catch my breath to answer her.

"Irene!" Honey-Belle yells. "Get over here! We're toasting!"

Irene makes her way over, rolling her eyes but laughing at Honey-Belle's enthusiasm. She hands me a water like it's second nature to her, and I realize I'm staring at her without meaning to. Her mascara is slightly smudged beneath her eyes; her skin is damp and glowing. Her cedar perfume swirls around us.

"Cheers to the Fighting Reindeer!" Honey-Belle yells. "We're definitely gonna win the championship this year! And extra cheers to our MVP, Scottie Zajac!"

I've never felt so important in all my life. People bang

on my back with such force that I almost double over. I even get a kiss on the head from Gunther. The cheering halts as people knock back their drinks. Then there's clapping and shouting and more congratulatory hands on me.

"Irene, show her some love!" Honey-Belle yells.

I turn with a skip in my stomach to see Irene gaping at Honey-Belle, but it only lasts for a second. She centers herself and pulls me in for an obligatory hug, the smirk in her eyes telling me that we should have expected as much. Her arms go tight around me and I pray she can't feel my pulse beating against her warm skin.

But it's not enough for Honey-Belle.

"Oh come on, Irene, put some feeling into it!" she chides. "Your girlfriend destroyed that game! Doesn't she deserve a kiss?"

Irene looks blindsided. My heart beats harder than it did on the court.

The crowd agrees with Honey-Belle. They're shouting at Irene to let loose, to show me some love. Danielle is frozen between laughter and shock. Charlotte Pascal looks poisonous.

"For fuck's sake, Irene!" Honey-Belle screams. "Seize the damn moment!"

Irene turns to me. There's a challenge in her eyes, but a question, too. It's like we're having a wordless conversation, and when I see her eyes flit to my mouth, I know what's going to happen before it does.

And I don't stop it.

Irene presses against me, wraps her hand along my neck. I feel it like I've never felt anyone's touch before. All I can see are her dark, blazing eyes, sure and steady, almost defiant.

She pulls me in and kisses me.

Something sparks in my belly, in my chest. Her kiss is gentler than I would have expected, but so firm, too. Her mouth is warm and soft. She tastes slightly of salt.

Irene pulls away and says something to the crowd, but I'm in a daze. My whole body is warm and buzzing.

The only thing my eyes can find is Danielle, standing there with her jaw hanging, and I know she can read the honesty in my face. I look away before she can see it too clearly.

Honey-Belle squeals with delight. She wrangles Irene into a hug that Irene tries to resist. I'm aware of people watching me, and I remember I'm supposed to look happy and in love. I force a smile and pretend like Irene has kissed me like this a hundred times before. Just the thought of that makes my head spin.

When Irene finally catches my eye, there's something in her expression I haven't seen before. I want to hold it and turn away from it at the same time. I overemphasize my smile and manage to say I'm getting another drink, but when I turn away I feel her eyes following me.

* * *

For the dozenth time this year, I wish I could go home with anyone else. But tonight, it's not because I hate her.

It's because I can no longer deny that I actually *like* her.

"Ready?" Irene asks, swinging her keys around her finger. It's a nervous tick that doesn't fit with her persona at all, and I want to tease her about it, but the words get stuck in my throat.

There's an unbearable moment of silence when we first slide into her car, but she switches her music on and plays the volume much louder than usual. It's a terrible song that I'm pretty sure neither one of us actually likes. We both do a lot of throat-clearing and seat-shifting as we wait at the first red light.

It feels weird to say there's any kind of normal with Irene, but if we were being normal right now, we'd bull-doze through this awkwardness. We'd force the subject of the kiss into life, even if it felt excruciating. We'd give each other shit about how weird we're both being.

But something has changed. It's a shift I can feel in the air between us. I want so badly to get back to our usual banter, but my tongue is leaden against my teeth.

It's not until we're parked in my driveway that Irene breaks the silence.

"So . . . that could have been worse."

I stare at the console. Whatever I thought she might say, it wasn't that. Was I hoping for something realer?

"I mean," she continues, taking a breath, "I guess they

needed proof at some point, especially after Charlotte's stupid antics. Plus, Honey-Belle's thirsty like that."

"Right."

The music plays on. The car hums beneath us.

"Um," Irene says.

I glance expectantly at her. "Yeah?"

She blinks across the space between us. I hate how attractive she looks with her dark eyes and full lips. I hate that it makes my heart flutter.

"You played great tonight," she says with a half shrug. She's trying to sound detached, but I hear the tremor in her voice.

"Thanks," I manage to say.

"Did it feel the way you hoped it would?"

What a question. I fantasized about winning the Christmas Classic a million times, but I never envisioned kissing Irene afterward. And I certainly never imagined I would *feel* anything kissing her.

"Yeah," I say breathlessly. "It was great."

There's a loaded silence between us. I can't stand it anymore. "So . . . see you later," I say, sliding out of the car. "Thanks for the—the cheering and everything."

"Goodnight," she says, trying to find my eyes. "And, you know, good game."

* * *

It's after midnight, but my family is still awake. They want to hear more about the game, to tell me every worry

182

and triumph they felt while I was playing, and for a few minutes it successfully distracts me. I bask in the warm routine of the five of us flopped on the couch together, Thora with her sass and Daphne with her giggling and my parents with their cheesy jokes.

But then my mom tells me how pretty Irene looked at the game, and my stomach loop-de-loops in the most surprising way.

"Yeah, she looked nice," I say vaguely. I try not to feel the echo of her kiss, but my lips are tingling so much I swear they're probably swelling in place.

"You look tired, Scots," Dad says. "Why don't you get up to bed and rest those sore muscles?"

I don't fight him on it. Upstairs, in the cool dark of my bedroom, I slip beneath my quilt and scroll through my phone to get my mind off things. The problem is, the exact opposite happens. One of the Cleveland triplets has posted a video of Irene kissing me.

And we look . . . *good*. We look real. We look like we fit together.

I feel breathless all over again.

But almost like a reflex, my next thought goes to Tally. She will no doubt see this. Will it pierce her heart, the way watching her kiss that girl at Charlotte's party pierced mine? Will she see the feelings written on my face? Will she believe I've truly moved on from her?

Should I even be thinking about Tally anymore?

"Did it feel the way you hoped it would?" Irene asked me in the car.

Maybe it did earlier tonight, but it doesn't anymore. Because I definitely never expected that only hours after beating Candlehawk in the Christmas Classic, I would fall asleep crying.

13

HOLIDAY BREAK BEGINS WITH A RAINSTORM.
It never gets cold enough to snow before Christmas, but
I guess *something* has to fall down from the sky. For two
days, rain lashes the windows and pushes our inflatable
snowman decorations onto the grass. We stay indoors
and feed our boredom with Christmas movies. When we
get tired of that, Thora insists we stage the holiday card
she wants to send from her family.

"You mean *our* family?" I ask.

"No, I mean Pickles, BooBoo, and myself."

She dresses in green velvet and lounges in front of
the fireplace with the cats in her arms. Daphne captures
three whole photos before Pickles scratches his way free.

When the weather finally clears, Danielle and I go
shopping for family gifts. Daphne tags along, which
I'm grateful for, because it means Danielle won't have
a chance to ask about Irene. We make our way around

town, hitting up the mall, the bookstore, and Balthazar's Antiques. None of us suggests treading into Candlehawk.

"Is Thora working today?" Danielle asks after we dip into a beauty store for some bath bombs. "We should go by The Chimney. I'm craving their fried pickles."

"I could go for a virgin piña colada," Daphne says. "Shopping is stressful. I need something to take the edge off."

"Yes, ma'am," I say, slinging my arm around her shoulders. Truth be told, I've been over this shopping thing for at least an hour. I've already picked out presents for Mom, Dad, and Thora, and now everything I see is starting to remind me of either Tally or Irene. I can't buy a gift for either one of them, though for vastly different reasons.

We slip into the warm, bustling tavern that is The Chimney just as the lunch hour is winding down. Thora spots us and signals to the hostess to put us in our favorite booth, the one by the jukebox. We slide into the high-backed booth and have a basket of fried pickles delivered within two minutes.

"Thora's the best," Danielle says, devouring the snack. "She always knows exactly what we want."

"She's people-smart," Daphne says astutely. "That's what Mom says."

"How did I miss that gene?" I ask.

"You're people-smart," Danielle says. "Maybe not, like, on a Thora level, but you're pretty sufficient."

"A ringing endorsement. Thank you."

Danielle shrugs. "Irene is the only person I know who's actually on par with Thora."

I say nothing, trying to keep my expression neutral.

"Is that why Thora doesn't like her?" Daphne asks.

I look around. "Did she say that?"

"Um." Daphne's ears turn red—a gene my sisters and I most definitely share. "I mean, I think she's just protective of you."

"Thora doesn't like anyone I date," I grumble.

As if on cue, Thora appears out of nowhere, carrying two nonalcoholic piña coladas for Daphne. "Did I hear my name?"

"No," I say, avoiding her eyes.

"We're talking about Scottie's love life," Danielle says. I glower at her across the pickle basket.

"Ah yes, her *love* life," Thora says.

"Why do you have to say it like that?" I ask.

"Because I'm not sure it involves actual love?"

My face burns. I grind my teeth and try not to lose my temper.

"Not even with Irene?" Daphne asks. Her smile becomes mischievous. "My friend's sister showed us that video of her kissing you at the Emporium. It was so romantic."

"That was . . . whatever," I say, keenly aware of Thora's eyes on me.

"*Was* it romantic?" Daphne asks breathlessly.

"No," I say shortly at the same time that Danielle says, "Yes." I flat-out glare at her, but she stares defiantly back.

"I just don't want Scottie to get hurt," Thora says pointedly.

"Irene's not going to hurt her," Danielle says.

"Can we please stop talking about me like I'm not sitting right here?"

Thora and Danielle settle, both of them sighing. Daphne pats my back and slides over her extra piña colada.

"Drink up," she says knowingly. "It will settle your nerves."

I inhale the sugary drink and let their conversation wash over me. My body feels all out of whack, like my emotions are sumo wrestling each other. I don't care how much Danielle brings her up: I *don't* want to talk about Irene. It's just too confusing. How can I be crushing on her and grieving Tally at the same time? Because that's what this is: grief. I may have thought I was finally getting over Tally, especially with the high I was on from basketball, but kissing Irene brought a rush of heartache to the surface. Her kiss was the first one I've had since my breakup, and even though it was great, it was *different*. It made all these feelings flood back.

I just wish I could box up my new feelings for Irene, tag the box with *Do not open until breakup grief is over*, and store it in my attic, out of sight and out of mind. I mean, I'm not even sure these flutters of excitement I'm feeling *are* a crush. I'm not thinking about Irene all the time like I did with Tally. I'm not obsessively checking her social media. I miss her, but I'm not bursting out of my skin with longing for her. I haven't even talked to her in days. Is that normal?

And beneath these confusing feelings, there's a mean little voice that pipes up whenever I imagine kissing Irene again. A voice that is deeply intertwined with the same insecurity Tally brought out in me.

Irene had your car towed. She humiliated you. She stood there callously while you cried.

How can I possibly reconcile having a crush on someone who bullied me? What does it say about my self-worth that I'm drawn to girls who hurt me?

* * *

On Christmas Eve night, my sisters bundle up in their peacoats while I throw on the fleece I insist is warm enough even though it's not. Mom wears her beautiful cream-colored coat and Dad sports his old brown jacket that smells like peppermint. We traipse out of the house and begin our walk toward Saint Gabriel's for the vigil Mass. The air is crisp and still, just cold enough to feel romantic.

Daphne points out the Christmas wreaths on the neighbors' doors. Mom and Dad huff at the Haliburton-Riveras' notion of decorating, which is a lone, ceramic candy cane hanging in their foyer window. Thora snaps a picture of Mom sticking out her tongue.

We turn onto the main road and walk past Irene's neighborhood. I try not to think about her, but it's like trying not to picture the color red.

The church is just beginning to fill up when we arrive. Poinsettias line the entryway and a wooden Nativity scene adorns the altar. The church smells like incense and old ladies' perfume, and the rumbling of voices is happy and warm. We slide into an empty pew toward the back and tug off our jackets.

"Oh look, Regina George is here," Thora says dryly.

"What?"

I follow her gaze to the opposite side of the church. Irene is kneeling in a pew with her family, wearing a jade sweater with her dark hair falling over the side. My blood warms; my breath catches.

"Didn't you know she would be here?" Thora asks.

"I didn't even know we went to the same church."

"Let's throw some holy water on her. Maybe she'll burst into flames."

Irene must feel me looking, because she turns her head and meets my eyes. I feel myself blushing, but I don't look away. She smirks and raises a single palm to say hi.

I raise my palm in return. Then I bow my head and

mime praying very solemnly. Even from across the church, I can see her rolling her eyes.

* * *

When Mass ends, I'm eager to leave so I can catch Irene in the parking lot. I've spent the last ten minutes thinking about what I'll say. I might be confused about my feelings for her, but that doesn't mean I'm gonna miss my chance to wish her a merry Christmas.

I shoot a look at my parents, wondering when they'll be ready to leave, but they're bellowing the last verse of "Hark! The Herald Angels Sing" like their lives depend on it. Finally, once the choir finishes and the majority of people have left, Mom and Dad pick up their coats and gesture for us to leave. I'm so antsy that I'm bouncing on the balls of my feet.

I needn't have worried, though. The second we get outside, I feel a tug at my elbow.

"Didn't know you were so into Christmas hymns," Irene says. She's standing alone, her family nowhere in sight. Her lipstick shines against the exterior lights.

I blink, trying to find my voice. "I am very devout."

"Uh-huh."

"Couldn't you feel my prayers wafting toward you? *Dear God, please bless my ruthless enemy on Christmas, even if she* is *a cheerleader . . .*"

"Hmm. I guess my prayer for you to get a better sense of humor didn't work." Her eyes twinkle as they roam

191

over my face. "Listen. Do you want to drive around and look at lights?"

"Oh. Um." I'm suddenly flustered. For some reason, my mind gets caught on the logistics. "I don't have my car. We walked here."

"I have mine." Her eyes take on that challenging look she had at the Emporium after-party. "We could get hot chocolate. My treat."

My family is watching us now. Thora has her arms crossed, but Daphne looks starstruck. Mom and Dad are beaming.

"Hi, Irene!" Mom says.

Now it's Irene's turn to be flustered. "Oh hey, hi! Great to see you. Merry Christmas. Feliz Navidad. Happy holidays."

"You're babbling," I say under my breath.

She looks pointedly at me. "Hot chocolate?"

"Um—yes. Mom, Dad?"

"Be home by midnight," Mom says, winking.

"Enjoy your romantic winter wonderland!" Dad says, but I'm already tugging Irene's hand and leading her away.

"Sorry about them," I mutter.

"I love them," she says easily.

Somehow we're still holding hands. I drop hers and clear my throat. We tuck ourselves into her car, where she blasts the heat and turns on my seat warmer. It feels familiar and new at the same time.

"I didn't know you were Catholic," I say as we pull out of the church parking lot.

"I didn't know you were, either."

"Both sides of the family. Irish and Polish."

"Both sides for me, too. My grandparents are from Kerala."

"Cool," I say, though I have no idea what that means. She smirks because she knows it. "How's that AP European History working out for you?"

"Shut up. I'll do some Googling later."

At Sweet Noelle's, she swings around the drive-through and orders two hot chocolates with whipped cream.

"I can pay for mine—" I say.

"Don't start," she says, pulling out her wallet. Her voice is almost tender, but she clears her throat and corrects it. "I have extra cash right now. Some nerd is paying me to date her."

"Ha, *ha*." I can't say anything else because she's catching my eye with a smirk that can only be described as *flirtatious*, and I feel like my stomach is full of sunbeams.

"Do you know the best street for Christmas lights?" Irene asks. She's driving with one hand, sipping from her hot chocolate with the other. Her nails are painted a perfect Santa Claus red. I wonder what would happen if I reached across the console and took her hand again.

"I do not," I say, trying to stay cool.

"Well, lucky for you, I do."

We end up on the other side of town, close to the square. Irene winds the car down one street, then another, in complete control of where we're going. I picture her family driving out here every year to see the lights. Is it a sacred tradition for them? Has she shared it with anyone else? Did she bring Charlotte here?

"Check it out," she says, turning onto the final street.

We're bombarded by a straight row of Christmas lights, so bright that the road itself is lit up from the reflection. At least a dozen houses are in on the magic, some of them draped in bright, solid gold, others bedazzled with flashing colored bulbs. It's overstimulating in the best way.

"Wow," I say, leaning forward in my seat. "Does Honey-Belle know this exists?"

"Who do you think showed me?"

"Should've known. It's totally her brand."

Irene laughs contentedly. "This is why I love Grandma Earl. We do what we want with zero pretense about it."

I look over at her. "Not everyone feels that way."

"They should." She says it with her usual conviction, her eyes on the dazzling display in front of us. "This place is special. The people are special. I feel it every time we cheer at a football game." She glances at me. "Or a girls' basketball game."

"Well played."

She pretends to bow. It's so corny, so unlike her, that I laugh out loud.

We inch the car forward, taking in each house as we pass. Irene decides her favorite is the twinkling ranch house with Charlie Brown cutouts that appear to be ice skating. Mine is a blinding two-story with reindeer silhouettes across the roof. The radio plays "Last Christmas" by Wham! and we reach to turn it up at the same time. Our fingers brush and I feel the electricity on our skin, radiant enough to power this street full of lights.

* * *

"Are you in any rush to get home?" Irene asks as we're driving back.

"No, why?"

"Let's stop at my house for a minute. I got you something."

My heart beats faster. "Like a gift?"

"No, like anthrax." She side-eyes me. "Yes, a gift."

We park in her driveway, a place I've been many times, and walk into her home, a place I've only wondered about. A disjointed part of my brain, the one that lives in an alternate universe where none of this ever happened, cannot process what I'm doing here, sneaking into Irene Abraham's house on Christmas Eve.

The house is warm and soft lit. The color scheme is different from my family's home: more sepia and tangerine, wood tones and marble surfaces. There's an ornate kitchen chest with a porcelain elephant centerpiece. I count two espresso machines on the counter. Irene pulls off her boots and places them on a shoe rack near the door, then gestures for me to do the same. A golden retriever pads over and Irene kneels down to rub her ears.

"Hi, Mary."

I laugh. "Your dog's name is *Mary*?"

She rolls her eyes. "My brother named her when he was learning about the Nativity. My dad calls her 'Holy Mary, mother of Dog.'"

"I'm obsessed with your dad. That bomber jacket he was wearing at church? Iconic."

She watches me for a moment. "Come see the tree."

She tugs on my wrist but quickly lets go. I follow her into the family room, where she sits on her feet next to the glowing Christmas tree. I hesitate before dropping down next to her.

"It's fake," she says. "My mom got tired of the needles."

"Beautiful, though."

I touch my finger to a golden light. It's warm, then it burns. I reach for an ornament instead. It's handmade from construction paper. The kind of thing a kid brings home from school.

"Oh my god," I mutter, finding the faded photo glued to the middle. "Please tell me this is you."

"Of course it's me. Look at that style game."

Little Irene wears a sparkly headband, polka-dot sweater, and toothless grin. She might be six or seven years old. There's no scar in her eyebrow, but her eyes are exactly the same.

"Enough of that," Irene says with a self-conscious laugh. "Here."

She hands me a perfectly wrapped box. I rip the paper as gently as I can, acutely aware of her watching me. When I open the case inside, I find a black, thick-banded wristwatch in the exact style I would choose for myself.

"I—"

"I kept the receipt in case you don't like it."

"No, I love it," I say breathlessly. "I don't have a watch."

"I know." Her tone shifts to something more familiar. "I thought you could use something to help you run on time."

Her eyes are dancing. I mean to look away from them, but the chance for that passes. I'm looking at her and she's looking at me and it's far too late to pretend otherwise.

She bites her lip. "Well—let's see how it looks."

She wraps the watch around my wrist. Her fingers on my skin are fire. I've never stopped to notice our hands together, the contrast of skin tones, the interplay of her polished rings and my bitten-down fingernails. She has a white scar near her knuckle that shines as clearly as the one on her eyebrow. Without thinking, I brush my thumb over it.

"Curling iron," she says. "Seventh grade." She twines our fingers together.

"My hands are sweaty," I whisper, like I'm trying to give her a reason to let go.

"No shit," she says with that sparkle in her eyes.

I stare at her mouth. I want so badly to lean in, but where would that lead? What would it mean?

"Scottie," she says softly. "Don't overthink it."

"Overthink what?"

"Kissing me."

I laugh unexpectedly, because it's the most Irene-ish presumption ever. "God, you're cocky."

"I'm right."

"I don't know what you want me to say."

"Say you'll go on a date with me. A real date."

It hangs there in the air between us. I search her eyes and she lets me. The sincerity in them scares me so much that I have to look away.

"Scottie." Her voice is a whisper. "I like you. It's crazy and unexpected, but there it is. Something is working here."

"You can't like me. That's not . . . we're not . . ."

"What?"

I shake my head. "This whole thing started because we hated each other, and then we got into a car accident and I paid you to be my girlfriend."

"Yeah, it'll make a great story for our kids. Will you lighten up? We're allowed to like each other."

I turn my head away. "I don't get it. You could have *anyone*."

"So could you, asshole," she says. "Why does anyone like anyone? We just do. It's pretty simple."

"But I'm—I'm a—"

"Ginger?" She tsks. "Yeah, it's surprising to me, too, but I did have a thing for Anne of Green Gables in second grade."

I laugh out loud. "Shut up."

She smiles. It's open and earnest and wanting. "I love when I get you to laugh."

We look at each other again. My heart is drumming beneath my sweater. Irene inches forward the slightest bit, and so do I, and we hesitate for only a moment.

"Don't overthink it," she whispers again.

Our mouths find each other easily. It's just as amazing as the kiss at the Emporium, but this time, it's only for us. She lays her hand along my jaw and kisses me like she means it, and I am breathless and weightless and dizzy at the very fact of her. Lips and tongue and teeth, her hair and her skin and her perfume, but more than anything, her very essence, her fire and flaws and that steely determination to be better, to always be better.

I don't let myself think about the things still unresolved: the tow truck and her cruelty and the hurt I can't reconcile. But even more tangled than that, the pain I've been carrying that has nothing to do with Irene and everything to do with the last girl I loved and the crater she left inside me.

"Are you okay?" Irene asks.

I pull back and paw the tears off my cheeks. "Sorry. Just—stupid emotions."

Her eyes flicker in the glow of the tree lights. "Do you wanna talk it out?"

We hover on the edge of something. It's so quiet I can hear my new watch ticking.

"Can I ask you something?" I say. "Are you over Charlotte?"

She tilts her head, searching me. I wonder if she can see the truth on my face: that I want her to say no. I want to know I'm not alone in this pain, this confusion. I want to know she understands how it feels to be falling in new love and bleeding from old love at the same time.

"Yeah, I am." She brushes my hair back from my forehead, her touch exceedingly gentle. "But you're not over Tally, are you?"

My eyes burn with more tears. I give her the only truth I can. "I want to be."

She swallows and nods solemnly. "What do you need?"

"I'm not sure."

"Sit with it for a second."

We breathe in the stillness. My emotions are crashing

all over the place. I trace my finger over her curling iron scar again, but before she can take my hand, I pull away.

"Can you drive me home?"

Irene's face falls. "Yeah, of course."

She gives me a hand off the floor. We keep quiet as we tug on our shoes, button our coats, pet Mary goodnight. We get back into her car and make the thirty-second drive to my house.

"Scottie," Irene says when I move to get out of the car.

"Yeah?"

"Take all the time you need. Everything's gonna be okay."

I give her the bravest smile I can muster. I'm not sure when I'll see her again. "Merry Christmas, Abraham."

She smiles sadly back. "Merry Christmas, Zajac."

14

MY SISTERS WAKE ME UP ON CHRISTMAS morning by placing BooBoo and Pickles on my chest. At first, coming out of my sleepy state, all I feel is the pleasant pressure of cat paws. But then Pickles tries to put his butt on my face.

"Ugh! Come on!" I yell, throwing off the covers. Pickles darts away and hides under my desk. BooBoo stays on the bed, licking his paws.

"Merry Catsmas!" Daphne says. "Do you think Santa Paws came?"

"That's right, BooBoo, we don't let anyone scare us away," Thora says, petting him where he lays sprawled on my extra pillow. "Come on, Scots, time to open presents!"

"Not in the mood yet," I say, turning away from them. "Let me sleep."

I don't want to get up and face the day, not when

I'm still heartsore from last night, but my sisters practically wrench me from the bed. Daphne jams a Santa hat on my head and the two of them lead me downstairs, where Mom and Dad are sipping coffee in matching pajamas.

"How cute do we look?" Dad says, spreading his arms so I can see the elf print on his green pajama top.

"Merry Christmas, honey!" Mom says, wrapping me in a hug. "Did you and Irene have fun last night? Did you kiss under some mistletoe?"

My cheeks flush, but not for the reason they think.

"You make a precious couple," Dad says. "Next year we'll get you matching pajamas, too."

"Can we stop?" My tone is sour even if I don't want it to be. I feel like I could cry any moment.

"Here, you little brat," Thora says, pressing a mug of coffee and a cinnamon cookie into my hand. "Chug that. Turn your Grinchy frown upside down."

We open presents in turns. Daphne gasps over her first perfume, a gift from Thora and me. Mom squeals over a new gardening hat Dad picked out for her. Thora actually tears up when she unwraps the hand-knit bonnets Daphne made for Pickles and BooBoo.

When I pick out a big, lumpy present, Mom leans forward in her armchair. "Ooh, this is our favorite!"

I shred the paper open to reveal a vintage denim jacket, copper buttons and all, with a white fleece lining along the top.

"Wow," I say, running my hand over it. "I really love—"

"Turn it around!" Dad says.

The back is embroidered with a cartoon basketball. In cursive script, the words *I Bounce Back* flow around it.

"We had it custom made!" Mom says.

"Isn't it *cute*, Scottie?" Thora says in a voice that means *Don't burst their bubble*.

I trace my fingers over the embroidered script. To my embarrassment, my throat grows thick and my eyes well up. The tears drop before I can hide them.

"Scottie?" Mom says. "Are you okay, sweetheart?"

It takes everything I have to get myself under control. I will *not* ruin Christmas morning by admitting my resilience has been a facade, that I literally bought this confidence they keep congratulating me for.

"I'm just very touched. Thank you, guys."

Mom and Dad beam at each other. My sisters trade a curious look, but they don't say anything. I force a smile and pull the jacket on over my pajama shirt. It fits almost perfectly.

* * *

The last three days of December are when the Earl-Hewetts knock down the price of their Christmas inventory, so Danielle and I make plans to shop the discount aisles at the Emporium. We're halfway down the specialty aisle, distracted by a Hanukkah sweater Gunther might like, when she says something that startles me.

"So . . . I saw Honey-Belle at the Munny last night, and she told me you and Irene are taking a break."

Her tone is heavy, like she's been waiting to drop this all afternoon. The air between us changes immediately. I lower the Hanukkah sweater and struggle to meet her eyes.

"Are you really gonna make me talk about this?" I ask. "*Here?*"

"Yes." She takes the sweater from me and places it back on the shelf. "What's going on? I thought you liked her. And she obviously likes you, too."

I swallow. "I do like her."

"But?"

I know she's not going to like this part. "But I'm still trying to get over Tally."

Danielle scrunches her face. "Really? *Still?*"

"Can you not shame me for this, please? I'm trying to be honest with you." My voice shakes. "I know you hate her. I know everyone does. I'm trying to hate her, too. But I *can't.*"

I slide to the floor, pulling my new denim jacket cuffs over my hands. The linoleum tile is cool beneath my pants.

Danielle slides down next to me. We stare ahead to the snow globes display in front of us. "You're right. That was insensitive. I'm sorry." She pauses. "I don't hate Tally. I just hate the way she's made you feel. I hate that everything you've done for the last few months has been a response to her. It's like you're not even your full self anymore. You're just this . . . *reaction*."

She sounds like Thora. *You've been a walking insecurity* . . . I keep my gaze on the snow globes and try to unclench my jaw. "Wow, D, great pep talk. Thanks so much."

Her eyes bore into the side of my head. "I'm not trying to give you a pep talk. I'm trying to give you the truth."

"You wanna talk about truth?" I round on her. "Fine. Let's go there. Let's talk about Kevin."

Her eyes bug out the slightest bit. "That's not a thing."

"It's absolutely a thing."

"Kevin's our *friend*. I can't just have feelings for him out of nowhere."

"You absolutely *can*, you're just not letting yourself. You have literally everything going for you. You're the captain of our team, you have amazing grades, and you're getting accepted to a million colleges, but you're holding back when it comes to Kevin even though he obviously likes you, too."

"You don't know that he likes me," she shoots back.

"None of us are gonna know until you ask him out. Stop being so afraid."

"Don't lecture me, dude."

"You've been lecturing *me*!"

Our voices have gotten heated. We pull away from

each other, huffing. Danielle's breathing is loud and angry. I can't stop grinding my teeth.

"Look," Danielle says finally, her tone even again. She crosses her skinny ankles. "You're right. I'm chicken-shit when it comes to Kev. I don't know how to do this. I'm not good at things that don't come naturally to me."

That makes me laugh, which breaks some of the tension. "*What?*"

"Dating!" she says. "I'm not good at dating! School is easy. Basketball is easy. College applications are actually *fun*. But how the hell am I supposed to figure out *romance* when it feels like a foreign fucking language?"

"Oh my god." I can't help myself; I'm still laughing. "You're totally that overachieving nerd who doesn't know how to be bad at something."

She drags a hand down her face. "Shut up."

"How can someone be *bad* at dating, Danielle?"

"It's been hard for you, hasn't it? I don't wanna get hurt like that."

That shuts me up. We go back to staring at the snow globes. An older woman in a purple beaded necklace skirts by us with her shopping cart, smiling like it's completely normal that we're sitting on our asses in the middle of the Emporium aisle.

"I'm sorry," Danielle says again. "It's just . . . sometimes it seems like dating Tally turned you into someone you're not. You were always so sure of everything, and then suddenly you weren't."

"Yeah," I agree, dropping my head into my hands. I'm not mad anymore. I know she's right. "That tracks."

"You do understand that she's bad for you, right? I mean, like, you can objectively see that?"

My chest is suddenly heavy. "I don't know how to let go of her."

"That's because she's made it impossible for you to move on," Danielle says gently. She pauses. "But you've made it impossible, too."

I look at her. We both have brown eyes, but Danielle's have always been a deeper shade, more solid than my watered-down color. Seeing them now makes me feel safe.

"What do I do?"

"You cut the cord," she says simply. "Whatever that means to you. If you have to block her number, do it. If you have to write an angry letter and burn it, do it. But you *have* to let go, dude."

My throat thickens the way it's been doing these last few days. "I don't know if I can. It's like . . . I'm holding on to this shred of her, and even though it's a bad shred, it's still *something*. The moment I let that shred go, I'll have nothing left."

Danielle scoots closer. She kicks her sneakers against mine. "You'll have nothing left of *her*, but you'll have yourself, Scottie."

I breathe in, breathe out. My knee-jerk response is to say *Myself isn't enough*, but I can't voice that aloud. I don't want my best friend's pity and I don't want to burden her with my grief. It's not her job to fill the hole inside my heart.

"Come on," I say, standing up. "Let's get a coffee. We promised Teddy a Sweet Noelle's pastry."

I can tell Danielle is concerned about me, but she doesn't push it. I don't bring up the Kevin thing, either. We get in her car and play our favorite eighties and nineties ballads playlist on the way to Sweet Noelle's, but I'm not really there. I'm deep in my head, trying to figure out how to let go of Tally.

* * *

I can't remember the last time I drove into Candlehawk. Probably over the summer, when Tally wanted to try that pop-up restaurant that sold overpriced ramen. I cruise down their pristine streets, knowing my hand-me-down Jetta looks out of place. The township is beautifully decorated for the holidays with string lights across the square and silver wreaths on the lampposts. It's elegant, tasteful, picture-perfect. The exact opposite of the street in Grandma Earl where Irene took me to see the lights.

I'm not sure where to park when I drive into the high school lot. Everything seems so formal and structured. There's a security guard driving around on a golf cart, but he doesn't say anything when I park in a random space near the front. The marquee is almost a twin of ours, except the message reads WINTER RESPITE—PLEASE ENJOY. I have a sudden, mischievous urge to mess with it, but I don't want the security guard to catch me. It's not why I'm here, anyway.

The basketball game has already started by the time I get inside. I planned it that way. I don't want Tally to notice me.

The stands are packed with Candlehawk fans. It's more crowded than I expected, even on New Year's Eve. I sneak up the side of the bleachers, past a well-groomed family and a college guy with a handlebar mustache. No one bats an eye at me, which is exactly what I want. For the first time in months, I have no role to play. I am free to sit here and simply watch the girl I used to love. I'm not sure this is what Danielle had in mind when she told me to do whatever it takes to cut the cord, but this *is* what I need, so it's what I'm doing.

Tally's hair is parted in twin braids. I remember a morning at her house, sitting on her bed in our pajamas, telling funny stories while her fingers instinctively braided her curls. Those were my favorite moments with her: When I had glimpses into the soft, simple, private Tally who wasn't aware of her habits and quirks. The version of her that could just *be*.

She's playing well today. Not the best I've seen her do, but still a strong performance. She sinks a few shots and snags a couple of rebounds. She looks completely at home, and I remember, with a bittersweet pang, that she is.

When the game ends with a decisive win for Candle-hawk, I slip down the bleachers and loiter off the side of the court. Tally and her teammates are shaking hands with their opponents. They linger afterward, telling jokes while they chug their water bottles. It's not until they head off to their locker room that Tally notices me.

She stops in her tracks. I stay planted where I am, hands at my sides, waiting. I'm not sure she'll come to me. I know it's her choice to make. But if she feels any ounce of the connection that I still feel, I know she won't be able to stay away.

When she finally heads in my direction, I let out the breath I've been holding. She lopes toward me in that easy, languid way she has. Something tugs at my chest.

"Hi," I say, hoping I sound more sure than I feel.

"Hi," she says hesitantly. "What are you doing here?"

She stares at me with those striking blue eyes, the ones that made me feel seen and known and loved like I'd never been before. My heart thumps. My breath catches. It's been months, but the sadness still hits me like a violent wave. I thought I'd pulled myself out of the water, especially after beating her in the Christmas Classic. Turns out I was just surfing between storms.

Tally's expression softens. She knows me well enough—she will *always* know me well enough—to understand the things I cannot say.

"Needing closure?" she asks.

I swallow. "Something like that."

She studies me. I let her.

"Come on," she says finally, gesturing for me to follow her. "The backup gym is probably free."

* * *

In the auxiliary gym, which is unsurprisingly nicer than Grandma Earl's main gym, we shoot free throws and layups. Tally is still warm from the game, but it takes me a few minutes to pick up the rhythm. I'm hyperaware of every movement she makes, every flick of her eyes, every twitch of her smile.

"You played really great in the Christmas Classic," she says suddenly. "You were, like, on fire. It was incredible to watch."

The compliment shoots through me like a blast of heat. It feels like when we first started dating, when everything she said made me feel special enough to hang the moon.

"Thanks. You were great, too."

She smiles wryly. "No, I wasn't." Her eyes flit over my face. "I always loved that intense side of you. I wish I'd seen it more when we were together."

My insides cool as quickly as they had warmed. How does she always manage to turn a compliment into a dagger? Why do I let her? And why doesn't it give me a strong enough reason to stay away?

"You did see it," I tell her. "You just didn't always like it."

Her mouth hardens. We're both quiet, and I'm ready to call it quits before I've even gotten what I needed.

But then she passes me the ball and says, "I miss Grandma Earl, you know."

I thrust the ball back to her. "You still live there."

"Yeah, but I mean . . . our school. I miss it. I miss the people."

Our school. She sounds genuine. I don't know what to make of it. "I thought you hated Grandma Earl."

She shoots a free throw. Misses. "I thought I did, too."

I grab the rebound and hold it to my stomach. She meets my eyes. There's a meekness in her expression I haven't seen in a while. The soft side she used to reveal only to me.

I pass the ball back to her. "How about we play something? P-I-G?"

"Okay."

She shoots first: an easy shot just below the basket. The ball sinks in. I step up to take the same shot. The ball bounces on the rim and tips in.

Her next shot is a hook shot. I've never been as good at them as she has. Whereas she makes the basket, my shot bounces off the rim.

"That's a *P*," Tally says, but she's not gloating. She says it matter-of-factly, like it could have just as easily been her. Or am I only imagining she says it that way? Maybe she *is* gloating.

We carry on, Tally setting the moves of the game until she misses a shot. Then it's my turn to set the pace. I sink a free throw. She follows suit. I line up to take my next shot.

"Do you really like her?" Tally asks out of nowhere.

I freeze, the ball in my hands. "What?"

"Irene," she says, like she has to force herself to say the name. "You started dating her so quickly. I thought— never mind."

"Tally, you broke up with me." I don't say it harshly. It spools from me like a question. Because this—*this*—is what I need to understand.

"I know," she says quietly. "But it wasn't because I didn't love you anymore."

I stop dribbling. My feelings are all over the place. My body is hot but my hands are cold. I need her to keep talking even if I don't *want* to need it.

"Transferring was the right thing for me," Tally says. "At least, I think it was. Maybe I won't know for sure until we're a few years out of high school, but at the time, it felt like the right decision. I didn't like Grandma Earl. I was floundering there. I felt like I needed—I don't know, a *push*. A chance to start over."

"But why?" I plead.

"Because I—" She shrugs her shoulders defensively. "I wanted something more than I was getting. I wanted to go somewhere basketball mattered. Where *I* mattered."

"You mattered to me," I say, my voice catching.

"Scottie, believe me. You were the only thing that made the decision difficult."

My heart splits. We stare at each other. Tally clears her throat and says, "It's your shot."

I take a deep breath and dribble again. My free throw sinks cleanly. Nothing but net. Tally sighs, and I point at my feet until she lines up in the same position.

Her shot misses the basket by a full foot, but she ignores it and turns to me.

"Scottie," she says, and *god*, I missed her saying my name. "I really, truly thought I was doing the right thing breaking up with you. I thought it would be too hard to switch schools and keep up a relationship. It didn't seem fair to you."

Neither one of us grabs her rebound. The ball rolls into the bleachers.

"Don't you think I should have decided that for myself?" I ask. "If it was fair to me?"

Tally pulls at the split ends of her braid. She looks up at me. "Do you wish we were still together?"

My throat feels tight. I have an aching need to reach out and touch her. Somewhere in the back of my brain, a small voice says *Irene Irene Irene*. But in my body, in my heart, all I can feel is this excruciating need to soothe this heartache.

"No," I answer truthfully. "But I don't know how to give you up, either. I'm trying and trying and it's killing me."

Tally's chest heaves. She moves toward me and wraps me in a fierce hug. It's tinged with yearning and grief and regret. I can't pull away from it. It's like pressing on a bruise and knowing it will hurt, but needing to feel the tenderness anyway.

When the tears leak out of my eyes, she wipes them with the back of her hand. "I'm sorry, Scottie," she whispers. "I really am. I never wanted to hurt you."

Is that true? Is she being genuine right now? Do I have to keep my guard up even though it's exhausting?

"I wish I could show you my world," Tally says. "Show you why I came here. It's the right place for me."

"I believe you."

She wipes my tears again. "You never answered my question. Are you really dating her?"

I look into those yearning blue eyes. In this moment, they're all I can see. "No." I pause. "Not right now."

Tally breathes deep. There's an eyelash on her cheek and I don't stop myself from brushing it away. Maybe this is okay. Maybe this is what I need.

"There's a party tonight," Tally says. "For New Year's Eve. Will you come with me?"

My body tenses, trying to tell me no, but my brain says *It's okay. Maybe this is the chance for resolution.*

What else can I say but yes?

15

THE PARTY IS AT SOME HIP, BOXY MONSTER of a house with floor-to-ceiling windows and decor straight out of *Mad Men*. It's the epitome of Candlehawk taste. I can just imagine what my friends and sisters would say if they walked in here. Danielle would give me that side-eye look she learned from her mom. Thora would wrinkle her nose like she was smelling a fart. And Irene would—

"Welcome," says a tall, brooding guy with a craft beer in his hand. I recognize him instantly. His chambray button-down looks intentionally wrinkled and his hair is deliberately windswept, held in place with some brand of fuckboy mousse. "I don't know you. I'm Prescott. This is my house."

He doesn't shake my hand, almost like our introduction hinges on what I can offer in return. *I know you don't know me. I'm Scottie. This is my ex-girlfriend.*

"Scottie," I say, giving him a nod.

"You go to Candlehawk?"

"No. Grandma Earl."

He laughs. Flat out *laughs*. Tally glances at me, puts her hand on my arm like I might say something—

"Aren't you dating a Grandma Earl girl?" I ask pointedly. "Or do you just block that part out when you're sucking face?"

"*Scottie*," Tally hisses.

Prescott regards me like a funny pet that just pissed on his rug. His eyes are bleary; he's already had a lot to drink. But then he starts to laugh again, tipping his beer in my direction.

"You're saucy," he says. "You can stay."

I have no idea what to say to that, but Tally drags me away before it matters.

In the center of the house, next to a fireplace that belongs in a fancy ski lodge, Candlehawk kids are waiting in line. I can't figure out why until I see a wall of vines with tiny candles and cacti dotting the shelves. It's a selfie backdrop. They're waiting in line to take pictures.

"So cool," Tally says. "It's, like, the perfect aesthetic."

A group of friends hand off their phones and gather in front of the selfie wall. One of the guys musses his hair, keeping his hand there like he's mid-movement. The girl next to him opens her mouth to laugh, but she doesn't actually laugh. She just holds the pose like she might. I feel like I'm in the twilight zone.

"We can get a picture later," Tally says, oblivious to my bafflement. "Drinks first."

She grabs my hand and I let her. We migrate to the kitchen, where several people do an obvious once-over of our outfits. Tally pretends not to notice, but she smooths her shirt beneath her leather jacket. She leads me to a counter full of liquor bottles and White Claws.

"Here," she says, pressing a can into my hands. It's not a suggestion. I think of Irene attending these Candle-hawk parties with Charlotte last year, and I can understand why she wanted to get drunk during them. But I also know where that led.

"I'm okay, actually," I tell Tally. "Um. My throat's been kinda sore. I'll just get some water."

Tally looks surprised, but she doesn't push me on it. She makes herself a mixed drink and takes a big gulp.

I'm pouring water from the sink when none other than Charlotte Pascal slithers up beside me. I feel her eyes on me like a laser beam.

"We have Pellegrino, you know," she drawls.

I take a pointed sip from my tap water. "I'm fine with this, thanks."

She narrows her eyes. "Why are you here?"

"Wanted to see how the other half lives."

She stares at me, unamused. "I can't imagine your

girlfriend is happy to know you're here with Tally Gibson."

It suddenly occurs to me how dangerous it is for Charlotte to see me here with Tally. She could spin this any way she wants. How did I think I could justify this?

"Irene knows I'm here," I lie. "I agreed to be Tally's designated driver."

Charlotte snorts. "That girl needs more than a designated driver."

"Who are *you* to judge?" I say pointedly, alluding to the DUI she and Prescott nearly got last year.

Charlotte's cheeks tinge with color. Her nostrils flare. "Why are you *really* here?"

"I just told you."

"Oh, don't be cute, *Scottie*," she hisses. She throws a contemptuous glance in Tally's direction. "You're here with the biggest wannabe I've ever seen, and you're telling me the queen bee doesn't care? Tell me, why are you 'dating' her anyway, especially after she pulled that shit with the tow truck last year? Or are you *also* so desperate for a ride to the top that you've blocked it out?"

My cheeks burn. I can't think of anything to say.

Charlotte gives me a haughty smirk. She dumps my water in the sink and slinks away.

* * *

Tally is drinking hard in a way that suggests she does this regularly. She's chatting with some girls I recognize from her team, but their eyes don't shine on her the way they used to. They seem to be looking for a way out of the conversation. When one of them changes the subject to her ski vacation, Tally goes quiet and steps closer to me.

"Why were you talking to Charlotte?" she asks. I can hear that yearning in her voice, that desperate need to be worthy. A combination of resenting me and living vicariously through me. Is that what I've been doing to her, too?

"She was talking to me. Listen, can we get out of here?"

"But we just got here," Tally says. She sounds drunk all of a sudden. "Don't you wanna meet my friends? Aren't you having fun?"

I look around. The basketball girls have ditched us. Everyone else is oblivious to our presence; one guy literally knocks Tally's shoulder and keeps walking. Is this how it's been for her lately? If I had known a week ago, it would have given me a sick validation. Now I just feel bad for her.

"How about we take a break, just for a minute?"

Tally looks around, too. I can tell the exact moment she realizes we've been shut out, because she adjusts her leather jacket and avoids my eyes.

"Come on," I say gently. "Let's find somewhere quiet and talk."

* * *

Upstairs, we find an open loft that serves as some kind of TV room. I guide Tally to sit on the couch with me, our knees barely bumping through our jeans. We face the bay window that looks over the dark backyard. Tally takes another swig from her drink. I study the expression on her face, the dullness in those once-bright eyes.

"Are you sure you're happy, Tal?" For once, I'm not asking for myself. I'm genuinely concerned about her.

"No. I feel like shit," she mumbles. "I don't like any of these people. I don't trust any of them the way I trust you."

That feeling of compassion comes over me again. I want to comfort her. I can't remember why I ever resented her.

"I hated watching that video," Tally continues. "You and Irene kissing at the Emporium. Felt like someone clawed my organs out. I couldn't stop watching even though it made me sick."

I breathe and take her hand to comfort her. "I know. I felt the same way watching you kiss that girl at Charlotte's party. It's been hard for both of us."

"I don't know how you moved on so fast. One second I'm talking to you after the demo game, and the next, you're dating this total bitch."

I flinch. My hand goes cold in hers.

"You became someone I don't know anymore." She swallows and wipes her eyes. "I thought I knew you. I thought we loved each other."

I have a sudden, strange sensation that I'm outside my own body. I've had nothing to drink, but my brain feels foggy and detached. How did I get to this place, sitting on the leather couch of this elaborate mansion in Candlehawk, actively trying to hurt the girl I loved and sacrificing my own integrity in the process?

"Tally . . . I should go. I don't belong here."

Tally shakes her head. Her drink sloshes onto the carpet. "No, Scottie, please stay. You're the only person I care about."

"No, listen, we should leave. This party isn't a good place for you." I give her hand a small tug, but she doesn't move.

Tally sniffles. She's legitimately crying now. "Do you still love me?"

I open my mouth, but nothing comes out.

"Please, Scottie?" she begs, her drunken eyes on mine. And then, before I can react, she pushes into me and kisses me. Hard.

At first I'm frozen. Then my body wakes up. I've fantasized about this moment a million times. *One last chance. One last kiss.* She tastes like liquor, but her lips are warm and familiar beneath mine. I press back against them. She opens her mouth and brushes her tongue against mine.

No. Stop. This isn't what you want anymore.

"Tally, I can't," I say, pushing her away. I wipe my mouth with a shaking hand. What the hell am I doing?

Why am I still sitting here? I'm desperate to go home, but I can't leave her. Not when she's this drunk. Not when she's this alone.

"Come on, Tal," I say, pulling her off the couch.

Downstairs, everything is rowdier than it was before, louder and less controlled. In the shadowy parlor, a group of people is bent over a coffee table, no doubt snorting something. In the main room, some guy is pissing on the vine wall as his friends laugh like hyenas.

I help Tally into her coat, guide her out the back door, and settle her in my car. She falls asleep immediately, and I feel a bittersweet pang when I glance at her in the passenger seat, the way I've done a million times before. I drive her home and nudge her awake on the street outside her house. She blinks awake, bleary-eyed and confused. She doesn't hug me; she merely nods and clambers out of my car.

16

DANIELLE SCHEDULES A WARM-UP PRACTICE
for the Friday before the new semester starts. It's a nice
way to ease back into school after the craziness of the
holidays, and I'm ready to have a basketball in my hands
and nothing on my mind except the game.

Until I walk into the gym and realize Irene has sched-
uled cheerleading practice for the same time.

It's the first time I've seen her since our Christmas Eve
kiss, and my initial glimpse of her is a moment where
somebody has clearly made her laugh, because her face
is one big, radiant smile. She's gotten a haircut—just a
few inches that shows in the length of her ponytail—and
she's wearing a vintage Tears for Fears tank over her
leggings. Even though she's sweaty and messy and not
wearing any makeup, my breath catches when I look
at her.

She notices me and a curious expression steals over her face. The corners of her mouth lift the slightest bit.

I start to smile back, but just then, the gym door bangs open. We turn to find the soccer team marching toward us, Charlotte Pascal at the front of the pack. She looks furious.

"What the fuck is this?" she says. "None of y'all are supposed to be here. I reserved the gym for soccer conditioning."

"Since when?" Danielle says. "Friday before the semester starts has always been basketball's day."

"Not this year," Charlotte says, hands on her hips. "Did you not check the reservation list?"

"Go run outside," Danielle says dismissively. She spins away from Charlotte and turns to our teammates. "All right, start with layups. Split up so we have rebounders."

She goes to pass Googy the ball, but Charlotte intercepts it, the ball hitting her palms with a sharp smack. The energy in the gym changes instantly. Everyone freezes.

Danielle looks ready to commit murder. "Give me the ball, Charlotte."

"No, *Coach*, I don't think I will," Charlotte says, guarding the basketball under her arm.

I want to strangle her. My teammates are seething. Charlotte's teammates are smirking, though some of them look uncomfortable.

"What's going on?" someone interrupts.

There she is. Irene in her element, high ponytail in place, blazing eyes roaming over the scene. My heart lodges in my throat.

"You're not needed here, *Ireenie*," Charlotte sneers. "This discussion is for *athletes*."

Irene's eyes sizzle. "Then it's a good thing we came over, *Char*. Because not only are we athletes, we're also *very* good at determining who to root for in these situations."

The air prickles with tension. Charlotte takes a step forward, basketball still trapped under her arm. Her focus is entirely on Irene.

"And who is it you're rooting for?" she asks in a deadly quiet voice. She turns around and gestures to me. "Your girlfriend?"

My heart beats forebodingly.

"'Cause I heard you're no longer an item," Charlotte continues. "At least, that's how it looked when I saw Scottie with Tally Gibson at my boyfriend's New Year's Eve party."

Irene's jaw twitches almost imperceptibly. Her eyes flicker toward me.

I do everything in my power to stop my body from flushing red, but it's no use. My skin is on fire as everyone looks at me. It's the exact signal Charlotte needs.

"Wait," she says in a faux surprised voice. Her mean eyes bore into mine. "I thought you said you *told* Irene that you were there with Tally." She spins around to Irene. "Didn't Zajac tell you?"

My body burns so hot I think I might pass out. Irene's cheeks have turned a patchy dark color. We lock eyes for a splintering second.

Charlotte pulls out her phone. "Lord knows we've had our differences, *Ireenie*," she says, "but for old times' sake, I'll do you a solid. It's only fair for you to know."

She drops the basketball carelessly and walks toward Irene with her phone. My pulse is hammering; I'm sweating like I'm in a nightmare. I have no idea what's on that phone, but I know it's bad.

Charlotte leans in toward Irene so no one else can see what they're looking at. It's easy to tell the exact moment Irene sees whatever the *bad* thing is, because her jaw locks and her mouth sets into a thin, firm line.

She looks up at me for a quick, searing second. Then she clears her throat.

"Practice is over," she says in a shaky voice. "Everyone go home."

She turns on her heel and walks off with her head held high.

* * *

I chase her down in the parking lot. She's completely alone, without even Honey-Belle to fuss over her. I catch up to her as she's slamming her duffel bag into her car.

"Irene! Wait!"

She turns to me with those dark, expressive eyes. My heart drops when I see they're full of tears.

"What, Scottie?" Her nose is dripping, but she doesn't bother wiping it away.

"What did she show you?" I ask in a small voice.

She stares at me as if deciding whether I'm even worth talking to. "A picture of you kissing Tally."

I go completely numb. Charlotte must have snuck up on us in the loft while I was trying to take care of Tally. What did she do, follow us up the stairs? Army crawl her way toward us in the dark? The thought makes me sick.

"Irene, it's not what it looks like. She was wasted and I was trying to help—"

"Why were you there in the first place?"

My mouth snaps shut. "Because . . . Because I . . ."

"I don't have time for this," Irene says, moving to get into her car.

"No—wait—please," I say, grabbing her arm. "I was falling for you and it scared the hell out of me. My feelings for Tally weren't going away and I—I thought if I got some closure—" I shake my head. "I went to see her and she invited me to Prescott's party. Things got out of hand. She got drunk and was totally miserable and—and I let her kiss me. But then I stopped it. I took her home just to make sure she was safe. I haven't seen her since."

Irene slumps against her car. "I can't be part of your mess, Scottie."

"No, but that's the thing," I say frantically. I don't want her to walk away from me. "I'm trying to figure *out* the mess! I'm trying to fix everything so I can be with you!"

She stares hard at me. "But you couldn't *tell* me that? You couldn't be honest about how wrapped up you were in your stupid, toxic pining and bullshit?"

"Don't talk to me like that," I say, my defenses rising. "Don't act like you're so much better at breakups when *your* ex is still pulling shit like she did just now—"

"I don't go *looking* for her to do that," Irene says sharply. "At least I've *tried* to cut her out of my life—"

"You didn't cut her out, she cut *you* out. But sure, good for you for keeping your dignity instead of backsliding. That doesn't mean you can stand there acting all high and mighty as if you've never done anything wrong in your life. You—towed—my *fucking*—car"— my voice is shaking now, and tears are falling from my eyes—"because you used to be just like Charlotte, picking on people simply because you could. That doesn't make you better than me. That doesn't even make you better than *her*—"

"Shut up!" Irene yells, slamming her door and barreling past me. "Shut up *right now*. You have *no* idea what you're talking about!"

She paces manically on the sidewalk, her eyes wild,

her whole body shaking. I have never, ever seen her like this.

And then she bends over and vomits into the grass.

"What the—?" I say, stunned.

Irene draws a slow breath, hands on her knees. She's silent for a moment, and I don't know what to do. "Did—" She swallows hard. "Did you know Prescott used to drive the same car as you?"

I blink. "What?"

She collapses onto the curb, wrapping her arms around her calves. "His parents took his Audi away after the drunk driving incident, so the 'spare' car he used when Charlotte first started dating him was a rental car. A green Jetta. When she invited him to that party last year, I lost my mind about it. I called a towing company and read them his license plate." She looks up at me, her eyes shiny. "But it wasn't his license plate. It was yours."

I can only stand there, buffeted by this reveal.

"I've been where you are, Scottie. That kind of crazy, flesh-eating pain that consumes every part of you. I understand wanting to get back at them. Wanting their attention, even if it's in a negative way. But the shitty thing is, that never helps you feel better. It just lands you in a worse situation, like towing the car of a perfectly nice girl who had nothing to do with the pain you're in."

The world goes quiet. I try to feel my body. My stomach is like ice.

"This entire thing was a mistake," Irene says, standing up. She leans against her car again, tears streaming down her face. A detached part of my brain says *Go to her*, but I'm frozen where I stand.

"Let's consider our arrangement finished," Irene says hollowly. "I'll return the money if you want it. You'll just have to give me some time to get a job."

A shard goes through the center of my body. That's not what I want, but I still can't bring myself to speak.

Irene opens her car door and settles into the driver's side. "You might wanna back up. I don't want to hit you with my car."

She pulls the door shut with a dull thud. The engine starts, the brake lights flash red, her car starts to move. I back up, numb from head to toe, and watch her drive away.

* * *

"Is everything okay?" Mom asks when I trail listlessly through the front door a full hour later. I meant to come straight home but ended up sobbing in my car until I felt light-headed. I'm grateful to have both my parents here, since Mom is working remotely today and Dad only worked a half day at the clinic. I know it's time to tell them everything, and I just want to get it over with.

I swallow. It takes everything in me not to start crying again. "I messed up."

Mom and Dad swoop over to me. Daphne looks up

from the couch, wide-eyed. "What's wrong?" Dad asks. "Are you hurt? Are you safe?"

"I'm fine," I say tonelessly. "But I've been lying about something."

My parents trade looks. "Okay," Mom says in her steady, soothing voice. "Let's sit down and talk about it."

Mom and Dad settle themselves on the couch together, a united front, and wait expectantly. I curl up on the couch across from them. Daphne places BooBoo in my lap, but before she can sit down next to me, Mom and Dad ask her to leave. She gives me a bewildered look and trudges upstairs to her room.

Once her door snaps closed, Mom and Dad focus all their attention on me. And before I lose my nerve, I start talking.

I tell them everything. The anguish I felt after Tally transferred. The attention I got when I carpooled with Irene. The plan I concocted to "date" her and the summer job savings I used to pay her deductible. The ruse I dangled over Tally's head. The deep confusion about my new feelings for Irene, and the feelings I still have for Tally, and whether I deserve to be loved by either one of them. And just when I've almost covered everything, Thora gets home from the lunch shift, takes one look at us in the family room, and asks, "Who died?"

Mom takes a deep breath. We all know she and Thora don't keep things from each other, especially not where

Daphne and me are concerned. It's a remnant from the time when it was just the two of them. I already know Mom will tell Thora about me even if I don't tell her myself.

"Come sit," Mom says, her voice carefully controlled. She turns and bellows upstairs for Daphne, who opens her door immediately.

My cheeks go hot. Telling Thora is one thing, but telling Daphne?

"*Mom*," I say meaningfully.

"We don't have secrets in this family," Mom says. "When one of us hurts, we all hurt."

I swallow and avoid my sisters' eyes as they settle in the family room with us. There's a protracted silence, but no one steps in to fill it. The focus is entirely on me. There's no way out of this.

I take a deep breath and tell the story all over again, finishing with the New Year's Eve party and the picture Charlotte showed Irene today.

When I'm finally finished, there's a ringing silence. Thora's jaw is tight. Daphne looks crestfallen. Mom breathes carefully through her nose while Dad rubs his mouth mechanically.

"That's pretty fucked, Scottie," Thora says finally.

"*Thora*," Mom reprimands.

"Thanks for those wise and compassionate words," I say thickly. I round on my mom. "Do you see why I didn't want to tell her? She's judgmental about *everything*."

"I'm being judgmental because this is not the Scottie I know," Thora snaps.

"Yeah, well, the Scottie you know was heartbroken and hurting, but you didn't want to hear about that. You only wanted to point out how shitty Tally was."

"Because she *was* shitty."

"From your perspective, maybe she was. But can you please consider that maybe I saw things worth loving in her? That before she broke my heart, she built me up into the best version of myself?"

"I don't get it," Daphne cuts in. Her voice is soft and quiet. "I've always thought you were amazing. Why did you need Tally to show you that?"

That's when I start sobbing again.

Mom and Dad meet me on my couch. Dad lets me cry into his shoulder while Mom strokes my arm. My sisters fold themselves onto the floor below us and wait. It's a piercing, intimate moment: the five of us packed together in a three-foot radius, the Christmas tree lit up in the background, Pickles pawing curiously at my socks.

By the time I stop sobbing, I'm sweating through my practice sweatshirt. Mom brushes the hair out of my eyes. Daphne squeezes my foot.

"It's heartbreaking for us to hear you say these things," Mom says. "Not just because we're disappointed, but because of the deeper issues going on here. When did you stop feeling worthy, Scottie?"

I sniff and turn away from her. "I didn't realize I

235

had." Thora gets up and brings me a tissue box, and I take one without meeting her eyes. "Tally left and it was like this giant hole opened up."

"In your heart?" Daphne asks.

I run my fingers up and down my sternum. "Everywhere."

Dad rubs his mouth again. "I think you lost yourself in Tally a bit."

"I didn't mean to," I say, still trying to get my breathing under control. "I loved her so much. I thought she was perfect. When I started seeing things I wasn't so sure about, I thought the problem was *me* and my way of looking at things. It felt like I couldn't tell the ceiling from the floor."

"You have good intuition, honey. You're allowed to trust it," Mom says. "And you are very, very worthy. You're worthy of love you feel good about. Not just from a girl, but from yourself."

"Mom's right," Dad says. "And we can tell you that all day long, but the belief has to come from you."

"But how do I do that?"

They're quiet, thinking.

"Mom," Thora says suddenly, "remember when you took up gardening?"

Mom smiles knowingly. She nods like she's giving Thora permission.

"I don't remember the divorce," Thora says. "I was only, like, three. But I do remember that Mom was always outside, planting in the dirt, and she always had the best smile on her face afterward." She grins at our mom. "Remember what you'd tell me?"

"Yes. You'd ask why I liked gardening so much, and I'd tell you that I was spending time with myself because I love myself."

"That always stuck with me. And when Buck came around, you still gardened just as much."

"It lit her up from the inside out," Dad says. He smiles at Mom the way he always does: like she makes the sun come out. "That's what love is, Scottie. It's letting someone be themselves."

I swallow down more tears. "I don't think Tally and I did that for each other."

"No."

"But I was so in love with her. I always had butterflies when she was around. I still kind of do."

"Are the butterflies entirely gentle?" Mom asks. "Or do some of them hurt?"

I bite my lip. My family nods knowingly.

"In my experience," Dad says, "butterflies aren't always the best compass."

"So you didn't have butterflies when you started dating Mom?"

Mom raises her eyebrows in a way that means *Be careful what you say here, buddy.* Dad merely kisses her hand.

"I thought there was no way in hell I'd end up with

your mom," he says. "We weren't each other's types. She was ten years younger than me, *much* better-looking, and she loved to put me in my place."

"And I had a five-year-old," Mom says. "And your dad didn't want kids."

"I *thought* I didn't. But let me tell you, something with your mother and me just worked. The more I saw her, the more time we spent together, she came to feel like home. Being with her was like a warm, cozy buzz." He pauses, and his eyes twinkle satisfactorily. "Not so much butterflies as bumblebees."

Daphne giggles. "Good one, Dad."

"And wouldn't you know, the more time I spent with Thora, the more I enjoyed being a dad. She was the cutest, spunkiest little kid I'd ever seen, even when she pushed our buttons."

Thora smirks, her chin in her hand.

"So before I knew it, we had not just one precious little girl, but three of them! And here they are, growing up too fast, learning how their hearts work."

Mom smooths my hair back from my forehead. I melt into her shoulder, sniffling and wiping my eyes.

"I really like Irene," I admit. "But I think I just ruined everything. There's no way she'll even look at me again."

Mom smiles wryly. "Don't count yourself out, sweetheart. Let the wounds breathe for a bit and see what happens."

"I'm tired of wounds. I still feel sad about Tally even

with all the work I've done to get over her. I feel like I gave her a piece of me I'm never going to get back."

"My sweet girls, let me tell you something," Mom says, looking around to each of us. "You will move through life and fall in love with many different people, and at some point, you will get your heart broken. It's unavoidable. The key is to not be afraid of the breaking. People break our hearts, but they create more room in them first, and that room makes it possible for us to become more ourselves."

"I don't think I've become more myself," I whisper.

"You can't always see the process when it's happening," Dad says. "But a year from now, you'll see how the pieces lined up. Give yourself time to heal, Scottie. Give yourself a break."

I nod, wiping my eyes. BooBoo jumps into my lap and purrs against my stomach.

"All right," Mom says. "That's enough heavy stuff for today. Time to let things breathe."

"Yeah, time to leave this bullshit behind," Daphne says unexpectedly.

"*Daphne*—" Mom starts, but when she sees the rest of us cracking up, she buries her face in her hands and laughs.

* * *

I wake up exhausted the next morning. It feels like all the heavy emotions I've been carrying these last few

239

months have finally knocked me down and told me to stay there. I feel some relief after talking with my family yesterday, but I also know I have a long healing path in front of me. Because that's the truth I have to face: It's time to meet my grief head-on and allow it to move through me.

There's a gentle knock on my bedroom door. Three people poke their heads in: Thora, Daphne, and, to my surprise, Danielle. They hover in the doorway, eyebrows raised like they're not sure what kind of state they'll find me in. When I pat my bed, smiles break out on their faces. My sisters snuggle up on either side of me while Danielle sits cross-legged at my feet, balancing a mug of coffee in her hands. Daphne hands me a coffee of my own in her favorite mug, the vintage Peter Rabbit one we've had since we were little.

"When did you get here?" I ask Danielle.

She wrinkles her nose. "Half an hour ago. Thora texted me. I showed Daph how to make coffee."

I smile my gratitude at Thora. It's easier to meet her eyes today.

"How's the coffee?" Daphne asks me. "Did we add enough cream?"

I lean into her. She smells like her floral shampoo, the one I only use when I run out of my own. "It's perfect, Daph. You're perfect."

Thora nudges me until I look at her again. "I woke up feeling like a bad sister," she says quietly. "It hit me what you said about how I never fully listened to your pain. I'm sorry, Scots. I shouldn't have been so quick to shit on Tally without understanding how you felt first."

I nod. "It's okay."

"No, it's not, but I'm glad we can always call each other on this stuff."

"I love our band of sisters," Danielle says, and we all laugh. "So . . . I heard about the New Year's Eve party. And the picture of you and Tally kissing."

"We filled her in," Daphne explains.

I risk a look at Danielle, afraid of what she'll think of me, but she merely looks concerned. "Are you okay, Scottie? Is Irene okay?"

I take a sip of coffee, considering the question. "Can I ask you guys something? What do you think of that scene in *Say Anything* . . . where he holds the boom box outside her window?"

"It's so romantic." Daphne sighs.

"Iconic," Thora says.

"He's a try-hard," Danielle says.

I point at Danielle. "That's what Irene thinks. She hates that part because she thinks it's a cop-out. That John Cusack, like, indulged in this cheesy gesture because he wanted to wallow in his feels. She says he should have made an effort to talk things out with Ione Skye instead."

Thora and Daphne frown, pondering this perspective.

"She's right," Danielle says simply.

"I don't want those hard conversations," I admit. "I'd rather stand outside her bedroom window and blast a love song."

"That definitely *sounds* more romantic," Daphne says, tapping her fingers against her chin, "but which one would mean more to Irene?"

I know the answer in my bones. "Ugh. The tough conversation."

"You've had hard conversations before," Danielle says. "You and Irene are always straight with each other. I mean, in a gay way."

Thora snorts and kicks her foot against Danielle's hip.

"You talk to her like you never talked to Tally," Danielle continues. "You're . . . you know . . . *you*."

I nod. "Yeah. And I wasn't me when I was with Tally."

"Right. Look, remember when people started turning out for our games and I freaked out and you said I couldn't have it both ways? Either I stopped caring that we weren't getting attention, or I learned how to play with attention on me? You were right, so now I'm gonna return the favor. *This* isn't you. The fake dating scheme, the messing with Tally's head, the sneaking around Candlehawk? Not even close to the real Scottie. The real you is authentic and genuine and grounded. She cares about people. Not the idea of them, but the people themselves."

We fall silent until Daphne turns to me. "No offense, but your best friend is smarter than you."

242

"Not offended." I smile and reach for my phone. "Hey, did Charlotte show anybody else the picture?"

"No," Danielle answers. "I mean, everyone put the pieces together that you were out with Tally and did something to upset Irene, so . . ."

"Yeah. Definitely sounds bad." I cringe. "Does the whole school hate me?"

Danielle shrugs. "They might?" She stares pointedly at me. "But I don't think you should worry about that right now."

I sigh. "Right. Authenticity. I'm just not sure I *like* the authentic me right now. She's a damn mess."

Thora sighs and slings an arm around my shoulders. "Look, Scots," she says gently, "if you're going to heal, you have to stop avoiding the hard shit. Trust that you can handle the bad parts of yourself. Trust that Irene can, too."

I bite my lip. "But what if she doesn't want to?"

"She'll want to," Danielle says. "If you trust me on anything, trust me on that."

* * *

When I call Irene the next day, I'm not sure she'll answer. She does.

And when I ask if we can talk, she says yes. I grab my keys and hustle out the door.

When I pull into her driveway, she's in the garage, shivering in a maroon hoodie with the collar cut loose, her glasses on, her hair in a messy topknot. My heart pounds beneath my denim jacket.

I take off my shoes when we enter the house. Mary the dog pads over and nuzzles into my thigh. A boy with Irene's eyes, maybe eleven or twelve years old, looks over from the wraparound couch.

"This is my brother," Irene says, gesturing toward him. "Mathew, we're going upstairs. Don't bother us."

Mathew scrunches his nose. "Are you two banging?"

Irene ignores him and hurries up the stairs. I follow her, trying to decode her body language. She doesn't seem angry, but it's like she's put up a wall between us. She's back to being untouchable.

Her room is just as I'd imagine it to be: clean, organized, effortlessly cool. The dark wallpaper suits her. The framed photographs are surprisingly old. I pick up a gold 4 x 6 frame showing young Irene with an older Indian couple.

"Are these your grandparents? Is this Kerala?"

"Good memory," she says flatly. She clambers onto the bed, stretches one leg out in front of her.

I hover uncertainly. "Can I—?"

She gestures wordlessly.

I seat myself across from her and stare into those dark, expressive eyes. My heart is in my throat. I want so badly to get this right.

"I could say sorry again, but I don't think that's what you want to hear," I begin. "I could make some sweeping declaration of love, but you deserve more than a boom box outside your window. Because you're right: that would serve *me*, not you."

She watches me intently. "So what do I deserve?"

"A million things." I look into her eyes, trying to show my sincerity. "But from me, you deserve honesty. I haven't wanted to be real with you about how messy and broken and confused I feel. I tried to keep you away by telling myself you were the popular girl who didn't care about me. But you *do* care about me. You care about a lot of things. You have a big heart and you're funny and headstrong. You're one of the most amazing people I've ever met."

I swallow and fidget with my jacket cuffs. "You've been authentic since the moment our cars hit. I'd like to be authentic with you, too." I clear my throat, and now I have to look away. "I'm not in a great headspace. I haven't been for months. Breaking up with Tally sliced me open in a way that embarrasses me, because I feel like I *should* be over her by now. I don't know how much of it's my fault. Like it's my fault for not seeing the red flags. It's *still* my fault for believing she has a good heart deep down. I know she's toxic. I really do. But I miss her in this way that physically *hurts*. It's like my brain gets it but my heart is lagging behind. I'm grieving even if I don't want to be."

I recap everything that happened over the last week: my conversation with Danielle about needing closure, my decision to seek out Tally at the Candlehawk game, my experience at Prescott's party. I even tell her about my conversation with my family the other day.

When I finish, there's silence. I notice my chest rising and falling, my breath moving in and out. Mathew is blasting the television downstairs.

"Do you still miss her?" Irene asks.

I take my time answering. "I miss who she used to be, but that person is gone. Maybe she never truly existed in the first place. You've been telling me all along that trying to get back at her wouldn't make me happy, and you were right. I've been competing with her but I've only been hurting myself. And I ended up hurting *you*, too. I never should have dragged you into this mess. That's the part that really kills me. I'm so sorry, Irene."

The shadow of a smirk crosses her face. "You didn't *drag* me into anything. I made the decision myself."

"Still. I should have been more self-aware. I should have stopped myself from developing feelings."

She shakes her head. "You can't control your feelings. If my big gay journey has taught me anything, it's that."

I give her a small smile. "True."

"I knew you were grieving. I knew you were in a bad place. I guess I just hoped that things had changed by now." She looks at me. "I'm sorry if I rushed you or pressured you."

"You didn't." I tentatively reach my fingers toward

hers. She lets me take them. "I want to date you. *Really* want to date you. But I'm not ready for that yet, and I don't want to give you anything less than my best self."

She nods. "I understand."

I meet her eyes. "Irene?" My voice has the slightest quake in it. "Why did you never tell me the truth about the tow truck?"

Her stare is piercing. "Because I was too proud to admit I'd made a mistake. I didn't know you and I didn't know how to explain myself to you, so I let you deal with the fallout instead of taking it on myself. I was a coward." She squeezes my fingers. "I'm so sorry, Scottie. For what happened to your car, but also for how it made you feel about yourself. Your family is right: You're amazing. You're more than enough. I hate that I made you question that."

I set my hand on her knee. "I'm sorry you were in so much pain."

"I'm sorry you still are."

"Will it really go away? Eventually?"

"Yes." She smiles sadly. "Look, I'll prove it to you." She reaches for her phone and scrolls until she finds a photo. "I know it's probably weird to show you this, but I stared at this picture every day for about six months after Charlotte started dating Prescott."

She hands it to me. It's a selfie of the two of them, Irene and Charlotte, kissing with their heads on the same pillow, their hair messy and intertwined. Irene is smiling the way she only smiles during cheer routines: like she's found the thing she was meant for.

"Oh." I feel a twinge of jealousy, but I remind myself this isn't about me; it's about Irene and her pain. "Does she know you have this picture?"

"No. We were drunk. I didn't find it until the next day."

"You look so happy," I whisper.

"I was." She scoots closer, lays her arm along my thigh. "I loved Charlotte with everything I had. I know she loved me, too. When I look at this picture, I can still see the best parts of her. I can remember exactly how it felt to love her."

I look up at her. "So how did you finally move on?"

"Time. Space. Acceptance." She searches my eyes. "And knowing that I deserved better."

I smile. We lean our foreheads together, breathing.

"I want to get to a place where I'm ready for you," I whisper.

"Just get to a place where you know how wonderful you are," she whispers back. "They're one and the same."

She gets up off the bed and pulls me to my feet. Before I can figure out how to say goodbye—for now— she grabs something off her dresser and presses it into my hand.

My basketball button.

I try to say something, but the words stick in my

throat. We stand there for a moment, breathing, giving this decision the space it deserves. Then I nod and walk away.

I don't cry when I get home. Instead, I pick up my basketball and run layups for an hour. I don't think about anything other than my own heart and the healing it needs to do.

Because before you can worry about who's in your passenger seat, you have to learn to drive yourself.

17

I NEVER ANTICIPATED HOW MUNDANE THE healing process would be. My next few weeks are filled with helping Mom in the garden, learning knitting with Daphne, and bussing tables for Thora at The Chimney. I wash dishes, practice free throws, and rank my favorite films on a list that my sisters argue over later. I help Danielle return Christmas presents and talk about my feelings without her prompting me. There is nothing glamorous about any of it, but I tell myself to keep going.

School becomes an absolute hellhole. Word has gotten around about Charlotte's accusation in the gym, and while no one has seen the picture she showed Irene, everyone has put the pieces together about us "breaking up" because I hung out with Tally. People are either giving me a wide berth or tossing me dirty looks in the hallways. My own teammates refuse to pass me the ball in practice. Only the Cleveland triplets are willing to hover nearby, but that's because they want quotes for the paper. It's a very sober, clarifying experience, to see how quickly people can go from adoring you to abhorring you.

Irene herself is cordial but distant, and I take my cues from her. We smile politely to each other in the hallways but otherwise keep to ourselves. Charlotte, of course, is happy to fuel the rumors about what went wrong between us. She plants more seeds about Irene's "fake" sexuality, but Irene stays above it all. I don't know whether that's because she doesn't care, or because she's extra focused on SAOY now that we're getting closer to nominations. I pray I haven't ruined her chances.

Danielle and the boys are unfailingly loyal. We sit in my car one afternoon and I tell them everything. Danielle already knows, of course, but it's a relief to finally explain myself to Gunther and Kevin. I confess the whole truth about the last few months, even though I'm still ashamed. I've told this story so many times now, but it doesn't get any easier. "I'm sorry for lying to you," I say, forcing myself to keep eye contact. "I'm sorry for getting so caught up in my ex. I feel like it took away from our senior year experience." I dab at my eyes. Danielle passes me a napkin from the glove compartment. "You guys are my best friends. I wanna make the most of our last semester."

Kevin leans forward and threads his fingers together.

"None of us is perfect, Scottie. Well . . . except Danielle."
He grins earnestly; she narrows her eyes playfully.
"Thanks for telling us the truth. I'm sorry you were
hurting so bad. I love you and I want you to be happy."

"Yeah, what he said," Gunther chimes in. "Besides,
I got to know Honey-Belle through this whole thing, so
how can I be mad?"

Danielle swats at him, and the laughter that follows
is exactly what I need.

The four of us spend every Saturday at the Chuck
Munny. On the night we plan to see *Love & Basket-ball*, Gunther brings Honey-Belle along and kisses her
in the concession line. I turn to Danielle and Kevin to
exchange glances, but they're not paying attention;
they're laughing at something on Kevin's phone. When
Danielle reaches forward to hit his arm with a flirtatious
little punch, Kevin's eyes light up. I pretend not to notice
when he insists on buying Danielle's root beer. I'm okay
with being a fifth wheel tonight.

When we're off from school in honor of MLK Day,
I sit cross-legged on my bedroom floor and read every
letter Tally ever gave me. Some of them make me cry. I
let the tears come and tell myself it's okay that my heart
is hurting. Once I've gone through them all, Thora and
Daphne help me burn them in the backyard. I breathe
in, breathe out, and watch the sparks of them drift away.

* * *

Spring sports begin near the end of January, because apparently January qualifies as spring. Each evening as I leave practice, I watch the soccer girls sprinting down the field, their lungs surely burning in the cold. The start of their season signals the closing of mine, which is hard to believe. It means we're nearing the end of my high school sports career. It also means we're only weeks away from the district championship, and based on Grandma Earl's winning record, it looks like we'll definitely be playing in it—and that Candlehawk, who remain undefeated except for their loss to us in the Christmas Classic, will be our opponent.

Danielle and I stay late after practice one night, passing the ball around while she works through a new play she wants to try with our team. We haven't seen Coach Fernandez in two weeks; Danielle has been leading the charge entirely on her own. Tonight she alternates between consulting the play on her phone, directing me through the steps, and disappearing behind Danielle Vision. I watch her with new eyes, in awe of the way her brain works.

"Did you ever finish your Common App essay?" I ask when we're walking to the parking lot. It's freezing cold outside; my breath clouds the air when I speak.

"Yeah, it's finished, but I haven't submitted it yet. Why?"

"What did you end up writing about?"

"This anecdote about my family visiting the Museum

of Bad Art and how Teddy went off on the tour guide about this octopus painting—what? What's that look?"

"Danielle, you have to write about coaching our team."

"I told you, I don't wanna brag. I don't wanna be all *me-me-me*."

I stop walking. So does she. We face off near our cars.

"What?" Danielle prompts, teeth chattering.

"I love you," I tell her firmly. "You're a force to be reckoned with. I think you should stop hiding from people."

She blinks. She looks completely dazed. "What?"

"You do realize that stepping up to coach your peers through a winning season is pretty extraordinary, right? Especially when you're still maintaining straight As? You should tell the college admissions people that. You should let them see you. The real, genuine you. Authenticity, remember?"

Danielle swallows and looks away, embarrassed.

"Try it," I plead, my arms shaking in the cold. "Just *try* the essay. I promise I'll tell you if it's too braggy. But, like, imagine if me or Kevin or Gunther wrote it! We'd brag about you the whole fucking time."

"You think Kevin would brag about me?"

I roll my eyes. "You tell me."

She gives me a crooked smile. "Yeah. He would."

"So you'll try it?"

She takes a deep breath. "I'll try it. I'll probably hate you the whole time, but I'll do it."

"Happy to be hated. It's kinda my thing lately—"

We're interrupted by a loud beeping over my shoulder. Someone is remote unlocking their car. We turn to see Irene pulling her duffel bag off her shoulder. She's wearing a ridiculously long parka.

I look back to Danielle. "I think I'm gonna—"

"Yes. Go."

She doesn't need to tell me twice. I hurry across the parking lot, my duffel bag bouncing over my coat. "Hey! Irene!"

Irene looks around. Her expression turns softer than I could have hoped for. "Hi. What are you still doing here?"

"Helping Danielle. It's getting pretty intense with the Candlehawk game coming up."

Irene stiffens, and I feel like an idiot for saying the C-word.

"Intense because it's the end of our season," I clarify. "Not because I care about winning anymore."

She tips her head, studying me. "Yeah?"

"Yeah." I smile at her. "So . . . nice coat. Aren't those for people in, like, Minnesota?"

She narrows her eyes. "They're for cold weather, asshole."

"*Arctic* weather, Georgia girl."

"I guess there's no chance of fixing your dumb sense of humor during this healing process?"

"Unfortunately, that wasn't part of the deal." I grin

until she rolls her eyes. It warms me to my bones. "Hey, so how are you? Are you ready for SAOY?"

"Yeah, I am." Her eyes have that familiar spark in them. "I was just making more posters with Honey-Belle."

"I've loved your posters so far."

"Suck-up." Her mouth twitches. "I guess you've heard Charlotte is back on her bullshit with all these rumors about me?"

I have to fight hard not to say something nasty about her. That's not what Irene needs. "Yeah. I'm sorry you have to deal with that. It's hard enough coming out. You shouldn't have to prove it to anyone."

"It's not your fault. She'd find another angle if she had to."

"Irene, can I ask you something?" I pause, letting the question formulate. It's something I've been wondering for weeks, but it's a delicate thing to ask. "That picture you have on your phone—the one of you and Charlotte kissing last year—why have you never showed it to her? To anyone? One look at that photo and Charlotte could never torture you again."

Irene stares at me. Her expression is very serious. "Is that what you think I should do?"

I search her eyes. It's clear she's had this idea before. Maybe even considered it.

"No," I say firmly. "I don't think you should do that. Do you?"

"No. I haven't and I never will."

I swallow down the lump in my throat. I look at her and wonder, is this how it feels to love someone for who they really are? Their core being, their compass, their resolve?

"Irene—you're a pretty incredible person." My voice is quivering with emotion. What is it with me gushing to people tonight?

Irene blinks. Her steely gaze settles. "I'm not, Scottie. I just try to do better than I've done before." She pauses. "Same as you."

We smile at each other. I don't want to end the conversation, but my body is numb with cold, yearning for the heat of my car. Besides, I have more healing to do.

"Good luck with SAOY," I say, backing away from her. "I'll be cheering for you."

* * *

In the first week of February, our principal finally makes the announcement: Nominations for Student Athlete of the Year will be announced at the end of the day.

"Holy shit," Danielle says as we're sitting in morning homeroom. "I wonder how Irene's feeling."

I look up from the final version of her Common App essay, which she submitted last week, where I've been reading about how nervous Danielle was before our season opener. She has somehow managed to write about coaching our team in a way that is both powerful and humble. I've only counted one self-deprecating remark, and she'd written it in parentheses, so I count that as progress.

"She probably feels the way she does before a routine," I say. "Anxious but excited."

Danielle taps one of her color-coding highlighters on the desk. "God, I hope she gets it."

"Me too." I run through the list of possible candidates in my head, trying to see who could knock her out of the running. She *has* to be nominated with everything she does for both squads, right?

At lunch, the nominations are all anyone can talk about. Gunther and Danielle confirm they voted for Irene during preliminary ballots last week, but Kevin refuses to say who he voted for. We bug him over and over, but it's no use; he keeps repeating "A man's conscience is his own private terrain," until Gunther squirts a ketchup packet at him.

By the time I get to Senior Horizons that afternoon, my stomach is in knots. I'm so nervous for Irene that I feel like it's *my* nomination on the line. But when I glance across the room at her, she is poised and steely as ever. It's not until we briefly meet each other's eyes that I recognize her nerves. I nod encouragingly until she nods back.

When the end-of-day announcements finally come on, our principal prattles on about useless minutiae, plus another empty warning about messing with the marquee, before he clears his throat and announces the SAOY candidates.

"*Darius Hart . . . Michael Lottke . . . ,*" he reads in his nasally voice. "*Charlotte Pascal . . .*"

There's a surge of applause from half the people in the room. Charlotte smiles and tries to look demure, but to me she looks like a deranged sociopath. I hold my breath, pleading for Irene's name.

"*Irene Abraham . . . ,*" our principal drones.

"YES!" I shout, pounding my fist on the desk. My face flushes red, but it doesn't matter: There's enough noise from the rest of the classroom to cover up my outburst. Half my classmates are shouting some variation of "*What?* She's a *cheerleader!*" while the other half are falling all over themselves to hug Irene. I forget myself and stand up to get a better look at her. She's beaming, her smile radiant, her eyes as joyful as the old school picture on her Christmas tree.

"And, lastly, with a record number of write-in votes . . . *Danielle Zander.*"

Time freezes. My heart explodes in my chest. One fragile millisecond of silence—Danielle's jaw falling open, her eyes wide and disbelieving—and then a roar of sound. People are shouting so loud my eardrums could burst. I'm wrapped around my best friend before I even realize it, and I'm squeezing her hands and yelling

"*You're nominated! You're nominated!*" More people rush over to hug her—band kids and theater kids and every type of average kid—and when it finally hits her, she shines like a goddamn star.

The classroom is absolute chaos, people running to Charlotte or Irene or Danielle—or sometimes all three—while Mrs. Scuttlebaum yells in vain for us to sit down. Our principal is still talking on the intercom, but he's nothing more than fuzzy white noise. And in the middle of the ruckus, in one lightning-hot moment, Irene meets my eyes and winks.

* * *

Later that day, after practice, the parking lot is rife with SAOY gossip. It's unseasonably warm for February, and people are using the opportunity to hang out by their cars. Music streams across the lot, courtesy of the baseball team celebrating Darius Hart's nomination. The soccer girls, fresh from practice, stretch on the grass near the marquee, which someone tweaked just this morning to read HAPPY VALENTITTIES DAY. Gunther and I sit on the trunk of my car, talking with Kevin, who just left the band room, and Danielle, who's so hyper she's bouncing on the balls of her feet. Again and again, we recap the moment her name was announced over the intercom. I'm bursting to go home and tell my family about it.

"Hey, Danielle, congratulations!" one of the band guys says as he passes by. He shifts his trumpet case and points to Kevin. "This guy has the *best* ideas. The second he told us he was writing you in, we all went for it. Anyway, good luck!"

Kevin flushes where he stands. Danielle blinks like she's not sure what she heard.

"You wrote me in?" she asks. Her voice is tender. It's such an intimate moment that I wish they could share it alone. Gunther and I trade awkward glances.

"Is that okay?" Kevin asks croakily. "I know I should've asked for your blessing, but I thought no one deserves it more than you—"

"Hey! Danielle!" Irene and Honey-Belle burst onto the scene. They smother Danielle with hugs; it takes her a moment to register they're there. "Congratulations! This is incredible!"

Irene's face is alight; she's genuinely thrilled. Honey-Belle is so happy that she looks ready to float away from the earth.

"Oh—yeah—thanks!" Danielle says, hugging them back. "Congratulations to *you*, Irene!"

"I never thought I'd have *two* friends nominated!" Honey-Belle squeals. She spins over to Gunther and smushes his face between her hands. "Can you believe it? It's like Christmas!"

Gunther grins like a total doof. "Coming from you, that really means something."

I don't realize I'm smiling so hard until my cheeks literally start to ache. I glance across the circle at Irene, who catches my eye and grins. It's already occurred to me that I'm going to have to pick between her and Danielle on the voting form, but right now, I don't care. There's too much to be happy about.

Which, go figure, is the exact thing I'm thinking when Charlotte Pascal slithers up with her cronies.

"Oh *god*," Danielle says, forgetting herself. "Come back later, Pascal, we're closed to bullshit right now."

My group snickers with laughter. Charlotte's cheeks color pink, but her vicious eyes stay planted on us. "I just wanted to congratulate you, Danielle. It's nice to see another hardworking female *athlete* nominated."

My classmates, sensing a bloodbath, start to gather round. The parking lot quiets. Our circle of onlookers grows.

"You can stop baiting me with that word now," Irene says in a bored voice. "We're celebrating, Char. You should be doing the same thing. Go have *fun*."

"I can't believe you got a nomination," Charlotte says in a slippery voice. "Especially when it's clear you were trying to leverage *gay* points for the sympathy vote."

A hush falls over the crowd. My pulse quickens warningly.

"I'm not interested in your opinion of my sexuality," Irene says smoothly. "I know who I am and how I feel."

"Yeah, see, that's just not adding up for me. I think you were using Zajac. We all remember the tow truck incident, Irene. How do you go from terrorizing the poor girl to showing her off like arm candy? But I know how calculating you can be. You're savvy enough to spin a story for your own gain. You took an underdog—an *obviously gay* underdog—and used her like an accessory to show that you learned your lesson, you could relate to everyone, you were a *poor closeted gay girl*—"

"That's a complete lie!" I say, losing my temper. "God, Charlotte, why are you so hell-bent on torturing her?"

Charlotte narrows her eyes like I'm an insect that has suddenly become interesting to her. "I'm hell-bent on proving she's a fraud. And so are you. I don't know what's in it for you with this whole scheme, but I do know you're faking it. You don't care about Irene. *You're* in it for something else entirely. And I can prove it."

She whips out her phone. Irene and I lock eyes. An infinite conversation passes between us.

"Yep, there we go," Charlotte says. "Let me just post this little development to Instagram . . ."

There's a heavy, protracted silence as everyone waits. Then one of the soccer girls looks at her phone and says, "Oh shit . . ."

In a flash, everyone is on their phone except for me, Irene, and our friends. We stay resolute as our peers gawk at their screens. The soccer girls roar with glee. The football guys elbow each other and laugh. The cheerleaders are silent as stone.

"Is that really true?" one of them asks Irene, thrusting her phone at her. Irene tries to look away, but the girl practically forces her to look. Irene's jaw tightens. She digs a hand through her hair.

In spite of myself, I pull out my phone and look.

Just as Irene said, it's a photo of Tally and me making out at the New Year's Eve party, time-stamped with the date and location. It's a little fuzzy from Charlotte zooming in on us, but there's no doubt who it is. The caption overlaying the picture reads *So Zajak was still hooking up with Gibson this whole time? I guess Irene really was just using her for show . . .*

Everyone is staring when I look up. My friends' faces are anxious. Everyone else's is judgmental and wary. They look from me to Irene and back again. It's dead silent until Irene finally speaks.

"You spelled Scottie's name wrong," she tells Charlotte, but her heart's not in it. She turns and looks past me to Honey-Belle. "Come on, let's hang those posters."

"I wouldn't bother," Charlotte says triumphantly. "You've showed your true colors. I doubt anyone will vote for you now."

There's an outbreak of murmuring and laughter. Irene looks stricken. I feel ready to throw up. This whole fucked-up thing is my fault. I can deal with the consequences for my own life, but sabotaging Irene's is something else entirely.

Gunther places his warm, stubby hand over mine.

That's when I realize I'm shaking. Irene and Honey-Belle retreat to their cars without a word, Charlotte and her entourage leave in triumph, and the rest of our class-mates disperse. Then it's just Danielle, Kevin, Gunther, and me, somber and silent by my car.

* * *

The next day, I seek out Charlotte after school. I literally chase her down the soccer field. I'll be late for basketball practice, but Danielle will understand.

It's just the two of us standing near midfield. Her teammates aren't out of the changing rooms yet. Charlotte regards me, hands on her hips, almost like she expected me to come find her. I take a deep breath and say my piece.

"I want you to leave Irene alone," I say without pre-amble. "Leave both of us alone."

Charlotte smirks, confident that she has the upper hand. "Or what?"

I shrug. "Or nothing. I have nothing to hold over you. I'm simply *asking* you to stop. I get that losing her made you sad or bitter or whatever, but for fuck's sake, find a healthier way to cope."

She stares at me like I've gone insane. Her laugh is mechanical. "Losing her? I don't know what you're talking about."

I stare at her. "Yes you do. You lost someone you loved, and you're not even sure what kind of love it was

in the first place, so now you're turning into a manipulative narcissist who can't stop craving Irene's attention."

Charlotte goes very, very still. "Whatever she told
you, it's bullshit."

"It's not." She looks ready to pounce, so I raise my
hands. "And before you freak out, you should know
that she told me in confidence and I'm not going to tell
anyone else. But I get it: You're hurting. You're acting
like a complete and utter asshole because you're in pain.
That's not an excuse, but still. I know how it feels to be
in love with someone and to lose her, and then make bad
decisions because you miss her so much. I've been there.
I get it. But I thought you should know it doesn't have
to be that way."

Charlotte blinks. "I don't understand your angle here.
You hurt her. You're no better than me."

There's the tiniest note of fragility in her voice. It
nearly bowls me over. I just stand there, trying to figure
out how to answer her. She's not wrong, but we are not
the same.

"Look, Scottie, whatever your deal is, I don't know
why you're trying to explain it to me," Charlotte says,
shaking her head like she can shake off this entire conversation. "It's the rest of the school you have to prove
yourself to."

"I don't have to prove anything. My feelings are
between Irene and me."

She smiles almost pityingly, like she's battle-worn and

I'm naive. "Don't be ridiculous. We have to prove *everything*. That's what I do every time I step onto the field. That's what you do every time you step onto the court. What we do when we walk these halls. What are we doing, if not proving ourselves?"

"Maybe we are," I concede. "But I think we'd all be much happier if we just believed each other."

Charlotte swallows. She looks like she wants to say something else, but instead she turns around and stalks off.

Her voice plays in my head all night. *We have to prove everything.* I think of Kevin trying to prove himself on guitar. Danielle trying to prove herself with test scores and leadership. Irene trying to prove herself to our whole school with one performance after another.

Irene on the sidelines, commanding attention, mirroring the crowd's feelings back to them . . .

And that's when it hits me.

I know what I have to do.

18

I FIND HONEY-BELLE BEFORE SCHOOL THE
next morning. She must pick up on my urgency, because
she stops reading her horoscope and gives me her full
attention.

"She's not mad at you," she says before I can even
open my mouth. "It just hurt her to see that picture
again. And it hurt her that Charlotte turned your fake
dating scheme against her."

I stiffen, realizing Honey-Belle knows the truth about our
whole charade. Irene must have told her after Charlotte's
antics in the parking lot.

"I'm sorry," I tell her feebly. "I hate that everyone
assumes Irene is the bad guy." I pause, lowering my eyes.
"For a while, I thought she was, too. Turns out she's
actually amazing."

Honey-Belle shakes her head. She seems disappointed,
but not surprised. "People just don't *see* Irene. They

see her looks, her charisma, her social status, but they don't see the way she cares about things. Cheerleading. Grandma Earl. *You*. Why are our classmates so willing to believe Irene would use you, but not willing to believe she's in love with you?"

My breath catches. "She told you she's in love with me?"

"Of course not." Honey-Belle stares at me impatiently. "I'm a free association thinker, Scottie. I'm reading between the lines here."

"Right." I bite my lip. "Look, I have an idea to fix everything, but I'm gonna need your help."

Honey-Belle assesses me. Her gray eyes seem to go right through me. "Are you over Tally? Like, *for real for real*?"

It's the first time I've been asked in a while, and I'm shocked to realize the answer now.

"Yeah." I smile, unable to keep from laughing. "Yeah, I really am."

Honey-Belle grins. "Then it's time we win back your girl. What do we need to do?"

"You and I wear the same size. Do you happen to have an extra cheerleading uniform?"

* * *

We have less than a week to pull everything together. First, I have to convince the cheerleading squad behind Irene's back. They're understandably wary of me, but

269

with Honey-Belle making my case, we're able to get them on board. They agree to help even though it means extra practice on top of their regular practice time. Next, I enlist my friends. I'll need both Kevin and Gunther's help to pull this off. Danielle even gives me her blessing to sit out the first half of the Candlehawk game. She says it with the authority of an official coach.

I sprint through the next few days on pure adrenaline and anxiety. School, then basketball practice, then secret cheerleading practice after Irene leaves each day. There's one evening where I'm convinced none of this will come together, but Honey-Belle hugs me and assures me the universe is working in our favor.

On the day before the district championship game against Candlehawk, I don't set foot in the gym. Instead, I leave school at the regular dismissal time and drive to the middle of town. Grandma Earl Eye Associates sits next door to the karate studio where I used to come when I was younger. No wonder the name sounded so familiar.

The receptionist greets me and asks for my appointment time. When I tell her that's not why I'm here, she frowns dramatically and says, "Oooh, honey, we don't need any more Girl Scout cookies. Dr. Abraham already bought twenty boxes." She looks seriously at me and recites the next part. "Dr. Abraham cares very deeply about supporting young women."

"Um—yeah. Funny you should mention that. I'm here to talk about Irene."

The woman's eyebrows jump. "Her daughter? Is she in trouble?"

"No. I'm a friend of hers, and I'd really like to speak with Dr. Abraham about something important to her. I can wait for as long as it takes." To emphasize the point, I plop down in one of the waiting room chairs and kick back like I have all the time in the world. I even grab a magazine off the side table.

The receptionist stands up. She eyes me as she crosses to the back office where Dr. Abraham must be. "Very determined," she says, almost like she's impressed. "No wonder you're friends with her daughter."

When she returns a minute later, Dr. Abraham is on her heels. "Scottie, what's this?" Dr. Abraham asks abruptly. "Is Irene okay?"

"She's fine. I just wanted to ask you something."

Dr. Abraham purses her lips. She adjusts a piece of hair that fell out of place. "All right. Follow me."

She leads me into an examination room. We sit across from each other almost like I'm here for a real appointment. I look distractedly around at the fancy equipment and wall diagrams, trying to steel myself.

"I'm confused about you being here," Dr. Abraham says, her shrewd eyes upon me. "Irene told me you two were on a break."

"We are." I clear my throat. "I'm hoping to rectify that tomorrow."

Dr. Abraham tilts her head. "Is this one of those prom-posal things? Are you here to ask for my permission?"

"No. But I would like to ask you to come to our district championship game tomorrow. Girls' basketball. We're playing Candlehawk." I sit up straight and look into her perplexed, beautiful face. "Dr. Abraham, did you know Irene changed the entire cheerleading schedule so the squad could cheer for our games instead of the boys'? She basically overruled her coach and got her entire team onboard. They started cheering at our games, and suddenly the whole school showed up to support us. Just because of her. Because of her initiative."

The shadow of a smile graces Dr. Abraham's face. "Yes, she's always been tenacious."

"She loves cheerleading. And she's *good* at it. It bothers her that you think it's a waste of time."

Dr. Abraham pulls back. She crosses one leg over the other and regards me with a stern expression. It doesn't scare me. I've seen the exact same look on her daughter's face.

"Do you think I don't understand how much cheerleading means to her?" Dr. Abraham asks.

"I don't know," I say mildly. "Maybe you do. But *Irene* doesn't think you understand. She doesn't feel like she can fully share this part of herself with you. Look, Dr. Abraham, I know I'm speaking out of turn here. I'm not trying to be disrespectful and I'm not trying to meddle. It's just that Irene means a lot to me, and I know it would make her incredibly happy if you would come watch her cheer tomorrow. She always acts like she doesn't need people's validation, and maybe that's true for the most part, but she *does* need yours." A sudden memory floats back to me. "I mean, she sleeps with that old shirt of yours like it's a teddy bear."

Dr. Abraham closes her eyes like she's trying not to smile. She exhales. Her body relaxes. "Yes, I do know that much. She tries to hide it from me, but I've seen it in her laundry pile."

"She's a lot like you."

"I know." Dr. Abraham nods in that way all moms seem to do. "She's an incredible girl. I'm very blessed."

"So you'll come tomorrow?"

She looks at me with something like amusement. "Yes, Scottie, I'll be there." She stands up and waits for me to do the same. As she steers me to the waiting room, she says, "Thank you for coming. I can see why she likes you." She smiles at me fully. "Nice to see that my cheerleader daughter has a personal cheerleader of her own."

"Thanks, Dr. Abraham."

"I'll see you tomorrow, Scottie."

It's not until I'm passing the receptionist's desk again

that I notice the small rainbow flag sticking out of the vase in the corner. "Is that yours?" I ask.

The receptionist spins around to see what I'm asking about. "No, Dr. Abraham put that there." She smiles knowingly at me. "She loves her daughter very much."

* * *

The championship game dawns on a cold, rainy Friday. I wake up with a feeling like I never went to sleep.

The school day passes in a blur. Everyone has game day fever, and while I've experienced this feeling during football season, I've never felt it to this degree, not even during the Christmas Classic. People are wearing reindeer antlers in class. Student government has taped up a banner with our team pictures on it. Danielle can't walk down the hall without our classmates hugging her. No one even mentions the boys' basketball team, which didn't qualify to play in the championship. For the first time in recent memory, girls' basketball is the talk of the town.

As 7:00 P.M. finally approaches, I'm shaking with nerves. Danielle gathers our team in the locker room and tells every single one of us why she's proud of us. Coach Fernandez is there, but she merely hovers in the background like a phantom. Danielle directs her to carry our water cooler out to the bench.

When we run onto the court for warm-ups, I wear

my jersey and a pair of lumpy old sweatpants to hide my outfit underneath. I join my teammates in layup drills and warm-up shots even though I'm not playing until the second half. I'll get my real version of a warm-up at halftime.

The bleachers are packed to capacity. Some people are actually standing beneath them because they can't find a place to sit. I scan the crowd for my family and find their line of red hair easily enough; they're waving posters and screaming my name. The Zanders are sitting in front of them with a giant Fathead of Danielle's face. Mr. Zander keeps making it dance.

It's harder to find Dr. Abraham in the sea of spectators, but I trust she's a woman of her word. She'll be here.

Funny enough, the last person I look for is Tally, over on the Candlehawk bench. I almost forgot she was playing tonight. I pictured this moment for months—the culmination of my dream to outdo her—and now that it's here, I feel nothing for her. The realization makes me laugh.

"What's so funny?" Danielle asks, jiggling her leg nervously.

"Nothing. Are you ready, Coach?"

Danielle gets that steely look in her eyes. "So ready. Are you?"

There's a tap on my shoulder. I spin around to find Irene standing behind me, glammed up in makeup and hair glitter, her cheer uniform impeccably pressed. She grins my way and I remember very suddenly why she was nominated for "Best Smile."

"Wanted to wish you luck," she says breathlessly.

It takes me a second to remember how to speak. "You too."

"I don't need luck." She smiles playfully. "I've got these routines down to a T."

"You don't say."

Her eyes are warm on mine. "Go kill it, Zajac."

"Show 'em how it's done, Abraham."

Minutes later, my teammates take their places at half-court. I watch nervously from the bench, still wearing my sweatpants. People seem to be confused about why I'm not starting. My family is whispering to the Zanders. Irene tosses me a questioning look, pom-poms tight behind her back.

The referee throws the jump ball and the game begins.

* * *

It's an evenly matched game for the first two quarters. Danielle is on fire, but so is the Candlehawk point guard. When we score, so do they; when they have a turnover, so do we. It's frustrating and emotionally exhausting, but I'm proud of our scrappiness. We look much different than we did four months ago.

The closer we get to halftime, the harder my heart pounds. I text Kevin over and over to make sure everything's all set. Honey-Belle keeps looking at me from the sidelines, her grin practically giving us away. The only unruffled one might be Gunther, but it's hard to say since he's hidden beneath the Fighting Reindeer costume.

The second quarter winds down. In the last minute of play, Candlehawk hits a three-pointer, and the red, tinseled half of the crowd groans. Candlehawk is now leading by five. My team tries to come back, but Danielle misses an inside shot.

And then the buzzer blares. It's halftime and my teammates come running off the court, frustrated and tired. But none of them heads for the locker room. They gather around me instead.

"You got this," Danielle says, smacking my arm. "Leave it all on the court, right?"

I take a deep breath and wipe my sweaty hands on my sweatpants. And then, using my teammates' bodies to shield myself, I pull off my jersey and sweatpants. Now it's time to wait for the signal from Honey-Belle.

The cheerleaders gather at the half-court line, ready to begin what everyone thinks is a normal halftime show. Irene stands at the front, strong and proud, ready to lead them.

Until Honey-Belle strides up beside her, grabs Irene's pom-poms, and throws them aside.

"What—?" Irene says, looking scandalized.

Honey-Belle says something to her. She tugs on Irene's

hands, pulling her away from the squad. Irene is resistant, looking for backup, stubborn as all hell. Honey-Belle drags her to the bleachers and seats her in the front row. By this point, the whole crowd is whispering urgently. No one knows what's going on.

Honey-Belle spins around, wiggles her hands above her head like antlers, and sprints back to join her squad in the middle of the court.

I take one last deep breath and wait for my cue.

Suddenly, deafening music blares from the sound system. Kevin came through with the audio.

Now I've had the time of my life . . .

I break through the wall of my teammates and run toward the cheerleaders. They part down the middle, giving me center stage. The crowd is suddenly screaming. They're putting the pieces together in one swift, dizzying moment: the *Dirty Dancing* theme, the routine we're starting up, and me, dancing like a fool in a regulation Grandma Earl cheerleading uniform.

But I'm only looking at one person.

Irene is flabbergasted. Her eyebrows are practically up to her hairline, her mouth hanging open, her arms flopped at her sides. For one horrifying second, I think I've gotten this all wrong.

But then she laughs. The crowd is roaring around her, I'm dancing like a complete buffoon to the *Dirty Dancing* song, and Irene Abraham is losing her shit laughing in the most unabashed, luminous way.

I grin and lose myself in the routine, concentrating on the steps Honey-Belle taught us. We mix the dance steps from the movie with some of the squad's best cheer routines, an homage tailored exactly to Irene's passions. My adrenaline has completely taken over, my cheeks are on fire, my heart is burning in my throat. I'm terrible, but I'm moving in sync with the squad, and they're all grinning like they're having an absolute blast. The whole crowd seems to be having the time of their lives. They're screaming their applause, all of them on their feet, even some of the Candlehawkians.

The Fighting Reindeer, a.k.a. Gunther, runs up to join us for the iconic movie moment. I take a deep breath and line up across from him, and the crowd's noise is thunderous. They know what's coming.

At that one, perfect moment of the song—the part where Jennifer Grey launches herself into Patrick Swayze's arms so he can lift her high above everyone—I run straight at Gunther and leap into his fuzzy mascot arms. We completely butcher it, of course: He lifts me in a kind of half pirouette as I scream with laughter, and we twirl around to make the most of it, and all I can hear is Honey-Belle shrieking with glee while the saxophone solo echoes in my head.

When Gunther sets me down, I straighten my skirt and turn to face the crowd. In a sudden rush, I understand exactly what Irene meant the day she told me cheerleaders regulate a crowd's emotion. I can *feel* their elation, their euphoria, their absolute delight. The song softens into the bridge, and I coax the audience down to a quieter decibel. I tap the lapel mic on my uniform and wait for Kevin to turn it on.

"Thank you for coming out to cheer on our Fighting Reindeer," I say, my voice booming around the gym. "I'm out here doing this cheesy dance because I have some cheesy things to say." I swallow and say the next part like I'm shooting a prayer of a three-pointer. "Irene Abraham, I wanna take you on a date."

The stands go haywire. People are literally jumping in their seats. Irene looks ready to pass out.

"I've been falling for you since the second you hit my car," I tell her, my voice shaking. "You are the most brilliant, passionate, infuriating person I've ever met. You make me feel seen."

I address the next part to the crowd. "And I've learned from doing *this*"—I gesture to the cheerleaders behind me—"that Irene is every bit as athletic as I suspected. So I don't care whether or not you vote for her for Student Athlete of the Year. I just want you to know she's worthy of it."

The applause is deafening. I swallow and look directly at Irene. She's wearing an expression I'm not sure I'll ever see again: completely dazed, like she's been caught off guard for the first time ever. But when I extend my hand toward her, something in her shakes awake. She springs up from the bleachers and dashes toward me with the whole school cheering behind her.

And suddenly she's in front of me, and her eyes are sparkling in that blazing, commanding way she has, and before I can catch my breath, she grabs my face and kisses me.

I'm vaguely aware of the crowd losing their minds, of Gunther whooping somewhere behind me, of Kevin looping the track so this moment can last forever, but the only thing truly registering is the feel of Irene's mouth on mine. She kisses me hard, and when she lets go, I literally have to blink to set my head straight.

"Let me show you how it's *actually* done!" she shouts, and before I can say anything, she's picking up the routine like she's been doing it all along. Of-fuck-ing-*course* she knows the steps to the *Dirty Dancing* song. I can only stand there, laughing in shock, as Irene and her squad finish out the routine to the delight of the thunderous crowd. And when the song finally ends, Irene leans into my lapel mic and says, "Now can we give y'all some *real* Fighting Reindeer routines?"

Irene and her squad seamlessly transition into their normal halftime show, riding the wave of the crowd's energy. Their routines are killing it. The crowd is loving it. I scan hundreds of faces and see joy and belonging and community.

One face sticks out to me: Dr. Abraham, standing

next to Irene's dad with Mathew on her other side. She's beaming with pride, with a mother's love, clapping along to her daughter's perfectly orchestrated cheer routines. My throat is suddenly thick.

When halftime is over, Irene takes my hand and leads me toward the locker room. She pushes me toward the door and says, "Get your uniform on. You are not sitting out for the second half of this game."

She doesn't have to tell me twice.

* * *

It really doesn't matter to me how this game ends. I'm so euphoric that I'm playing like a little kid, purely for the fun of it, practically oblivious to the competition. I assist Danielle with three different jump shots; she assists me with a steal that turns into a layup. It's easily the best time we've ever had playing together. Even when I shoot an air ball in the third quarter, I merely laugh and keep playing.

One moment stands out to me: Tally getting fouled in the fourth quarter. She trips over Googy in the midst of a desperate drive to the basket. When she hits the floor and begins to cry, I don't hesitate to run over to her. I crouch next to her, offering my hand. She refuses to take it.

"I don't understand," she cries, wiping tears away.

The words that come out of my mouth aren't planned. "It's just a game, Tal. Shake it off."

I shrug and run off, leaving her gawking on the floor. The game doesn't resume until the Candlehawk coach subs her out.

In the final few minutes of the game, we're neck and neck with Candlehawk. My competitive drive overtakes me again. Stress is rolling off Danielle in waves. The tension in the gym is palpable.

"We have to stop their point guard," Danielle pants during time-out. "She's their biggest scorer. I can't keep up with her."

"She's not great with free throws," I say. "We have to keep fouling her."

"That means Danielle would foul out," Googy says. "You've got four already, Danielle. One more and you're out of the game."

"I know," Danielle huffs. "I'm trying to figure it out."

An idea strikes me. "Hey . . . what if I guard her instead? I only have two fouls. Plenty to spare."

Danielle frowns at me. "And I take your girl?"

"Exactly. On offense we'll still play shooting and point, but on defense we'll switch. If I get fouled out, it doesn't matter. You're our best player, Danielle. You have to stay in."

Our teammates look at each other. The ref blows the whistle.

"Okay," Danielle says.

The last three minutes pass quickly. I guard the Candlehawk point guard and draw two fouls when she's trying to shoot, but the strategy works: She only makes one out of four free throws. Candlehawk is now up by only two points.

At just over a minute to go, their point guard drives to the basket. I sprint after her and block her shot. My hand never actually touches hers, but the ref calls a foul. My fifth and final one. I've officially fouled out of the game. The crowd boos in anger.

"It's all good," I tell Danielle as I head to the bench. "Stay focused. You can win this."

Forty-five seconds to go. Thirty seconds to go. Candlehawk still leading by two. I can't sit still on the bench; I spring up and bounce where I stand. Coach Fernandez is screaming, but no one is listening to her. All eyes are on the court.

Fifteen seconds to go. Danielle bringing the ball down to our side of the court. Ten seconds to go. Googy trying to get open for a pass. Five seconds to go. Danielle trying to shake her defender.

And then, in the final seconds, it happens.

Danielle breaks free and shoots the most beautiful three-pointer. It sinks cleanly through the net with a perfect, satisfying *swoosh*.

The buzzer blares. The gym is an explosion of noise. Bodies start pouring out of the stands and I am running off the bench and Googy is hanging all over Danielle and crying. I throw my arms around them and kiss my best friend on her sweaty head, and suddenly I'm crying, too. We're a sauna of heat, bodies pressing in from all sides, and my family is there and Danielle's family is there and Gunther has thrown off his mascot head and is yelling with the reddest face I've ever seen.

People are grabbing Danielle, shaking her, pounding her back. She's practically lifted off her feet. Then suddenly Kevin is there, and his arms are around her, but before he can do anything else, Danielle pulls him in and kisses him.

I am sobbing. At least, I think I'm sobbing. It's impossible to hear my own voice. My sisters are holding on to me, and Daphne is staring at Danielle and Kevin like they're in a movie. Mrs. Zander is shrieking with glee while Mr. Zander stands dumbfounded next to her, his cheeks reddening by the second, until Mrs. Zander grabs his hips and pulls him into a dance. It's so humid and I can't breathe and it's the best feeling in the world.

There's an arm around my waist, a press of lips to my cheek.

"Congratulations," Irene says in my ear. "That was some spectacular fouling out."

I turn in her arms, hold her face in my hands. "Would you believe the last one wasn't even real? I didn't even hit the girl's hand!"

"Mmm, I'm gonna call bullshit on that. You claimed you didn't hit my car, either."

"I hate you," I say. Then I kiss her and kiss her and kiss her.

19

LIFE SETTLES INTO A CALMER PACE OVER the next week. With the season over, and the trophy won, my afternoons are suddenly free. I spend the time hanging out in the parking lot with Irene and our friends.

On a brittle late-February afternoon, Irene shocks the five of us into silence when she casually announces she's dropping out of the SAOY competition.

"Are you out of your mind?" Danielle asks.

"Irene, you can't do that," I plead. "You've been working toward this for months. *Years*, even."

The boys stay quiet, but Honey-Belle says, "Let's hear her out. I trust Irene's intuition."

Irene smiles. "Well, I hadn't even told *you* this," she says, kissing my temple, "but my mom had this big talk with me last night. Her office is filming a new commercial soon. She wants the squad to be in it."

Honey-Belle's eyes light up. "The squad?"

"The squad. *Me.*" Irene looks ready to burst. "She wants me to come up with a catchy cheer for Grandma Earl Eye Associates."

"Oh my god!" everyone says at once.

"Only problem is, what rhymes with 'associates'?" Gunther asks.

"Invertebrates," Kevin says seriously.

"Okay, let's worry about that later," Danielle says. She turns to Irene. "You said yes, right?"

"I got up and spelled it out." Irene pretends she has pom-poms in her hands. "*Y-E-S!*"

"God, you have a heinous sense of humor," I tell her while our friends crack up.

"But here's the bigger news," Irene says, leaning into me. "She said even if I can't get a cheer scholarship to Benson, that we can still work something out. I can help in the office this summer while her receptionist is on a cruise to Majorca. I'm going to Benson no matter what."

"Irene, that's amazing!" Honey-Belle squeals.

"So I'm dropping out of SAOY," Irene continues with a shrug. "I don't need it anymore. I don't *care.* Besides, I want Danielle to win." She looks seriously at her. "I need you to beat Charlotte."

Danielle stands at attention. "It would be my honor."

* * *

The day Danielle wins Student Athlete of the Year is the Friday before my eighteenth birthday weekend. Our principal announces her win during a special ceremony in the gym, with Danielle, Charlotte, and the remaining two candidates seated behind him. No one is surprised to hear Danielle's name called, but nearly all of us are surprised when Charlotte throws her chair off the stage in a fit of rage. Even her friend Symphony can't calm her down. In the end, Mrs. Scuttlebaum has to bodily drag her to the nurse's office. That's how we find out that Scuttlebaum used to be a professional rodeo cowgirl.

Danielle's SAOY victory isn't as ground-shaking as her buzzer-beater against Candlehawk, but everyone is still thrilled for her. Kevin gives her a dozen red roses. Honey-Belle makes her a flower crown. Gunther secretly cuts off the Fighting Reindeer's tail for Danielle to save as a keepsake.

All in all, the end of that school day is pretty anti-climactic. We're happy, but it's a comfortable kind of happy. Tonight, the six of us are having birthday dinner with my family, and then we're going to the Munny for a triple date to see *Sixteen Candles*. Irene has already made us promise to debrief about the problematic parts afterward. I don't think I've ever seen Kevin and Danielle so excited. They literally made notecards so they wouldn't forget any of their discussion points. Danielle says they made out in his car first, then took turns trading highlighters. They're disgusting.

It's a beautiful March day when we break free of the

senior locker hall and wind our way to the parking lot. Irene hasn't joined us yet; she told Honey-Belle she had to email the Benson cheerleading coach first. It's weird to hear college names dropped into every conversation now. Irene talks about Benson all day long. Kevin has already gotten into Morehouse. Gunther has his sights set on Kennesaw State, and Danielle got into Vanderbilt. I'm still planning on Georgia State; I can picture myself down in the city. The only one of us who doesn't mention college much is Honey-Belle, but that's because she wants to take a gap year. She's thinking about becoming a doula. Gunther had to look that one up when she told him about it.

We're strolling lazily toward the parking lot, Danielle and Kevin holding hands, Gunther and Honey-Belle wrapping their arms over each other's shoulders. It's not the group I would have expected to finish out my senior year with. It's better.

The early spring weather is gentle and calm. Golden sun on our hair, birds chirping timidly. The marquee has read PROM NEXT MONTH all week, but someone messed with it so it now reads PROM SEX MONTH.

There's a steady beat of music coming from the parking lot. We turn the corner and head to our cars, and suddenly the music is blaring. A thumping drumbeat. A lone figure standing by my Jetta—

It's Irene, hoisting an old-school boom box above her

head, wearing a trench coat over her cheer uniform. *So much cuter than John Cusack.* I laugh with my whole heart, because what else can I do?

My friends don't look surprised: They hang back and watch me approach her.

Irene grins, bites her lip. She dials the volume down and sets the boom box on the roof of my car. That's when I realize she's not even playing the right song. It's not "In Your Eyes." It's the Fine Young Cannibals song we listened to during our first week carpooling together.

I grin and press into her. "Why the song change?"

She rolls her eyes. "Because the other one is so fucking cheesy. 'She Drives Me Crazy' is much more our vibe."

"Where did you even get this boom box?"

"Balthazar's Antiques. Five bucks. The guy had to show me how to use it."

"Incredible," I say, threading our fingers together. "But aren't you allergic to romantic performances?"

Irene smirks. She raises that eyebrow, the one with the scar I love so much. "Not when they're done for their own sake. And not when it's your birthday weekend. Besides, I can't let you outdo me."

"Uh-huh," I say, leaning into her.

She kisses me. Our friends start to whoop in the background.

"You're something else," I tell her.

Her eyes dance. "I really am, huh?"

"Shut up."

I pull her close by the fabric of her trench coat and kiss her again. When the song starts to fade away, Irene holds a hand to my mouth, spins around, and restarts the track. I laugh out loud.

"Have to set the mood?"

"Obviously," she says, and she kisses me again.

You would think, based on the fact that I've watched the *Say Anything . . .* boom box scene a million times, that I wouldn't have bumblebees in my stomach when my cheerleader girlfriend reenacts it for me in the school parking lot.

You would be wrong.

ACKNOWLEDGMENTS

I HAD SO MUCH FUN WRITING THIS GOOFY, campy, ridiculous book, and I couldn't have done it without a whole community of support.

Mekisha Telfer, you deserve a trophy for being the best—and most patient—editor on the planet. Thank you for pushing me to make this manuscript the best it could be. Thank you especially for loving "sweet baby Irene" as much as I do.

Marietta Zacker, this book wouldn't exist without your initiative. Thank you and I love you.

To the whole team at Roaring Brook Press, including Avia Perez, Veronica Ambrose, Christa Desir, Susan Doran, Lindsay Wagner, and Morgan Kane: Thank you for your careful, attentive work. Aurora Parlagreco, thank you for your beautiful cover design.

Steffi Walthall, your cover art is better than anything I could have imagined. Thank you for being so intentional and compassionate with these characters. Thanks for talking through ideas with me. You're a truly special person.

To my family: Thank you for carrying me through the writing of this book, especially with everything else we had going on. Mom, Dad, Freida, Sean, Michael, Annie, and Quinn P, you are my whole world. I love you guys.

Shout-out to my godfather, Uncle Tommy, for inspiring the famous "Chuck Munny" cineplex. I hope this book brings readers even half the joy you bring our family.

Adrienne Anne Tooley and Jenny Cox-Shah: Where do I even begin? You are two of the greatest gifts in my life. Thank you for reading every draft and offering ceaselessly generous feedback. I love you and I think you're both geniuses. So proud to be writing sapphic stories alongside you. Black hearts and sour beers for days.

Jasmyne Hammonds, thank you for your careful reading, thoughtful notes, and overall cheering. I'm honored to call you a friend—and now an editorial sibling!

Irene is one of my favorite characters I've ever written, and it was important to me to understand her family background, cultural context, and way of looking at the world. I am enormously grateful to my Indian and South Asian friends who were so generous with sharing their time, personal experiences, and perspectives as I sought to build Irene's inner and outer world. Thank you a million times over to Nithya Amaraneni, Annie Jacob, and Jenish Joseph. Extra heapings of thanks to my always-frenemy and sometimes-lover, Sana Saiyed.

Andrea and David Alexander, thank you for inspiring Danielle's family (and surname) and for generally being the best. Thomas Hicks and Ellyn Zagor(g)ia, thanks for braving the rain at that local high school football game. You are the best research buddies (And shout-out to Thomas and Todd for lending your names to Gunther and Kevin!). Kate Austin, thanks for letting me pick your brain about being a queer cheerleader (queerleader?) and for being such a light to the LGBT community.

Sarah Cropley, you are an extraordinary beta reader, librarian, and friend. Thank you for accompanying me through three books now! Claire Gibbs, my favorite teen beta reader, thanks for your careful and thoughtful feedback on early drafts. Kathleen F. F. Rhoads, thanks for keeping my basketball references tight and for being my person. (Eessababiesss!) Meaghan Quindlen Hanson and Jessy "Bubba" Quindlen, thanks for being test readers and fangirls. Rima Salloum, I already know I'm gonna ask you to draw Scottie and Irene based on how awesome your LTTP and HNITS character portraits were, so thanks in advance. Lisa Vincent, Cassie Gonzales, and Kimberly Hays de Muga, thank you for your feedback on my earliest drafts.

To all the booksellers, book bloggers, librarians, educators, readers, and writers who make this community so loving and rich: Thank you from the bottom of my heart.